CW01496070

BRIGHT ONE

A MOTHER'S SACRIFICE
A DAUGHTER'S FATE

BOOK ONE

A NOVEL BY
LISAJOY SACHS

HISTORIUM PRESS U.S.A.

BRIGHT ONE

This is a work of fiction inspired by historical events and family stories. Names, characters, places, and incidents are products of the author's imagination or are used fictitiously, with some names changed to protect privacy. While certain historical elements are based on true events, the narrative has been fictionalized to explore themes creatively and is not a literal account of history.

HARDCOVER ISBN: 978-1-964700-41-0
PAPERBACK ISBN: 978-1-964700-40-3
EBOOK ISBN: 978-1-964700-39-7

First Edition

Historium Press, a subsidiary publishing house of
The Historical Fiction Company
New York, NY / Macon, GA USA
www.historiumpress.com

To those who dare to hope in the face of despair, who find resilience in their struggles, and who dream even when the world feels unkind. To the survivors whose stories carry legacies, and to the memories that remind us to never forget. This is for you.

TABLE OF CONTENTS

PART II

ADVANCED PRAISE

In pre-World War II Czernowitz, Romania we follow the unforgettable journey of Jetti, a Jewish mother in the storm of rising antisemitism and personal sacrifice. If you're looking for a story that embodies resilience from the very first page to the last, this book delivers it beautifully. Jetti's journey is far from easy, marked by loss, heartbreak, and challenges that would break most people. But what makes her story so compelling is how she refuses to let those moments define her. Instead, we watch her rise from each setback with her daughter and unshakable determination. This story is rich with moments of profound hope and tender love, in particular with the friendships she forges. It's a story of healing, of learning to trust again, and of finding light even when everything around you feels dim.

— **Vanessa Keck,** *Chapters and Charm* **book blog**

Moving, haunting, devastating and hopeful. A truly beautiful tale of sacrifice, resilience and love. *Bright One* takes us on an emotional journey as Jetti Finkelthal, a Jewish mother, navigates the devastating losses, hope for the future, changing attitudes and the rise of antisemitism in pre-WWII Romania. It is a moving story of sacrifice and a mother's love, forcing us to consider the simple question, what wouldn't a mother do for her child? Inspired by Sachs' own family, the characters of *Bright One* are brought to life on the page in a way that is both beautiful and haunting. Sachs' storytelling is vivid, powerful and deeply emotional. *Bright One* draws you in as you follow Jetti from the return of her husband during WWI, her journey of grief and loss in the years after, her fears for the future and her heartbreaking choice to send her daughter away in a desperate attempt to save her life in a world she no longer recognizes. A stunning debut novel from LisaJoy Sachs.

— **Alycia Baker, Bookstagrammer**

Lisajoy Sachs' debut novel, *Bright One*, is a captivating and moving work of historical fiction—an impressive entrance onto the literary stage that is sure to establish her as a new voice to watch in the genre... Sachs delivers this poignant story with elegance, empathy, and a vivid sense of time and place. Her ability to blend historical detail with emotional depth makes *Bright One* both an intimate family saga and a powerful testament to survival. I, for one, am eagerly awaiting the next installment, where we get to follow Berta on her own journey, when it arrives. If *Bright One* is any indication, Sachs is only just getting started. Five Stars - hands down!!

— **Jon Bowman, ARC Reviewer**

A truly captivating read that pulls you in and stays with you long after the final page. Lisajoy Sachs masterfully captures the unwavering dedication and strength of a mother as she faces unimaginable hardships. Every emotion is vividly felt through the author's careful and evocative descriptions, placing you right in the heart of each scene. It's an inspiring and deeply moving story that lingers in both mind and heart.

— **Ellen Paddison, ARC Reviewer**

Bright One is a family heirloom as much as a novel. Each chapter feels like an act of remembrance, stitching together fragments of history, memory, and love into a whole that is both heartbreaking and hopeful.

— **Susan D. Levitte, author,** *Secrets in the Woods*

PREFACE

The story of how my grandmother Berta escaped the Holocaust began long before I ever thought of writing it. It started with a collection of boxes; dusty, heavy, and brimming with history. She carefully preserved these boxes over decades. When she passed away in 2004, these boxes became her parting gift to me. Inside were letters from my great-grandparents dating back to the early 1900s, even before O'ma was born. Her original birth certificate, her divorce *Get*, and a well-preserved ship passage from Palestine to New York were among the ephemera. These documents, some yellowed with time, sparked more than curiosity. They ignited a deep need to understand the lives of those who came before me. The documents and letters revealed not only the story of Berta's escape and survival but also the broader journey of an entire family navigating a world that was often unkind.

Yet the story didn't live in those papers alone. It was carried by the voices of the people who loved her. Berta's cousin Kurti, who took his last breath in 2015, brought their shared childhood to life with vivid recollections. Rivka, whose name I've changed for her privacy, offered insight through her letters, each one brimming with detail and emotion. My Uncle Lee, who died during the Covid 19 pandemic in 2020, added his perspective, as did my aunt, my mother, and father, who helped fill in some of the missing pieces. Together, their stories reminded me that our history isn't just about dates or events, it's about the lives lived, the choices made, and the bonds that carried us through.

At the heart of these memories and letters was Jetti, Berta's mother and my great-grandmother. The post cards from Jetti were unlike anything else in those boxes. They were raw, filled with grief, encouragement, and an indomitable will to protect her family.

Through her few words, I came to know not just a mother navigating impossible choices but a woman of extraordinary strength, surviving in a world that sought to break her. Her resilience was a light in the darkness, a reminder that even in the most harrowing times, love and determination could endure.

Uncovering these stories allowed me to see reflections of my own life. These weren't just tales of a distant past; they were threads woven into my family's present, shaping how we love, how we endure, and how we relay the consequence of what came before us. I came to understand the lingering effects of their struggles: the adversity of displacement, war, death, and survival that ripple through generations. In those stories, I recognized the pain of generational trauma; subtle but persistent, and alongside it, an extraordinary grit. My grandmother's story is one of rebuilding, of finding joy and purpose even in the face of unimaginable loss.

This book is the first in a series inspired by her life, set against the backdrop of a world in upheaval and transformation. It is a testament to tenacity, the enduring power of family, and the choices that define who we become. While these stories are deeply personal, I have faith that they carry universal truths about the human spirit and the bonds that tie us all together.

Thank you for opening these pages and reading with me through this journey.

Sincerely,

Lisajoy Sachs

PROLOGUE

There are stories so painful, so weighted with loss, that speaking them aloud feels nearly impossible. And yet, they must be told —passed gently from one generation to the next, woven into the fabric of consciousness, spoken even when the words shake with sorrow.

This is one of those stories.

It is rooted in truth, drawn from the lives of real people—my family. For the sake of privacy and the safety of those still living, some names have been changed. But the core of this story remains untouched. It is a legacy of love, courage, and survival.

It begins with Jetti Finkelthal, my great-grandmother. She was a woman of vigor and unwavering love. One of nine siblings, she was a steady light at the center of her family. Before the Second World War, her pursuits revolved around the people she cherished most, and the sanctuary they forged together. But war has a way of tearing through even the strongest bonds.

After the Great War, Jetti's life turned down roads no woman should ever have to face. But she did not walk them alone. With the strength of her family beside her, she found the courage to endure what seemed agonizing. Together, they carried one another through grief, uncertainty, and sacrifice.

One of those paths led her to leave behind a legacy for those she would never meet—especially for the "Bright One" in her life. A legacy not born from solitude, but from love. A love that was fierce, unwavering, and deeply rooted in the bond of those who stood beside her.

History does not bend for love, and war does not pause for family. Faced with agonizing choices and unimaginable loss, Jetti held fast to the future the only way she could: by making a sacrifice no mother should ever have to make. Sometimes, keeping love alive means paying a price far greater than anyone should be asked to tolerate.

This book is the first in a series that honors a legacy of survival, courage, and defiance. It is not only Jetti's story, it is a testament to what it means to endure. To choose love over fear. And to carry memory forward, no matter how much it hurts.

My great-grandmother Jetti's determination echoes through generations.

It lives in me now.

And through these pages, it will live in you too.

PART I

Chapter One:
Unchosen Future

Joel Wolf Linker stepped off the train onto the frostbitten platform in Czernowitz, Romania on December 9th 1917, early in the morning, the first day of Hanukkah. A thick gray sky loomed over the city, blanketing it in a frigid silence that seemed to mirror his own trepidation. Visible clouds of breath escaped between his lips as he stood motionless, his small pack weighing heavily on his shoulder, staring at the streets he had once known intimately. The city had changed, just as he had. The vibrant boulevards of the past felt eerily subdued, their lively inhabitants replaced by a muted stillness, a testament to the shadow the war had cast over the world.

As Joel began his walk, a sudden wave of emotion overtook him, making his chest tighten and his vision blur with unshed tears. He blinked them away, and they immediately froze to his scruffy beard, like miniature icicles on tree branches. He pressed on, his boots crunching against the snow-covered cobblestones. His family was no longer here to greet him. They had fled to New York shortly after he left for the war, abandoning the home of his childhood and the warmth of their embrace. It was a pragmatic decision, one of survival, but the thought left him feeling untethered. Now, all he had to hold on to was the hope of finding the wife he had married three years ago. He was queasy about Jetti waiting for him in her family's home, but hadn't heard anything about the family since he left.

Joel and Jetti had married in June 1914, a union arranged by their families, a bond not just of love but of necessity. Both the Linkers and the Finkelthals were prosperous Jewish families, rooted in the traditions and commerce of Czernowitz. Their marriage symbolized the fortification of two dynasties, a pact to weather the storms of an uncertain world. Joel had been called to serve in the army shortly after their wedding, leaving his young bride behind mere weeks after they had spoken their vows beneath the chuppah. The recollection of that day, of solemn promises and joyous celebration, felt like a distant dream.

The flashback of her face, framed by the glint of the summer sky on their wedding day, was etched into his mind like a treasured photograph. He remembered her smile, the way her hands trembled slightly when they touched his cheek on the morning he departed for war. Yet, even in its practicality, Joel had found tenderness in their brief time together, a feeling he had carried with him through the darkest days of the war.

The war had stripped Joel of much. In the trenches, he had lived among the decay of death and the putrid stench of mangled bodies that lay rotting in the mud, their faces frozen in final agony. He had seen men reduced to fragments, their cries haunting Joel long after their death. The mutilated bodies of the wounded and dying still followed him in his dreams, an endless chorus that played in his mind during the still hours. He had witnessed comrades torn apart by artillery fire, their blood soaking into the frozen earth, and he had felt his own humanity erode with every life lost. The war had reduced him to a creature of survival; he no longer had the innocence and ambition that once defined him.

He had survived, but at a cost. The boyish optimism he previously wore like a second skin had been replaced by a heavy, weary understanding of life's fragility. Joel had spent the last three years in a world defined by foxholes and death, but now, after months of arduous travel following the collapse of Romanian supply lines in October, he was finally home.

Each step brought him closer to her, but doubt clung to him like the grime of the battlefield. He had missed Jetti fiercely, her laughter and fearlessness haunting his thoughts during long nights in the dismal barracks and bloodied fields. The vision of her smile had been his solace, an aurora piercing the suffocating darkness of war. Yet, as Joel meandered through the city streets now, the certainty he once held faltered. War had tested them both, leaving scars he couldn't yet measure. What if Jetti no longer recognized the man she had married? What if he couldn't recognize himself?

He thought of her fortitude, her unwavering endurance that had always been his anchor. Jetti had been resourceful, practical, and fiercely determined, qualities that had reassured him when he left, she could endure whatever hardships came her way. He pictured her tending to the roses in the garden behind her home, her hands deftly weaving life into the seasons yet to come. But now, that belief was clouded by his own doubts. Could she hold faith in the man who had returned, broken and unsure? And more troubling, did he even deserve the faith she had so steadfastly placed in him?

As Joel approached the mansion, his steps slowed, each one weighted by a mixture of longing and unease. The grand estate loomed ahead, its elegant facade softened by his years away. The gray clouds of dawn were retreating, their somber veil lifting to reveal a sky touched with the pale blue promise of sunlight. The first golden rays slipped through, illuminating the fine details—frozen ivy creeping along the stone walls, the glint of brass on the ornate knocker, and the intricate carvings framing the imposing doorway.

The sight of the mansion stirred conflicting emotions within him. It was a place he used to find solace in, a sanctuary filled with laughter and security. Yet now, it stood as a threshold to the unknown, a space between his past and a future he feared might reject him. His hand trembled as he reached for the knocker, its cold metal biting into his palm. The rhythmic pounding of his heart seemed almost deafening, and he wondered fleetingly if its frantic beat might be heard through the heavy wooden door.

Doubt clawed at him, settling heavily on his chest, threatening to unmoor his determination. He swallowed hard, the lump in his throat thick and unyielding. The musical chatter of birds, emboldened by the clearing skies, seemed an almost cruel contrast to the turmoil within him.

Gathering his courage, Joel closed his eyes for a brief moment, willing himself to steady. Would he be able to sustain her scrutiny? Could she look past his scars etched across his face? Could she endure the demons he carried home in silence? These questions repeated in his mind, each one a jagged edge. He exhaled, his breath shaky but resolute, and lifted the knocker, knowing the answers would come only with the opening of that door.

When the door opened, the world seemed to hold its breath. Standing before Joel was not the woman he had longed for but a young girl he didn't recognize. She couldn't have been more than fourteen or fifteen, with short brown hair, cut in a modern, almost boyish style that seemed startlingly different from what he remembered of Czernowitz fashion. The girl's sharp, inquisitive eyes regarded him for a moment, and then a wide grin spread across her face as if she'd pieced together who he was.

"Sir, you're Mr. Linker, aren't you?" she asked, her voice brimming with excitement. Joel nodded, his voice crackling in his throat as he murmured, "Yes, I'm Joel Wolf Linker."

"Oh, she'll want to see you! Wait here.... no, no, come with me to the library!" the girl exclaimed, grabbing his arm with surprising force, pulling him inside.

Joel barely had time to drop his worn bag by the door before she was leading him down the wide, polished hallway. Her enthusiasm was contagious, but Joel's heart pounded with a mix of anticipation and anxiety.

"You've been gone so long," the girl chattered as they walked, her words tumbling out as though she couldn't contain them. "We've heard so much about you. Oh, wait till Mrs. Jetti sees you!"

She ushered him into the library with a dramatic flourish, gesturing for him to sit. "Wait here. I'll fetch someone!" With that, she dashed out of the room, her footsteps clicking against the marble floors.

Joel stood in the doorway for a moment, overwhelmed by the opulence of the library before him. The room was nothing short of magnificent, a testament to the Finkelthals wealth and refinement.

Towering mahogany bookshelves lined the walls, each crammed with hundreds of books in a dazzling array of languages; Hebrew, German, Romanian, French, English, and others he couldn't identify. A rolling tall ladder was attached to the upper shelves, hinting at the library's depth and the importance the family placed on knowledge and culture.

The floor was covered in a lush, richly woven rug, its intricate patterns of crimson and gold reminiscent of far-off lands. In the center of the room stood an ornate writing desk, its surface inlaid with delicate floral marquetry. The chairs surrounding it were upholstered in deep emerald velvet, their carved arms and legs gleaming with gold leaf. Above, a grand chandelier hung from the high ceiling, its crystals catching the weak winter sunlight that streamed through the tall arched windows. The scent of old paper, polished wood, and a hint of something floral lingered in the air, comforting and elegant.

Joel ran his fingers along the spine of a nearby book, the leather smooth and cool beneath his touch. He felt out of place in this grandeur, a soldier wearing the strain of war in his tall boots and threadbare coat. Before he could dwell too long on his unease, the door opened again, and a flurry of movement interrupted his thoughts.

He had lived here for the brief three weeks of their marriage, yet standing inside the mansion now, he could hardly recall it being this grand. Had the passage of three years transformed it so dramatically, or was it his memory, dulled by time and shadowed by all he had endured? Or perhaps it was simply that he had changed, his perspective shaped by years of hardship, making the once-familiar now feel distant and imposing.

The kitchen staff bustled in, carrying a tray with a sterling coffee pot, a small pitcher of milk, and two porcelain cups and saucers. They set everything down on a low table near the fireplace, their faces alight with curiosity and barely contained excitement.

"Please, Mr. Linker, sit," one of them urged, pouring him a cup of steaming coffee. The aroma filled the room, rich and inviting.

Joel sat, gripping the delicate cup in hands roughened by years of war. The heat seeped into his fingers, but his mind was elsewhere. He stared into the swirling mix of coffee, milk and sugar, wondering where Jetti was.

The staff exchanged knowing glances, whispering among themselves about the long-awaited reunion of these two lovers. Joel caught snippets of their conversation, words of surprise, excitement, and even a hint of mischief. It was clear they knew who he was, and they were just as eager as he was for the moment when Jetti would walk through that door.

For now, Joel waited. The library's elegance surrounding him, offering both comfort and a poignant reminder of the life he had left behind. The ornate grandfather clock in the hall marked each passing second, its steady ticking echoing like a slow, relentless march. Despite the ache of waiting, there was something about this space, the collection of books, or its promise, that made him feel as though he stood on the threshold of something extraordinary, something that might finally mend the fractures left by war.

Chapter Two:
Flutter of Heart

Time seemed to stretch unbearably, each tick amplifying Joel's anticipation. His palms were damp, his heartbeat loud in his ears, when at last, Jetti appeared in the doorway. She took his breath away, her presence radiant and dreamlike. Her periwinkle dress flowed gracefully to her ankles, the silken fabric catching the golden morning streaming through the tall windows.

The hue of the dress seemed to embrace her, highlighting her delicate skin. Her blonde hair, styled in cascading waves, framed her face with effortless perfection, each strand illuminated as if painted by a master's hand. She seemed to shimmer with an ethereal beauty, a vision so strikingly real it felt almost impossible to behold. Joel's heart clenched; she was here, luminous and unbroken, and more beautiful than he had ever dared to remember.

Behind her, the grand library spread in a stately display of mahogany bookshelves that reached toward the ceiling. Dust motes floated in the beams of sunlight, their lazy drift a stark contrast to the tempest of emotions in Joel's chest. His pulse quickened, and for a moment, time itself seemed to halt. Jetti stood there, poised, her hands resting at her sides, the space between them charged with years lost and words left unsaid.

Joel's throat tightened, his longing a tangible thing, as though the vast, book-lined room could scarcely contain the depth of it.

Jetti stepped back slightly, her eyes scanning Joel with a mix of disbelief and wonder. The man before her was not the Joel she had once known, the young, carefree boy who had been so eager to take on the world. That boy had been full of energy, his laughter infectious, his eyes alight with the spark of endless possibilities. But the man who now stood before her, his head slightly bowed, was someone entirely different, a stranger, yet somehow still hers.

Looking over his face, taking in the changes that time and war had wrought. His once-smooth skin was now marred by scars, one that traced a jagged line just above his brow and another, smaller but no less telling, along his cheek. His beard was thick and unkempt, streaked with hints of silver strands that hadn't been there before. It framed his face, making him look older, harder, and almost unrecognizable. Yet it wasn't just his physical appearance that had changed. The brightness she had always loved in his eyes, the mischievous glint that hinted at his endless optimism, was gone, replaced by a weary dullness that made her heart instantly ache.

Jetti noticed how thin he had become, his frame wiry and muscular from years of hard labor and little sustenance. His shoulders, though broader than she remembered, slightly stooped, as if carrying an invisible weight too heavy to bear. His hands caught her attention, once smooth, they were now rough and calloused, the hands of a man who had fought and survived in ways she could only imagine. She wanted to reach for them, to feel their harshness and let him know that she understood, even if only a little.

His uniform was worn and threadbare, its fabric faded and patched in places, telling a story of long marches and countless nights spent in the cold. The edges of his coat were frayed, and the buttons mismatched, hastily sewn back on during some distant moment of respite. He smelled of cigarettes and damp earth, an odor that spoke of trench life and the endless rains that had soaked his very soul. Yet despite the wear and tear, there was a medal pinned to his chest, a small, shining emblem that caught a shimmer. She didn't know what it was for, but she felt a swell of pride and sadness all at once, knowing it came at a cost she could barely fathom.

Jetti's gaze landed on his boots, scuffed and caked with dried mud, the soles worn thin from countless kilometers. He shifted his balance awkwardly under her scrutiny, his hands clenching and unclenching at his sides. She could see how tightly he held himself, as if bracing for rejection. The sight of him made her heart ache with a sharp, sudden tenderness.

She took a step closer, her voice trembling. "Joel," she said, her hand reaching up but hesitating just before touching the scar on his face. "You've... changed."

He flinched slightly at her words, his eyes lowering in shame. "I'm not the man you remember, Jetti," he admitted, his voice low and gravelly. "The war...." He stopped, shaking his head as if the words were too unwieldy to speak.

Jetti tilted her head, her hand finally brushing against his cheek, feeling the roughness of his beard and the coolness of his skin. "No," she whispered, her own voice thick with emotion. "You're not the same. But you're here. You came back to me."

As she looked into his eyes, searching for any trace of the boy she had married, she realized something profound: the man before her, scarred and weary as he was, had survived. He had endured horrors she would never fully understand, and yet he had returned to her. Though the brightness she remembered was gone, replaced by shadows of pain and loss, she believed…hoped…that the man he had become was someone she could love.

In that moment, she decided. She would love him not in spite of the changes but because of them. Because he was Joel, her Joel, and they would find a way to rebuild what had been broken, together. She let her hand fall from his face to his chest, resting over the medal pinned to his coat. "You're home," she said again, her voice steady now. "And that's all that matters."

Joel nodded, his lips pressing together as he fought back tears. "I am," he whispered. "And I'll never leave you again."

Her head rested against his shoulder, and Joel buried his face in her hair, inhaling the familiar scent of lavender. It was a scent that had remained in his subconscious mind through years of war, a fragile thread connecting him to the life he had left behind. The floodgates of his emotions opened, and he clung to her as if letting go would mean losing her all over again. Tears streamed unchecked down his face, soaking into his beard. His voice, hoarse and broken, escaped in a whisper. "I missed you," he murmured, his words trembling with his anguish. "Every day, every moment... I didn't know if I'd ever see you again."

Jetti pulled back, just enough for her eyes to meet his. Her hands, steady despite their slight tremor, cupped his bearded face. Her thumbs brushed away the tears streaking the top of his cheeks, though her own tears flowed freely. The tenderness in her touch was almost too much for Joel to hold.

His eyes roamed her face, drinking her in as if she might vanish if he looked away. Her cheeks were flushed, her delicate features sharper than he remembered, etched with the serene strength of someone who had endured. Yet, to him, she was more beautiful than ever. Her independence, her unwavering grit, it shone through every part of her, illuminating the darkness he had carried for so long.

"I wasn't sure if you'd still want me," he confessed, his voice barely above a whisper. His eyes dropped, unable to hold hers, shame pooling in their depths. "After everything I've seen, everything I've done... I'm afraid I'm not the man you married."

Jetti's hands remained on his face, anchoring him. Her expression soothing, her lips curving into a bittersweet smile. She shook her head, her blue-green eyes shimmering like the ocean at dawn. "Joel," she said, her voice steady, "you came back. That's all I've ever wanted. We'll face the future. You and me."

Her words pierced through the armor he had built around his heart, soothing wounds he hadn't realized were continuing to bleed. He nodded, unable to speak, his throat tight with emotion. Joel couldn't help but feel its significance, a reflection of his own journey from the darkness of war back to the embrace of home.

Before they could say more, the staff entered with a silver tray. Joel's eyes glanced toward it, momentarily pulled from the intensity of the moment. The tray was crammed with marzipan pastries, exquisitely crafted into delicate shapes, roses, stars, and crescents with almonds pressed into them, each glistening with a dusting of fine sugar. Jetti's favorites. The sweet almond perfume filled the room, blending with the aroma of the steaming coffee brought in earlier.

The staff placed the tray carefully on the table before retreating, their faces alight with anticipation. Joel glanced at Jetti, who stared at the pastries with a mixture of longing and sorrow. Neither of them moved to eat. The emotions between them were too raw, too overwhelming to allow for such simple comforts. But Joel's stomach growled, a stark reminder of the years of deprivation he had endured.

Tentatively, he reached for his cup of coffee, that had gone tepid now. He lifted it to his lips, and the first sip was like a revelation. The smooth, rich coffee, sweetened with milk and sugar, flooded his senses. It was nothing like the bitter, gritty concoctions he had grown used to in the trenches. He closed his eyes, letting the flavor spread through him, grounding him in the present.

Finally, unable to ignore his hunger, Joel picked up one of the pastries, a crescent-shaped one dusted with sugar. It felt almost wrong to bite into something so beautiful, but he forced himself to take a small bite. The marzipan's almond-rich sweetness melted on his tongue, the outer crust providing the perfect delicate crispness. The taste was exquisite, a luxury he hadn't known in years. And yet, as he ate, the guilt crept in. How could he, a man who had seen so much suffering, allow himself to enjoy this?

The room's opulence, its plush rugs, towering bookshelves, and gleaming furniture, pressed down on him with an almost suffocating weight. He felt out of place. His hands, rough and hardened, looked as though they belonged to someone who had clawed his way out of the earth, not someone sitting in a room so grand. He felt like an imposter.

Joel set the half-eaten pastry back onto the porcelain plate, the delicate crunch of the sugared crust giving way to a clink as it met the china. The sweetness that lingered on his tongue now felt excessive, almost cloying, and his stomach churned, not from hunger, but from the uneasy burden of his thoughts.

He glanced at Jetti, who was seated across from him, her delicate fingers resting on the edge of her cup. Her expression was unreadable, her sapphire eyes fixed on him with a subdued intensity that only deepened his unease. He could feel the questions she wasn't asking, the emotions she was holding back. The wealth that surrounded them, the opulent furniture, the intricate Persian rug underfoot, the glittering crystal chandelier overhead, seemed to mock him.

The guilt gnawed at him, relentless and unyielding, but it wasn't alone. Beneath the surface, resentment simmered, sharp as the memories he tried to bury.

His family had once thrived in Czernowitz, their wealth born from years of meticulous work in the mercantile trade. Their grand home, though not as extravagant as this mansion, had stood as a testament to their success, a place of community and laughter, where the aroma of his mother's cooking intertwined with the bouquet of the rose garden that bordered the front walk. That life, so vivid in his memory, was now nothing more than ashes of the past. It had been abandoned, left behind when his parents and sister fled the country as the war swept over Europe like an unrelenting tide.

He had stayed behind, clinging to a sense of duty or perhaps stubbornness, but their departure felt like more than necessity, it felt like a betrayal. Years passed without a word, their absence as arduous as the reticence that followed artillery fire. Only the faintest whispers reached him - 'New York'. A city spoken like a half-remembered dream, a destination that carried the promise of safety he had never known. He tried to picture them there, in a city he couldn't imagine, living a life he couldn't comprehend. He thought of his mother's delicate hands smoothing down the hem of her skirt, his father's booming laugh filling a room, his sister's shy smile. Had they managed to preserve these pieces of themselves in a new world?

The thought of their survival brought a surge of solace, but it was overshadowed by a deeper ache. While they built a new life, carving out a future far from the horrors of war, he had been left behind, swallowed by violence and loss. The scars of that abandonment ran deep, woven with the ones carved by the battlefield. Their absence wasn't just a void, it was a wound that festered, leaving him to wonder if the connection they once shared could ever be mended.

His attention fixed on Jetti, a picture of grace against the firelight. She seemed so at home in this house, her movements effortlessly in sync with its lavish elegance. It suited her with its polished floors and immaculate halls reflected in her poise and perseverance. She had carved out a life here, weathering the war in her own way, tending to the world that had remained while so much else had crumbled. Her force was palpable, a steady presence in a world that felt fractured to him.

He wondered how much she had sacrificed to keep it all intact. Did she stay up late at night, consumed by worry, only to face early mornings, carrying the burden of it all? This house, this city, this country, they weren't just her home, they were the anchors of the life she had fought to preserve. To ask her to leave it all behind felt like asking her to abandon pieces of herself. And yet, he couldn't shake the feeling that her choice came with a price, a connection she might never express out loud.

The hesitation between them felt alive, the fire's crackle the only sound in the room. Jetti's hand rested on the edge of the table, her fingers gently picking the embroidered edge of a napkin. Joel's hand subconsciously drifted to the medal pinned to his coat. Its coldness pressed against his chest, a reminder of things he hadn't yet told her, things he wasn't sure he ever could.

Chapter Three:
The Medal

The only thing he could do at the moment was stare at Jetti and see her, indulge in the beauty of the woman who was his wife. Her eyes, those extraordinary blue-green eyes, met his, and Joel felt as though he were gazing into the depths of an aqua sapphire. They shimmered with a clarity and brilliance that seemed otherworldly, like something plucked from the treasures of royalty. Her expression revealed a mysterious blend of tenderness and determination, an intensity that had captivated him from the moment they first met as children. The color was neither entirely blue nor green but danced between the two, shifting with the light and her mood. It was the kind of beauty that poets would struggle to describe, the kind that made the ordinary world feel distant and dull in comparison.

Jetti's features were delicate but well-defined, her high cheekbones giving her an almost regal air. Her pale skin, kissed with a pink flush from the winter cold, was smooth and unblemished, as if untouched by the hardships of the world outside. Her lips, enticing and full, parted slightly in surprise as she took in the sight of Joel sitting before her. He saw the slight quiver in her chin, a sign of the emotions she was trying to steady, and it made his heart ache with a mixture of guilt and longing.

She was wearing a simple dress of periwinkle blue, the fabric hugged her slender frame in a way that suggested both modesty and distinct confidence, a reflection of her nature. There was a peaceful nobility about her, an inner essence that seemed to radiate outward and fill the space around her.

Joel felt his chest twitch as he looked at her, overwhelmed by the sheer beauty of the woman before him and the albatross of the years they had spent apart. In her eyes, he saw questions and answers, longing and fear, love and uncertainty, all the things he had carried within himself during his time away. For a moment, he could only stare, as if afraid that speaking would shatter the fragile magic of the moment.

The restraint hung heavy between them, unspoken words lingering in the air. The tension was palpable until Jetti, with a sensitive voice, broke it. "Joel," she said, her tone filled with curiosity, "what is that medal from?"

Joel looked down at the striking decoration pinned to his chest, the glint of bright white polished silver catching the edges as he shifted. His fingers brushed over it, his mind momentarily drifting back to the muddy, blood-streaked battlefields. He looked up to meet Jetti's eyes, and for the first time in a long while, he allowed himself to speak of the horrors and heroism that had defined him in her absence.

"It's a medal called the *Croix de Virtute Militara*," he began, his voice thick with the gravity of the past. He could see her brow furrow slightly as she tried to comprehend the name, and he hurried to explain further. 'It's not well-known, because so few are given out, but it was awarded to me for bravery during the war... for acts of valor in combat." He paused, the words feeling foreign on his tongue. He wasn't sure if he was explaining it to her or to himself.

Jetti's focus deepened as she leaned in, her eyes never leaving his. "It sounds important," she said, her voice a mixture of awe and concern.

Joel nodded, though the pride he might have once felt in the medal was now tempered by the experiences it symbolized. "It's a Romanian medal," he continued, his fingers tracing the edges of the cross. "A Maltese cross, with King Carol I's profile on one side..."

'CAROL I DOMN AL ROMANIEI'
'VIRTUTE MILITARA'

"On the back side it says Military Virtue." He paused, the metallic gleam of the medal in the dim room reflecting his mixed emotions. "It's, um... silver. Because... well, since I'm Jewish, they... I was only awarded the second class medal. For, you know... lower-ranking officers. But it doesn't feel... important anymore. Not like it did when they first pinned it to me. Now that I'm home it just feels like a reminder of everything I've lost."

Jetti's eyes dropped to the medal, and she studied it carefully, as if trying to understand the magnitude of what it represented. The Maltese cross, with its pointed arms, seemed to shimmer, and she noted how Joel's rough hand rested so carefully over it. "It's beautiful," she said gracefully, her voice barely above a whisper. "So much history, so much sacrifice in something so small."

Joel shifted in his seat, uncomfortable under her observation and the flood of memories that the medal stirred. "The ribbon," he continued, his voice thick with emotion, "is striped... green and blue. It's worn over the heart, as a symbol of the courage it took to earn it... but I don't wear it with pride, not truly. Not since the day they gave it to me. Because every time I look at it, I remember the men who didn't make it back. And the war, Jetti... it was nothing like I imagined it would be when I first left Czernowitz. Nothing like the stories of honor I grew up with."

The grandfather clock in the hallway started chiming for the eleventh hour, the sound filled the space between them. She seemed to understand without needing to ask the weight the medal carried. The way it rested against his chest, directly over his heart, wasn't just symbolic of the bravery it represented. It was where Joel felt the loss most acutely, the loss of innocence, of the boy who had once been eager to embrace the world, of the future he had once imagined with her.

"Joel," she said softly, her eyes holding his with a tenderness that made his throat dry. "You've been through so much. You've seen so many horrors, yet you still returned to me, to us. That's more bravery than any medal can ever represent."

21

Joel closed his eyes briefly, feeling the burn of delayed tears. "I didn't feel brave. I just... I just wanted to come back. I had nowhere else to go," he continued. "When I was drafted into the army," he began, his words slow and deliberate, "I knew it would be hard. But I wasn't prepared for just how much a man could take, and still survive." He glanced at Jetti, her eyes locked onto his, a mixture of concern and admiration etched across her face.

Joel leaned forward, his voice low and steady as he began to recount the memory. "I can't believe it was only a few weeks ago," he said, his eyes clouded. "The cold and snow came early, covering everything in white. It wasn't just freezing, Jetti... it was the kind of bitter cold that burrows into your bones, no matter how many layers you wear. Our toes were frostbitten, blackened, and swollen inside boots that barely held together. When we stopped to rest, the snow muffled everything around us, but it couldn't cover the groans of men too weak to move or the stench of death that clung to us, and never left."

He paused, his mind drifting as if he could see the forest stretched out before him. "The forests seemed endless, the trees towering above us. Ice coated the branches, weighing them down, and the ground was uneven, slippery, and treacherous. Every step felt like a gamble… one wrong move, and you could twist an ankle, or worse. At night, the wind howled through those trees, knocking down branches and icicles to the ground. It drowned out almost every sound, except the crunch of footsteps on the snow was always there, a constant reminder that we were still moving, and alive."

His tone softened, a foreboding emotion creeping in as he continued. "We scavenged what we could for food, and when we found fatwood, it was like finding gold."

He glanced at her, noticing the curiosity in her expression. "Do you know what fatwood is?"

Jetti, completely entranced in the story, shook her head and plainly said "no".

"It's a type of resin-soaked heartwood from dead pine stumps or fallen trees. We'd have to cut the branches close to the trunk to get

22

it, no matter how frozen it was. It burns hot and fast, even in the snow. That fatwood saved us, letting us build fires when we needed them most. Fires to keep us from freezing, to cook whatever scraps of food we managed to scrounge up."

Joel's lips curled into a thin smile, though his eyes remained serious. "When we weren't marching through the forest and could make camp, those fires became our refuge. We found small ways to distract ourselves, simple card games if someone had a deck, dice carved from bits of wood, or even just guessing games and stories. We tried anything to keep our minds off the hunger, the cold, and the fear. For a few moments, we could pretend life was normal, laugh like we used to. But it never lasted. The laughter always faded, and the reality would creep back in. We were starving, Jetti. Just a bunch of young boys, retreating through those forests with nothing but sheer will holding us together."

He looked at her, his voice apprehensive. "I don't think I ever stopped moving because I was afraid of what would happen if I did. That cold... that silence... it had a way of swallowing you whole."

Joel's tone grew heavier as he continued. "I made the decision to leave the camp in search of food..." he said. "I spoke Russian fluently because my father had insisted I learn it when I was a boy, saying it would be useful one day. That, along with a pair of borrowed street clothes, allowed me to blend in. I looked like any other starving civilian, not a soldier. But it was dangerous. Looking back now, I see how reckless it truly was."

He paused, drawing a deep breath, as if summoning the strength to relive it. "I walked through the forest until I found a snow-packed trail of footprints; the cold that day was biting into my face like little needles. I was so hungry, I decided to follow the trail. The wind was brutal as it blew through the trees, hiding the sound of my footsteps as I trudged along the path. After what felt like hours, I saw it... a small hut tucked into a clearing."

Joel's hands moved as though sketching the image for her. "It was a verderer's hut, the kind used by forest wardens. Rough logs were stacked high with moss and clay packed into the gaps to block winter cold and wind from getting in. Smoke drifted out of the chimney, promising warmth... and maybe food. I got closer, but just as I was about to step onto the porch, the door creaked open. My heart nearly stopped. I threw myself behind a stack of firewood; I could feel my heart pounding... it was so loud Jetti, I was certain they would hear it."

He leaned forward, his voice lowering as the tension in his story mounted. "Two men stood at the door. I assumed the first was the verderer, and the second was unmistakably a Russian soldier in uniform. I stayed frozen behind that woodpile, the cold creeping into my limbs as I strained to hear their conversation. The soldier warned the man not to leave the hut for three days. My blood ran cold when I realized what he meant... the Russians were planning to destroy our camp and kill us."

Joel's jaw tightened as he continued, his words quickening. "That's when it all started to make sense. We must have had a spy at our camp, maybe several. My mind raced back to the three new men who'd joined us a few weeks before. Their uniforms... they could have been stolen, stripped from the dead. The pieces fell into place, and I knew I had to get back to warn the others."

He paused, regrouping his thoughts. "I stayed crouched behind that woodpile for at least two agonizing hours. The cold was unbearable, every muscle in my body screaming to move, but I couldn't risk it. On top of that, it was starting to get dark. If they'd found me, Jetti..." His voice faltered for a moment. "I wouldn't be here now. They would've shot me without a second thought. And our camp... it would've been obliterated."

Joel straightened, his voice steadying as he recounted what followed. "When I finally made it back to camp, it was already dark. I'm lucky I found my way back at all. I told my commander everything I'd heard. There was no time for hesitation. The three suspected spies were rounded up, tied together, and stripped of their uniforms. They were given nothing but filthy cloaks, forcing them to feel the icy air, a cruel reminder of their betrayal. Out of fear of being killed, they admitted they weren't part of our troop. It was harsh, but it was survival."

He met her eyes then, his voice lower but no less intense. "We quickly dismantled the camp that night, moving through the midnight forest. The continuing snowfall muffled our footsteps, but every creak of a branch or snap of ice sent waves of fear through us. We continued walking for two days, despite being completely exhausted, avoiding every road, every trail, praying we wouldn't stumble into a Russian patrol. And somehow, by sheer luck and the grace of that overheard conversation, we made it. All sixty of us. We crossed into Transylvania alive."

Joel's expression was raw. "I've thought about that night so many times since, wondering how close we came to the end. And I keep asking myself... was it luck, or something more?"

Jetti's eyes shimmered with suppressed tears, her hands clutching the folds of her dress tightly as Joel recounted the aftermath of his perilous journey.

"In Transylvania, we heard about the attack that would have decimated our camp," he said, his voice steady. "My comrades called me a hero. But truthfully, I didn't feel like one. I'd acted out of desperation, not bravery. If I hadn't overheard those plans, it would've been over for us all. I just... did what anyone would have done."

Jetti leaned closer, insistent. "Not everyone would have had the courage, Joel. You risked your life, and because of you, sixty men made it back. That's not something to diminish."

Joel lowered his head, the firelight casting darting shadows across his face. "The Romanian army seemed to agree," he continued, a visible note of wonder in his tone. "They awarded me this... this medal. Can you imagine? A Jew, awarded such an honor in times like these, it feels unreal."

Jetti reached for his hand, her voice trembling with emotion. "Unreal? No, Joel. It was justice. Recognition for your bravery. They saw you for who you truly are."

25

Joel nodded, a moment of pride lighting his eyes as his thumb brushed over her knuckles. "But it wasn't just the medal, Jetti. They gave me something else, something I never expected. They told me that when I returned to Czernowitz, I would be promised the title of Postmaster."

Jetti's gasp filled the room, her eyes widening in disbelief. Her voice trembled as she whispered, "Postmaster? Joel, that's... incredible. Do you understand what that means? How rare it is to hold such a title?"

A smile broke across Joel's face, the corner of his mouth edging upward. "Rare doesn't even begin to describe it," he said, his tone laced with a mix of pride and astonishment. "A Postmaster isn't just a title, it's responsibility. I'll oversee all postal operations, ensuring mail flows seamlessly, managing workers, keeping communication alive across the region. It's a position of immense trust and respect, Jetti. I never imagined they'd see me as capable of something like this."

Her voice steadied, her pride shining through her tears. "It's not just about trust, Joel. It's about who you are. They see in you what I've always seen in you, a man of integrity, resilience, and courage."

Joel's lips lifted in a subtle smile, his expression touched by her words. "Maybe they do..." he murmured, his voice thick with gratitude.

Jetti squeezed his hand tightly, tears now streaming freely down her face. "You've always been extraordinary, Joel. Finally, the world is catching up to what I've known all along."

He looked at her, his eyes glimmering with a mix of humility and determination. For a moment, the oppression of the world around them seemed to lift, replaced by the possibility of something brighter. "Maybe," he said, his voice filled with aspiration. "Do you think we can try? To build something new, something better, in this broken world?"

Jetti's tears turned to a radiant smile, her hand never letting go of his. "With you, Joel? Yes. I believe we can."

He continued to describe the award ceremony, his comrades cheering and clapping him on the back as the medal was pinned over his heart.

"It was overwhelming," he said. "To see the pride in their faces, to feel that I'd truly made a difference. The celebration that night was modest, but we shared what little we had. We toasted with watered-down spirits… and for a moment, we forgot the war. We forgot the cold and the hunger. We were just men, alive… together, and grateful."

Joel paused, his voice dropping. "My commander offered me a chance to come home," he said, his eyes meeting hers. "On December 2nd, I boarded the first train to Czernowitz. It felt odd, sitting in an indoor compartment after my years at war and the past months starving in the freezing forest. But all I could think about was you; so, I came here."

Chapter Four:
Unexpected Parcel

In the privacy of their shared moment, as Jetti's eyes sparkled with admiration, Joel felt a strange, gnawing unease settling deep within him. Her belief in him, in them, was so absolute, so unwavering, that he almost believed it himself. Almost. But in the back of his mind, a small voice whispered doubts he could not shake.

He tried to push the thought away, focusing instead on the daintiness of her hand in his. Yet, the feeling persisted, a growing conviction pressing down on him. Am I lying to her? The question, complex and unrelenting. He was saying the things he thought she wanted to hear...that they could build a life, that they could find happiness in the mansion surrounded by her family. But was it the truth? Deep down, Joel feared it was not.

What he truly wanted, though he could hardly admit it to himself, was to leave. To go to New York. To find his family, wherever they were, and piece together the life that had been torn apart by war.

The truth was, he barely knew Jetti. Their courtship, such as it was, had been brief and overshadowed by the storm clouds of war. He'd written her a few simple postcards when he could, clinging to the idea of her as a beacon of purpose, but letters weren't life. They weren't the messy, complicated day-to-day reality of living with another person, of really understanding them.

The thought unsettled him further, and his focus moved to the empty menorah over by a window, and the long shadows stretching across the floor. He had wanted to love her, had tried to hold onto her kindness, her laugh. But now that he was here, the mansion looming around him, the noise of her siblings down the halls, Joel felt out of place. He wasn't sure this life was what he wanted.

He wanted to tell Jetti the truth but feared the hurt it would cause; she seemed so happy. The last thing he wanted was to extinguish the optimism in her eyes. For now, he swallowed his unease and forced a small, hesitant smile, though his heart felt wearisome with everything he wasn't telling her.

The chime of the clock broke, marking one-o'clock. Joel shifted in his seat, his stomach rumbling loudly, a reminder of the hours that had passed since he had last eaten. Across from him, Jetti glanced his way, her face concerned as she read the discomfort etched into his features. "You must be hungry…" she said, rising from her chair. "Come with me. Let's see if the kitchen has anything ready… more substantial than pastries."

Joel followed her out of the library, the room giving way to the cooler, dimmer corridors of the mansion. As they walked, she tried to fill the emptiness with conversation, but he could barely focus on her words. He felt like a guest overstaying his welcome. Jetti moved with the ease of someone who belonged, leading him down a maze of hallways that seemed to stretch endlessly.

When they reached the kitchen, it was as though they had stepped into a haven of comfort. The air was rich with fresh bread and simmering broth, wrapping around Joel like an old, familiar quilt. The cook, an older woman with silver-streaked hair tucked neatly beneath her kerchief, stood at the counter slicing bread with practiced precision. Nearby, the young maid who had let Joel in earlier was wiping down the stove, humming something familiar to herself. Jetti greeted them both effortlessly, her voice carrying the ease of someone perfectly at home.

Joel stood in the doorway, his hands stuffed deep into his coat pockets. He glanced around, his eyes catching on the steady flames in the hearth and the tidy rows of jars lining the shelves. It was a picture of security, of abundance…worlds away from the stark hunger and bone-chilling cold he had just come from. His discomfort must have been obvious because Jetti turned to him, her brow furrowing slightly before she motioned to the long wooden table at the center of the room.

"Joel," she said, her tone leaving little room for argument, though it softened with a hint of care. "Please, sit down. This is your home now. You're not a guest here, so stop acting like one."

He hesitated, the words catching him off guard, but the obvious authority in her voice nudged him forward. He shrugged off his coat, hung it over a nearby chair, and took a seat at the table, his movements stiff and uncertain. Jetti, already busying herself, glanced at him again and added, "That's what this marriage was supposed to do Joel, for both of us. It's meant to give you safety, a place to belong, to feel steady."

Her words landed with an unexpected clarity, and Joel sat a little straighter, though his hands rested awkwardly on his knees. He watched her move around the kitchen, uncovering a dish of roasted chicken, ladling steaming bowls of borscht, and slicing thick, crusty pieces of bread. She worked efficiently, her movements brisk yet purposeful, filling the table with enough food to make Joel's stomach churn with both hunger and guilt.

He stared at the spread. The scene was tantalizing, the sight of the rich borscht and perfectly cooked chicken almost overwhelming, but he couldn't bring himself to reach for any of it. This abundance, this comfort... it felt foreign. Indulgent. His mind drifted back to the trenches, to gnawed bones and thin, watery soups, to the frostbitten nights when a raw potato felt like salvation. This feast seemed impossibly extravagant.

Jetti slid into the seat beside him, her hand brushing his arm gently to break his reverie. "Joel," she said, her voice low but insistent. "This... this is what our family wanted for us. When they arranged this marriage, it wasn't about tradition or appearances. They saw the way the world was turning. They knew the dangers people like us would face. This wasn't just about keeping up propriety, it was about survival. They wanted you to have this. A home. A family. Somewhere to come back to."

Her words settled on him heavily, her steady scrutiny piercing through his doubts. He swallowed hard, his throat parched. His eyes looked between the food and her earnest expression, and for a moment, like he understood what she was offering, not just a meal, but a lifeline. A promise that he didn't have to face the world alone.

A knot of resistance sat heavily in his chest. The thought of leaning into this comfort, of allowing himself to belong here, felt perilously close to betrayal. Betrayal of the men he had left behind, of the hardships that had shaped him. He glanced at her, her expression a mixture of expectation and determination. She wasn't asking. She was telling him to accept what was his. To accept her. And though he wasn't sure he could yet, he found himself nodding, her certainty the only steady thing in the swirl of his doubts.

The kitchen was lively with the fiery crackle at the hearth and the rhythmic clinking of utensils. Joel finally reached for a piece of bread, his fingers brushing against the warm crust. He broke off a small piece, his movements hesitant, as if the act of eating here was some kind of surrender. Jetti smiled, her eyes watching him with subdued patience.

As he took the first bite, the taste of home; savory, yeasty, and impossibly rich, washed over him, and for a moment, his thoughts faltered. The bread was a stark reminder of everything he had lost and everything he might have in the future. He chewed slowly, the flavors fusing with the ache in his chest.

Jetti's voice was low and measured. "Joel," she said. "I know it's hard for you to be here. To believe you deserve this." Her hand rested on the table, close but not quite touching his. "But you do. And it's time you start seeing it for yourself."

Before he could respond, the sound of hurried footsteps pattered down the hallway. Anka, the young maid, appeared in the doorway, her breath short as she clutched a carefully wrapped brown paper parcel in trembling hands.

"It's for you, sir," she said, her voice barely above a whisper. "It just arrived."

Joel's stomach tightened as he reached for the parcel, its significance unwieldy even before he unwrapped it. Whatever was inside, he knew it might shatter the fragile moment they had just begun to build.

Chapter Five:
Echoes from New York

The parcel felt heavier than it should have, as though it carried more than paper. Wrapped in coarse brown butcher parchment and tied with rough twine, it had a small handwritten note tucked under the bow. The ink, partly smudged but legible, read in elegant, curling cursive:

Postmaster Joel Wolf Linker

Joel stared at it, his breath hitching. The sight of his name written so formally, so deliberately, unsettled him. Word must have spread quickly about his arrival at the mansion, which surprised him. Czernowitz wasn't large by comparison to other cities in Bucovina, but it moved with its own rhythm of chatter and knowledge, as if the streets themselves carried news from door to door.

Jetti watched him closely, her brow furrowed with concern. "What is it?" she asked, her voice calm but edged with unease. Her eyes darted to his face, reading the subtle shift in his expression as he gripped the parcel. She thought she sensed fear, though it was faint, like a shadow dancing in candlelight.

Joel didn't answer. Instead, his fingers found the twin ends of the twine, pulling them loose with a practiced motion, like untying shoe strings. The knot unraveled easily as the bow fell away. He lifted the paper, his movements careful, almost reverent, as though he already understood the importance of what lay inside.

When he saw the contents, a shudder of recognition seized him.

Neatly stacked within the parcel were letters. Dozens of them, their envelopes worn but intact, some with stamps faded from age. Each composed with familiar handwriting, addresses written with care, though marked by the desperation of their sender.

These were letters from his family in New York.

Jetti leaned closer, her hand brushing his arm lightly. "Joel?" she prompted. "What is it?"

He didn't respond immediately, his eyes scanning the envelopes as though trying to convince himself they were real. His family had fled Romania over three years ago, scattering to safety while he went to the front lines of war. On the battlefield, there had been no way for them to reach him. They had written anyway, pouring their words onto pages, sending them to his abandoned childhood home in the hope that someday he might return.

The current Postmaster, thoughtful and resourceful in ways Joel couldn't fathom, had kept the letters. Knowing the house stood empty, the old man had piled them in the general office, waiting for the day Joel might come to collect them. For over three years, the letters had sat untouched, small relics of a connection Joel thought he had lost forever.

And then, the Postmaster had heard rumors… Joel Linker was back. He was at the Finkelthal mansion, no less. The man, curious and thorough, made inquiries. When he learned of Joel's marriage to Jetti in 1914, he didn't hesitate. Carefully packing the letters into a single parcel, he entrusted them to a young errand boy, instructing him to run them to the mansion immediately.

Joel traced his fingers over the edges of the envelopes, his chest tightening as emotions he hadn't allowed himself to feel surged forward; relief, concern, grief, and the ache of years spent at war. He glanced at Jetti, who was watching him intently, her worry converting into understanding.

"These," he said finally, his voice thick with emotion. "These are from my family."

Jetti's hand rested on his, steadying him as the room seemed to close in, the force of the letters pressing down on him with of all the years they represented.

Joel held the letters in his hands, pulling the rest of the brown paper off to reveal the entire stack of envelopes. The power of their significance was almost too much to stomach. He glanced at Jetti, her steady presence grounding him in the moment.

"These… these letters… they're from my family," he said again, his voice hushed this time, as if speaking too loudly might shatter the fragile moment.

Jetti nodded. She placed her hand over his, her touch gentle but firm. "Joel," she said, her tone careful, as though she didn't want to intrude on the delicate emotions in the room. "Why don't you finish your meal, and then go to the library? You should have a little privacy to read the letters. Take the time you need."

He looked up at her, surprised by her suggestion. "Jetti, you don't have to leave," he said, though his voice lacked conviction. Part of him wanted her to stay, but another part, the one that had carried so much solitude for so long, felt an overwhelming need to face this moment alone.

Her lips curled into a confident, reassuring smile. "This is your family, Joel. Your connection to them has been waiting for years. You deserve a private space to feel whatever you need to feel." She stood, brushing a hand over her apron absentmindedly. "I'll be in the suite upstairs if you need me, just call for Anka, she will come get me. Take all the time you need."

Joel swallowed hard, his throat tightening. "Thank you," he said, his voice barely audible.

Jetti waited a moment longer, her eyes searching his face as if ensuring he was truly all right. Then, with a graceful nod, she turned and left, her footsteps padding against the wooden floor... leaving Joel alone with his letters.

Chapter Six:
Trepidation

That evening, while Joel remained tucked away with the bundle of letters... reading, rereading, his absence stretching long, Jetti moved through the house like someone tracing old steps in a familiar dream. The parcel had changed something between them, shifting the air with questions neither had dared voice. She'd left him to the solitude he clearly needed, but in doing so, she'd wandered into her own uneasy reflections. All afternoon, the memory of their earlier conversation looped through her thoughts, more for what hadn't been said than what had.

Determined to create a sense of normalcy, Jetti had intently instructed the staff to prepare their suite. She wanted everything to feel right, not just for him, but for both of them. This was meant to be their fresh start, a safe place to land after so much hardship. The suite was an attempt at offering him comfort, though in the recesses of her mind she worried it might feel like too much, too soon.

When Joel finally emerged from the library, the letters in his hands, Jetti didn't press him. She didn't ask what they said or how they had made him feel. Instead, she offered him a reassuring smile and gestured toward the staircase. "It's late," she said. "Let's go up."

The house was silent as they climbed the back narrow staircase from the kitchen, the pronounced creak of the wooden floorboards the only sound accompanying their ascent. The air felt heavy, laden with Joel's clandestine disposition. Jetti walked a bit ahead of him, her hand grazing the worn wood banister as she tried to appear composed. Joel followed, his thoughts a swirl of the letters, the memories they had unearthed, and the uncertainty of what lay ahead with Jetti.

When they reached the suite, Jetti pushed the door open and stepped aside to let him enter first. Joel hesitated on the threshold as he stepped into the room. The walls were adorned with delicate tapestries, the rugs underfoot were lush, and the dancing flicker of candlelight glinted from a large beeswax pillar on the mantle. The bed, draped in fine linens, seemed impossibly large and inviting. The sweetness of honey and smoke hovered in the air, a detail Jetti had arranged to calm his nerves, or perhaps her own.

Joel's feet faltered as he stepped inside, a wave of trepidation washing over him. The opulence was almost too much, a stark contrast to the bleakness of his past three years. The barracks, the battlefields, the desolation—they had stripped him down to his barest self. This room, this comfort, felt foreign now, a reminder of a life he had almost forgotten. And yet, it was familiar too. He had lived here before, briefly, in the earliest days of their marriage. He remembered the hurried passion of their first night together in this very room, a night that felt like a lifetime ago.

Jetti watched him carefully, her hands clasped in front of her. "It's the same as it was," she said. "I asked the staff to put it back to the way it was. I thought it might feel like... like a piece of what we had before."

Joel nodded, though his chest felt constricted. He crossed the room slowly, his fingers brushing the edge of the desk where he used to sit and watch her undress. The letters weighed heavily in his hand, a physical reminder of the people he'd left and the life he'd been unable to return to. He set them down carefully, eyeing the top envelope as if it might whisper untold secrets to him.

Jetti approached with measured steps, her presence calm and composed, though her eyes held a deep concern. She rested a hand on Joel's arm, the gesture neither pushy nor overly cautious, but simply a reminder that she was there. "You don't have to say anything," she said, her voice even and steady. "Not about the letters, not tonight. I only want you to know that whatever they hold, whatever you're carrying... you don't have to do it alone."

Joel stiffened under her touch, not out of discomfort but because the words struck closer to home than he cared to admit. He nodded, not trusting himself to speak. The thought of sharing the contents of the letters with her felt impossible—not because he didn't trust her, but because some parts of his past were too tangled to explain, too burdensome to place in her hands.

He turned to face her fully, his eyes searching hers for something he couldn't quite name. Reassurance, perhaps, or permission to remain guarded for just a while longer. She watched steadily, unflinching without expectation, and in that moment, her strength reminded him why he had admired her so deeply before the war. She wasn't asking for answers. She wasn't demanding his secrets. She was simply reminding him that she was here, no matter how long it took.

"I know," he said finally.

Jetti's lips curved into a wistful smile, and she dropped her hand back to her side, as if to give him space to process. "Good," she replied, her tone calm but not dismissive. She stepped back, her movements unhurried, as though allowing him to find his footing without feeling rushed. "This is your home now, Joel. And no matter what those letters say, that doesn't change."

Joel watched her for a moment, appreciating her restraint. It was clear she wasn't trying to push him or pry, and yet the certain assurance in her voice felt grounding. He glanced at the letters sitting on the desk, their edges illuminated by the candlelight. They seemed to nag him with the weight of everything his family took with them, tethering him to a past he wasn't ready to share, and a future he knew nothing about.

Jetti turned toward the hearth, adding another log to the low flames. The heat spread slowly through the room, a palpable tension between them. Joel let out a slow breath, his shoulders relaxing, though his thoughts remained tangled in the emotions stirred by the letters. He wasn't ready to let her in, not yet. And he wasn't sure when, or if, he ever would be.

The muted air between them stretched, not entirely comfortable, but no longer sharp or strained. It carried the energy of grief, memory, hesitation, but also something more human. Jetti didn't try to fill the space with words or touch. Instead, she simply stayed close, letting it settle between them like a fragile truce. She understood, perhaps better than he expected, that what he needed tonight was not conversation or consolation, but the steady presence of someone who wouldn't press, wouldn't push, wouldn't ask him to explain. She gave him room to breathe, even if just barely, to possibly begin again.

Chapter Seven:
Puncheon

Joel's regard drifted to Jetti, her presence both calming and unnerving. She stood near the hearth, her movements unhurried, her silhouette enhanced by the embers of the firelight. In the hours they had spent together since his arrival, he had come to believe, with certainty, that she had never strayed. He could see it in her eyes, clear and steady when they met his own. In the cadence of her words, in the way her body unconsciously leaned toward his, there was a loyalty that was unshakable. And with every sign of her faithfulness, the impact of his own guilt pressed harder on him.

The thought of touching her again stirred something deep within him, a pang that was as much emotional as it was physical. He remembered the feel of her skin, tender beneath his fingertips, the way her presence had once ignited a fire in him that was more than mere desire. This wasn't just longing, it was a yearning to rebuild the connection they had shared before the war, to bridge the chasm that time and distance had carved between them. But that yearning only magnified the shame he felt for his own transgressions.

During the war, his moments of weakness had led him into meaningless encounters; fleeting, hollow dalliances with women whose faces blurred together in his mind. They were never about love or even true passion, just a desperate attempt to escape the loneliness, the fear, the constant edge of death. Yet, every one of those moments now felt like a betrayal when he looked at Jetti. Her unwavering devotion was a sharp contrast to his own failures.

Joel's eyes roamed the room again, seeking an anchor to steady his turbulent thoughts. The canopy bed, draped in fine linens and accented by plush pillows, exuded comfort and security. Lavender lingered on the sheets, intertwining with the sweetness of the candles. It was a scene so removed from the barren trenches and the grim realities he had lived through. The suite was a testament to permanence, to wealth, to a life he wasn't sure he deserved anymore.

And yet, it also frightened him. This was different. This was sacred. The awareness of her touch, her faith in him, and the bond they had once shared made his failings feel sharper, deeper.

Joel swallowed hard, his eyes returning to Jetti as she glanced back at him. Her face, serene yet curious, was free of the burdens that haunted him. But how long would it stay that way?

The creak of the floorboards beneath her feet as she stepped closer snapped him from his thoughts. For a moment, he allowed himself to envision, that perhaps, in this room, with this woman who looked at him with trust and care, there was a chance to start anew. But the letters sitting on the desk whispered otherwise, their words a reminder that the past was never truly gone.

He looked at the massive bed again, the feather mattress was impossibly lush, almost cloud-like, with overstuffed pillows that invited rest. At either side of the bed were sheepskin rugs, their plush texture a stark contrast to the cold, hard ground he had grown accustomed to.

In the corner of the room stood a magnificent tub, its shape and size commanding attention even amid the lavish surroundings. Fashioned from a French oak puncheon barrel, it had been expertly sawed in half and polished to a soothing, inviting sheen. The water within it brimmed nearly to the edge, steam curling lazily into the dimly lit air, illuminated by the amber radiance of the fireplace. Joel's eyes rested on it, both intrigued and awed by its history and presence.

From his own background and experiences, Joel recognized the rarity of such a piece. French oak puncheon barrels were a hallmark of luxury, designed with the utmost craftsmanship and traditionally

44

reserved for aging the finest French wines. Joel's memories from before the war, and even during it, offered fleeting glimpses of barrels like these, though most of those he had encountered during the conflict had been abandoned or destroyed, their purpose forgotten amid the chaos.

This particular puncheon was different, a survivor that had been carefully brought to this place and repurposed with reverence, he thought much like himself. It's staves, bound tightly with iron hoops, displayed the unmistakable touch of a master cooper's hand. The golden oak, once smooth and unblemished, now carried the rich stains of its past life. Deep burgundy shadows and purples hinted at the exquisite wine it once held. Joel's fingertips itched to trace the grain of the wood, to feel the texture that told its own clandestine story.

Transporting such a treasure from the heart of France to Romania would have been an expensive and laborious undertaking. His thoughts wandered as he imagined the logistics: the careful packing, the journey across borders, and finally, its arrival in this sanctuary where it had been received with the same reverence that defined the Finkelthal way of life. He suspected the barrel might have been originally procured for a grand celebration, perhaps a wedding or an important family gathering, occasions that merited only the finest of European wines. He glanced around the room again, the opulence confirming his suspicions about the family's taste for the extraordinary.

At some point, the barrel had been retired from its duties as a wine vessel and transformed into the tub before him. Joel marveled at the precision required to saw the puncheon in half without compromising its integrity. The interior had been smoothed and polished, treated with hard wax and possibly linseed oil to create a satin-like finish that repelled water yet preserved the wood's natural beauty. He imagined the aroma of Burgundy wine, a sweet, heady scent within the damp humidity of the room, a sensory reminder of the barrel's storied past.

Joel's eyes held on it, his thoughts weaving between admiration and melancholy. Such a tub would not have been made alone, its other half likely resided elsewhere in the sprawling mansion, a twin to this work of art. Together, they spoke to the family's resourcefulness in reimagining something functional into an object of luxury. The care and intention behind it mirrored the ethos of the household: even the simplest things were elevated to something extraordinary.

The puncheon itself, with its grand proportions, seemed almost to beckon him. The curvature of the staves created a deep, welcoming basin, its dimensions generous enough for someone to fully submerge and lose themselves in the hot water. The darkened iron hoops framing the tub gave it a sense of sturdy elegance, reminiscent of the ribs of a great ship, while the oak's grain glowed richly in the interplay of firelight and candlelight. It was a piece that carried history within it, a witness to the lives and events it had touched.

To bathe in this vessel was to steep oneself not just in water but in legacy. Joel's thoughts wandered to Jetti, to the life they were meant to build together. The luxurious surroundings contrasted sharply with the barrenness he felt inside, and yet there was something about the tub's transformation, its journey from humble utility to opulent indulgence, that resonated with him. It was a reminder, both painful and beautiful, of what was possible if one dared to dream beyond hardship.

The fragrance of lavender soap wafted from a small milled bar on a nearby table. He could tell it was Jetti's soap, familiar and intimate. Rolled towels were placed neatly nearby, ready for use. It was clear that Jetti had thought of everything, but Joel couldn't shake the tight knot of anxiety.

"Did you want me to bathe first?" he asked, his voice low, almost hesitant.

Jetti turned to him. "I just want you to feel at ease," she said, though the longing in her voice was unmistakable. She stepped closer to him, her presence inviting and grounding.

Her words were tender, but he felt exposed, uncertain, and undeserving of her kindness. And yet, he couldn't deny the hunger in her actions, the way her hands trembled slightly as she began to unbutton her dress. Slowly, she undressed before him, letting the silky fabric fall to the floor, her body illuminated by the glow of the fire. Without breaking eye contact, she slipped gracefully into the bath, the water rippling around her.

Joel stood frozen, unsure of what to do. He watched as she leaned back in the water, her skin luminous, her hair curling at the ends from the steam. She smiled at him, patient and inviting, but he hesitated.

"Come," she said, her voice laced with both reassurance and desire.

Reluctantly, he began to undress, peeling away the layers of clothing that felt like armor. When he finally stepped into the tub, the water overflowed, spilling onto the floor. Jetti laughed, the sound pure and musical, as she stepped out and wrapped herself in a towel, drying off while he settled into the bath.

For the first time, she truly saw him, his body gaunt and skeletal, his translucent skin stretched over bones that had carried him through war. Her breath seized in her throat. She hadn't expected him to look so fragile, so unlike the strong, youthful man she remembered. The sight frightened her, but it also deepened her purpose to try to comfort him, to love him.

On the other side of the room, she had placed a straight razor, shaving soap, and a small basin of fresh water. A three-part mirror sat atop a dressing table, reflecting in the candlelight. She preferred he would use them, though she wouldn't mind his beard, it just made him look so much older than his actual years. Joel seemed to understand her wish. He bathed, shaved, and dried himself with methodical precision, as if performing a ritual that grounded him in this unfamiliar space.

The room was soundless except for the crackle of the fire and the rhythmic ticking of a clock on the mantle. Joel stood near the edge of the bed, his posture uncertain, his hands fidgeting with the towel wrapped around him as if he were unsure what to do with them. Even now, after all they had shared, Jetti could sense his discomfort. It was in the way his eyes volleyed between her and the floor, the way his bony shoulders seemed to carry a gravity heavier than the three years they had been apart.

But her longing for him was undeniable. She had waited so long for this moment, for the chance to be close to him again, to remind him of the love they had once shared. Without hesitation, she stepped toward him, her movements slow and deliberate, her eyes never leaving his. The towel draped around her slipped from her shoulders, pooling at her feet. She stood before him, unguarded and unashamed, her body illuminated by the firelight.

For a moment, Joel simply stared. He took in every detail—the elegant curve of her hips, the delicate line of her shoulders, the way her skin seemed to shine in the flitting light. She was more beautiful than he remembered, and the sight of her stirred a feeling deep within him, something he hadn't allowed himself to feel since he left. His hands twitched, but he didn't move, afraid that if he touched her, this moment might shatter like a fragile mirage.

Jetti reached out first, taking his hand in hers, her touch steady and reassuring. She guided him to the bed, her heart pounding in anticipation, though her movements were calm and composed. She lay down, her body sinking into the feather mattress, and looked up at him with a mix of tenderness and longing. A seductive smile played at her lips as she whispered, "Joel, come here."

He hesitated for only a second before joining her. His hands, roughened by years of hard labor and hardship, hovered over her skin as if afraid they might hurt her. But when he finally touched her, it was with a gentleness that took her breath away. His fingertips traced the curve of her waist, the delicate line of her collarbone, memorizing her as though she might slip away.

The tension in his muscles was pronounced. Jetti could feel it in the way his body moved, slow and cautious, as if every movement carried a reminder of the war. And yet, there was something else, a kind of devotion in the way he touched her, as though she were something sacred, something worth cherishing after all he had seen and survived.

Their bodies moved together in a rhythm that was unhurried, their intimacy less about passion and more about a deep need to reconnect. Joel's breath was blissful against her neck, his whispered apologies barely audible, though she felt each one as if it were a consolation to her soul. She ran her fingers through his hair, murmuring his name repeatedly, letting him know that he was here, that he was safe, that she was his.

The act wasn't about climax or fulfillment in the usual sense, it was about rebuilding something that had been fractured, about finding each other again in the inconspicuous spaces between grief and love. Jetti could feel his need, not just for her body, but for her presence, for the comfort and devotion he had been denied for so long. And though she didn't reach her own release, it didn't matter. This was for him.

As they lay together afterward, their breaths slowing in unison, Joel rested his head against her chest, his arm draped protectively across her. She held him close, her fingers tracing small circles on his back, grounding him in the moment. The room was noiseless once more, save for the steady beat of her heart beneath his ear, a sound he hadn't realized he'd missed so deeply.

Jetti pressed a kiss to his hair, her voice barely a whisper as she said, "You're safe now… Joel. You're home… With me."

In that moment, Jetti hoped he believed her, even if she knew it would take time for him to feel it. For now, she held him tightly, vowing to make this place, this life, something he could truly call his own.

Joel and Jetti lay entwined in each other's arms, their bodies fitting together like pieces of a fragile puzzle. The blaze of the fire cast a radiance over the room, a cocoon against the encroaching chill of winter outside. They didn't say much, but it wasn't uncomfortable, as though words might shatter the tenuous peace they'd found in the intimacy of the moment.

When the first stars began to twinkle in the inky sky, Anka slipped into the room, her steps hushed on the thick carpets. She moved efficiently, stoking the fire to keep it alive through the cold night ahead, replacing the bedpans with a practiced hand, and finally extinguishing the candles one by one. Their smoke curled upward in thin tendrils. Joel watched her from the corner of his eye, his face unreadable, as Jetti stirred but did not let go of him.

Even as the room fell into the evening, cloaked in shadows broken only by the darting movement of the fire, Joel's mind refused to settle. The loyalty of Jetti's embrace should have been a comfort, yet his thoughts wandered relentlessly. The letters, resting just a few feet away on the desk, seemed to vibrate with an unknown potential, anchoring him to a life that breathed half a world away. New York... vast, bustling, and ever-moving... loomed in his mind like a distant horizon, its relentless progress an unsettling contrast to the stillness of this moment.

Here, in the embrace of Jetti's arms, surrounded by the privileged luxury of their suite, the world outside felt impossibly far. And yet, he couldn't shake the sense that it was shifting, reshaping itself in ways neither of them could yet comprehend. The magnitude of the unknown pressed down on him, even as her steady heartbeat reminded him, for now, he was home.

Chapter Eight:
Longing

That night Joel's thoughts were far from restful. Somewhere, distant from this opulent suite, in a city he had never seen but prayed toward countless times during the war, British forces captured Jerusalem, bringing an end to four centuries of Ottoman rule. For Jews around the world, it was a moment of profound historical significance, a spark of conviction in a time steeped in despair.

But Joel's mind wasn't on Jerusalem, or the broader fate of his people. Instead, it was tethered to the letters resting on the desk, mere feet away. They felt alive, charged with invisible dominion that tugged at him even as he lay in Jetti's arms. New York... the city where his parents and sister had started anew... loomed in his thoughts like an uncharted horizon. It felt impossibly inaccessible, yet its relentless march forward seemed to echo through the room.

As Joel lay in the massive canopy bed, the luxurious silk sheets felt almost alien against his scarred, calloused skin. The ornate candlesticks glinting in the firelight, lavender in the air, even the plush sheepskin rug beneath his feet earlier, all of it seemed to mock him. He had fought tooth and nail to survive the war, to return to Czernowitz, to Jetti, but this life of wealth and comfort was not the same one he had fought for. It felt foreign, like a costume he was expected to wear, and the letters were a stark reminder of the distance between this life and the one he had left behind before the war.

Yet, as his eyes landed on Jetti, her body illuminated by the fire, his heart ached in a different way. She stirred beside him, her hand tightening slightly on his chest in her sleep. The simple gesture tugged at something deep within him—a yearning to belong, to make this life work, if only for her. She had given him so much: a place to rest, a promise of stability, a chance to rebuild.

He leaned down and kissed her forehead, though doubts gnawed at him. As her breathing steadied and the room fell into a quiet rhythm, Joel closed his eyes, but the darkness offered no peace. The letters pulsed in his mind, relentless as a low buzz, their presence impossible to ignore. His family's voices clung to him, persistent words that refused to fade, haunting inside his head like ghosts he couldn't outrun.

The next morning, Joel woke slowly to the golden beams of dawn streaming through the velvet curtains. The embers in the hearth cast a comforting feeling over the room, elevating the musk of their shared intimacy. For a moment, he allowed himself to savor the sensation, the simple luxury of waking in a bed far removed from the hard ground of the trenches.

He shifted under the sheets, his muscles sore in a way that reminded him of the intimacy they had shared the night before. He glanced to his side, where Jetti lay curled in sleep, her hair spilling across the pillow in radiant waves. Her face was serene, and her presence filled the room with a calm that eased some of the tension in his chest.

But the letters intruded again, their presence unavoidable. Joel slipped quietly from the bed, his bare feet meeting the cool sheepskin rug. He moved to the hearth, adding a few logs to the embers until the fire roared back to life. The flames made shadows dance against the ornate furnishings, but his eyes kept darting to the desk. The letters sat there, neatly stacked, waiting.

He slowly climbed back under the covers, careful not to wake her, the comfort and warmth of the mattress embraced him like a cloud. He realized, with a touch of wonder, that he'd never slept so

52

well in his life. The horrors of the war and the uncertainties of his future had been momentarily eclipsed by the simple luxury of rest, and he allowed himself to savor the sensation for just a moment longer.

Jetti was asleep beside him, an emotional sigh escaping her lips as she rolled toward him. Her hand reached out, finding his arm and pulling it around her and tucking it under the weight of her full breasts. Joel felt her desire against him, the curve of her body pressing into his chest, and her plump round buttocks.

She shifted, and he felt the unmistakable press of her desire with the small of her back against his stoic manhood. She turned her head just enough to meet his eyes, a sleepy smile gracing her lips.

Without words, they moved together, their bodies finding an easy rhythm that spoke of trust and longing. This time, their love-making was a little hurried but tender, each touch and kiss laden with a growing familiarity. Joel marveled at her passion, the way her body welcomed his as if it had always been meant for him.

Jetti held nothing back, even as she felt her own release remain just out of reach. It didn't matter. She felt his climax, his shuddering surrender, and it filled her with a profound sense of connection. She wanted to hold onto this moment, to keep him inside her, not just physically but in every possible way.

When it was over, they lay intertwined once more, their breathing entangled in the blissful intimacy of the room. Jetti closed her eyes, her heart swelling with a love so deep it nearly brought her to tears. She quickly fell back asleep into a dream state of never-ending love.

Joel held her close, his doubts and fears momentarily removed by the passion of her embrace.

He too closed his eyes, but the image of the stack of letters seared into his mind, their edges yellowed from time, the ink on the outside faded but still legible. Each envelope was a bridge to a world he had never seen, a world he hadn't even imagined, until now. The words his family had written gnawed at him, feeling heavier than any pack he had carried during the war.

Joel could almost hear his sister's voice in his head, the way she used to read aloud from her favorite novels, her tone always lilting with curiosity and meaning. He imagined his father writing them, his hand sturdy, deliberate, as though each stroke of the fountain pen carried a secret promise. And his mother's letters, filled with careful reassurances, her words wrapped in love and worry, the same way she used to wrap him in her shawl on cold winter mornings.

The thought of his father came to mind, not as a memory but as a question: what kind of man would he expect Joel to become in this new world? His mother's letters were filled with plans, her careful words nudging him toward a future of possibility. His sister described the bustling streets of New York, their potential as vast as the skyline. He could almost see it, not the ticking of his father's old watch, but the churning of factory wheels, the buzzing of electric bulbs, the pulse of a city constantly in motion. It wasn't the past he was stepping back into, it was a future rushing toward him.

The letters felt like blueprints of a life not yet lived, a road map to something unknown but vital. They were harbingers of a future he could scarcely imagine, fragments of a life waiting for him across the ocean. They spoke of a family who had found a way to move forward, who had carved out something new in a world far from the devastation he had known. They weren't reminders of what was lost, but whispers of what could be built, possibly a bridge to a life he hadn't yet dared to dream. They spoke of promises louder than any battlefield, yet carried an anchor that tugged at him with equal parts fortitude and dread.

Jetti stirred about an hour later, the promising morning filtering through the cracks between the drapes, painting the room with a flash of light. She stretched out lazily, the sheets warm and comforting against her skin. The musk of Joel clung to the linens, a reminder of his presence. She closed her eyes briefly, her heart weightless as she thought of the intimacy they had shared. Butterflies fluttered in her abdomen at the thought of his touch... the way his hands had moved over her with such tenderness, the closeness they had found after so much time apart.

Smiling, her hand drifted across the bed instinctively, reaching for him.

Her fingers met only cool, empty silk sheets.

The realization hit her like a sudden gust of wind. She sat up abruptly, her heart quickening. Her eyes darted around the room, searching for any sign of him. The clothes that had been folded over the chair were gone. The boots by the hearth... gone. The fire smoldering in the grate seemed to mock her, its orange flame doing nothing to ward off the chill creeping over her.

Her gaze snapped to the desk.

The letters were gone too.

Joel was gone.

Chapter Nine:
Shadows of Time

It had been ten days since Joel had vanished, leaving no note, no explanation...just an aching void in Jetti's heart and the cruel certainty that he would never return.

She lay motionless in her oversized bed staring at the thick canopy above, its plush feather mattress swallowing her slight frame. The linens, once crisp and fragrant with fresh lavender, were now crumpled and damp from the millions of tears that seemed to seep endlessly from her eyes. She could not bring herself to leave the cocoon of the bed, the only semblance of safety she felt in a world that had suddenly become unrecognizable. The bed that had once been a place of trust and intimacy now felt like a prison, the linens uncomfortable against her skin.

Each passing moment stretched unbearably, every tick of the clock a cruel sound that had settled over the house. The familiar chimes that once marked the rhythm of meals, of laughter, of footsteps down the hall—now they only reminded Jetti that she was alone.

The rooms that had once pulsed with life and motion felt hollow, their stillness deafening. The brush of her skirts against the floor, the creak of the stairs, even the hushed closing of the door—all of it felt too loud against the absence she carried in her chest. Her days folded into nights like a shroud, and time lost its shape, melting into one long ache.

This pain... this kind of anguish... was far worse than the years she had waited during the war. Then, at least, she had purpose. She had courageousness. She had imagined Joel riding trains across Europe, imagined him reading her letters by a lantern. There had been fear, of course, but it was wrapped in love and the belief that he would come home to her. And he had. Bruised and changed, but he had come back.

But this... this desolate vanishing, was different. He hadn't disappeared into war this time. He had walked away. Left with no explanation, no letter, no goodbye. And that kind of abandonment didn't wound like a bullet; it poisoned slowly, seeping into the corners of her soul, into the way she stirred her tea or tied back her hair.

She found herself returning to the vision of him in the kitchen when he first showed up, his hand placed firmly on hers, his eyes searching... but for what, she hadn't known. And now she feared she never would.

That unknown, that hollow space where answers should have been, hurt more than his absence of those war years ever had. Because this time, he chose to leave.

And she had to learn how to stay.

She had not eaten properly in what felt like weeks; the few bites of bread she forced herself to take were only to stave off the unbearable dizziness that came with starvation. Even then, the bread tasted like dust, its texture dry and unyielding, crumbling in her mouth without offering solace. Food, once a source of joy and connection during lively family meals, had become meaningless. It brought no comfort, no energy, only a hollow reminder of her isolation.

Anka, her ever-dutiful young maid, came daily to tend to her mistress in ways that no longer felt routine but necessary for survival. She soundlessly emptied the bed pans, the indignity of which Jetti barely registered, and stoked the fire with logs to keep the chill at bay. The enchanting embers in the hearth seemed out of place in the cold, lifeless room. Anka stayed longer sometimes, her hands smoothing the edges of blankets or rearranging the books Jetti had abandoned. Her presence was a thin thread of humanity in the void, but Jetti could not bring herself to acknowledge it. She lay unmoving, her back to the room, staring at the jumpy shadows cast by the flames on the walls.

Occasionally, she could hear muted voices through the oak door. Her oldest brother Aaron, her sisters, and some of the house staff would come to Anka and inquire about her well-being. Their concern carried on hesitant whispers, filtering through the thick wood like unwelcome sirens. Jetti refused to see any of them. She sent Anka to shoo them away, her orders brief and cold. The thought of their pitying glances and well-meaning platitudes made her stomach turn. She knew what they were thinking, speculating about why Joel had left, wondering if she had somehow driven him away. She could hear it in their voices even if they didn't say it aloud. The value of their perceived judgment only deepened her shame.

Her grief was a relentless tide, pulling her further from the world with every wave. She felt like a ghost haunting her own life, tethered to a reality she no longer wanted to face. Even the firelight, bouncing cheerfully, seemed to mock her misery.

Anka's attempts to coax her into bathing or taking tea were met with disregard. The maid's gentle "Please… just a sip, Mrs. Jetti," or "Let me brush your hair, just for a moment" only amplified Jetti's despair. Each act of care felt like a spotlight on her unraveling, a reminder of how far she had fallen. Anka's compassion, though genuine, felt like an intrusion, a sharp contrast to the emptiness she clung to.

Jetti could not face the world outside her door, nor could she face herself. Each day spent in the bed felt like surrender, and yet she lacked the ability or will to fight.

The bath, once a centerpiece of indulgence and self-care, now loomed in the corner like a forgotten relic of another life. Its polished oak curves glimmered faintly in the dim light, a haunting reminder of the joy it had once brought her. How she had loved sinking into its depth, the water laced with oils and flower petals, the steam curling around her as if to shield her from the world. Now, the thought of filling it, of undressing and stepping into its embrace, felt like scaling an impossible mountain. It wasn't just the effort it required; it was the confrontation it demanded, with her body, her reflection, her reality.

She couldn't even bear to face the mirror that hung above the washstand, its gilded frame mocking her disarray. She knew without looking what she would see: a hollow-eyed shadow of the woman she once was. Her cheeks, once rosy and full, would be gaunt and pale. Her lips, now cracked and dry, no longer smiled with the confidence they once held. Her eyes, rimmed with shadows and raw from days of relentless tears, seemed hollow, as if her grief had drained their brilliance. They carried the deafening ache of someone bearing sorrow too painful to voice, a truth she wasn't yet ready to acknowledge.

Her hair, once her crowning glory, had become an unmanageable tangle. The blonde locks that Joel once twirled around his fingers were now matted at the back of her head, knotted beyond recognition. Each strand seemed to cling to another in defiance, forming a nest of neglect that mirrored her inner turmoil. The floral scent that once clung to her pillow was now overpowered by the stale odor of her unwashed skin.

The room itself had begun to decay alongside her. The roses in the vase on her bedside table, once vibrant and fragrant, had withered dry, their petals curling inward as if retreating from the air. Their once-sweet perfume dissapated, ruined by the stagnant smell of the unventilated space. Even the winter sunlight streaming through the curtains seemed muted, unable to pierce the armor of her grief. Each fading rose, each crumbling petal, was a cruel reminder of the passage of time, a time she felt utterly powerless to reclaim.

Jetti's thoughts were a storm she could not escape, an endless whirlpool of questions and doubts that dragged her deeper with every passing moment. Each thought struck like a hammer, relentless in its precision. What had she done to drive Joel away?

Was there something in her demeanor, in her words, that had pushed him to abandon her? She replayed their last conversations in her mind, dissecting every phrase, every nuance, searching for any trace of discontent. But the answers eluded her, slipping through her fingers like grains of sand.

Her memories, once a source of comfort, now betrayed her. She thought of the nights they spent wrapped in each other's arms before he went away to war, their whispered confessions, their shared dreams. Had it all been a facade? Had he ever truly loved her, or had she built their life together on a foundation of illusions?

She pictured his face, the way his eyes had crinkled when he smiled, the love in his touch... and then the cold emptiness of waking up alone. Her love, which she had once thought a sanctuary, now felt like a prison, its walls closing in around her.

Was it her fault? The question gnawed at her, cruel and insistent. Had her love suffocated him, clinging too tightly to a man who needed freedom? She scrutinized every moment they had shared, every gesture she had made. The thought that she might have been the architect of her own heartbreak sent a fresh wave of anguish crashing over her.

The guilt was unbearable, an undertow tide that threatened to drown her. It pressed against her chest like a massive boulder, a crushing force that left her gasping for air. She could feel it in the pit of her stomach, in the ache of her muscles, in the throbbing in her temples. It was a pain unlike any she had known, searing and all-consuming. She tried to push it away, but it was unyielding, relentless, a shadow that refused to be banished.

Her mind offered no respite, no escape from the torment. Every path of thought led her back to the same unbearable question: why?

Chapter Ten:
Dowry Chest

Jetti sauntered to the corner of the room where the dowry chest sat, an elegant and imposing sentinel of her shattered dreams. The dark walnut wood gleamed in the morning light slipping through the retreating clouds, its intricate patterns of ivory and mother-of-pearl catching and reflecting the glowing rays of sun. It was a masterpiece, crafted years earlier at her father Jacob's request, fashioned by one of Vienna's finest hands. Though not built expressly for her, time had marked it as hers, a chest that seemed always destined to cradle the treasures of her womanhood. She had once been proud of it, taking solace in its presence as a tangible proof of the life she had worked so hard to build, a life that had seemed full of promise and security.

In the early days after Joel's departure, the chest had been a strange comfort. She would sit before it, letting her fingers trace the cool, polished surface, reassuring herself that its contents were untouched. That he had taken nothing seemed to her, at first, a sign that he had not betrayed her completely. But as the days turned to weeks, the chest began to change in her eyes. No longer a comfort, it became an accuser, its delicate lid holding secrets she could not face. Each treasure inside, the strands of pearls like drops of moonlight, the silver candlesticks that shone even in dim shadows, the vibrant gemstones her brother Milton cut with precision tucked into velvet pouches, mocked her with their permanence. What once symbolized intent and a shared future now seemed to carry her failure, their beauty a cruel reminder of everything that had slipped away.

She remembered kneeling before the chest on their wedding night over three years ago, her hands trembling with excitement as she showed Joel its contents. She had carefully explained the significance of each piece: her grandmother's sterling silver candlesticks, polished and engraved with delicate patterns; the pearls she had worn that very day, their gilded clasp set with a radiant yellow diamond; the leather purses filled with gold coins, meant to build a foundation for their life together. Joel's smile had been discerning, but also amused, and now she wondered, had he been laughing at her even then? Had he already been planning his escape, even as she shared her family's legacy and her deepest desires?

Jetti knelt before the chest once more, her trembling hands hovering over the latch. Inside were relics of a promise now broken, each item imbued with history and meaning, yet hollowed out by Joel's absence. Her heart sank when she realized the chest was untouched. He hadn't taken a single thing. If he had, she might have clung to the notion that he intended to use the treasures to build a future for them both in New York. But this? This was abandonment in its purest, cruelest form. No note, no whispered farewell, no message left with the staff. Just an empty bed, a hollow ache in her chest, and a beautiful box filled with treasures that now felt like ashes in her hands.

He had taken her love, her trust, her dreams of a shared future, and left her with nothing but this exquisite chest, a cruel relic of a union that had crumbled before it even began.

Jetti drew her knees to her chest as fresh tears spilled freely down her cheeks. The dowry, meant to be a lifeline, a symbol of stability, now stood as a mocking reminder of all she had lost. She was a married woman in name alone, her husband vanished without a word, leaving her to face the world and herself with nothing but an unbearable emptiness no riches could ever fill. The chest sat untouched and unopened, its treasures locked away like the future she had once believed was hers. To lift its lid would be like tearing open fresh wounds, and Jetti knew she would not survive the avalanche of sorrow it would unleash.

Chapter Eleven:
Heart Ache

The silence of the mansion clung to Jetti like a winter cloak, stifling and merciless. She longed for Joel's presence, the sound of his voice, the steady rhythm of his footsteps filling the empty hallways. Instead, all she heard was the rustle of the wind outside and the irregular patter of snow against the shuttered windows. The world beyond the mansion felt impossibly far away, a distant reality she no longer belonged to.

Occasionally, muffled voices drifted up from downstairs. The staff speaking in hushed tones, their words indistinct but padded with curiosity and speculation. Jetti didn't need to hear them clearly to know what they were saying. She imagined their pitying glances, their whispered conversations about Joel's sudden disappearance and what it meant for her. The thought of their judgment filled her with an aching shame, sharp and bitter, even though she tried to ignore it.

Her brothers and sisters had tried to reach her, knocking with great care on the door of her suite, their voices sedate and hesitant. "Jetti, please," Aaron had said, his tone laced with worry. "Just let us in." Another knock, more insistent this time, came from Nurit, who always spoke too fast when she was worried. "We just want to talk, Jetti. You don't have to be alone."

But she had refused them all, her voice barely a whisper as she told them to leave. The sound of their retreating footsteps only deepened her pain, their presence gone as quickly as they had come.

Even their attempts to reach her felt like intrusions, breaking the fragile stillness she had wrapped around herself like armor.

Yet that stillness offered no comfort. It was suffocating, filled with muted words and unanswered questions.

By the third week, her despair solidified into a cold, inescapable certainty: Joel was not coming back. The realization pierced her like the edge of a finely honed blade, sharp and unrelenting. And yet, within the pain, a strange clarity emerged. There was no point in hoping anymore, no use in waiting. He was gone. She was alone. She would remain so.

Even with this knowledge, she found herself unable to move. Her body felt leaden, as though the bed had become an anchor. Rising seemed impossible, an act of defiance against the crushing pressure of her grief.

Anka was determined and finally reached the end of her patience. She stormed into the room one morning, holding a tray of food and a pitcher of tepid water. The sight of Jetti, pale and gaunt, her once luminous skin now dull and lifeless, ignited a fire of worry in her chest. The woman she had cared for like a sister was wasting away before her eyes, the vibrant life drained from her body. The maid set the tray down with a forceful clatter that cut through the oppression.

"You must eat something, miss," she demanded, her tone unyielding but laced with genuine concern. "You'll starve yourself to death, and for what? He is not here, but you are. You must live."

Jetti's hollow eyes shifted toward her but gave no acknowledgment. It was as though her body remained present, but her soul had retreated to some unreachable place. Anka loudly sighed, lifting a fresh pastry from the tray. It was golden and flaky, filled with sour cherry preserves and a hint of rosewater, a recipe meant to bring comfort and sweetness. She pressed it into Jetti's hand. "Just one bite," she urged. "For me."

Reluctantly, Jetti obeyed, her fingers trembling as she raised the pastry to her lips. The first bite felt like chewing stone and sand, the tartness of the cherries turning bitter on her tongue. It reminded her too much of Joel, of the honeyed words he once whispered to her the day he came back. *'I'll never leave you again.'* The memory lodged in her throat, choking her as if they were shards of glass. She forced herself to swallow, each bite heavier than the last, until the pastry was gone, leaving her with a hollow ache that only deepened her pain.

The maid's sharp eyes heartbroken as she watched Jetti struggle. "There now," she murmured, brushing crumbs from her lap. "You've eaten, and that's a start. But this will not do. You cannot stay like this."

Anka set the tray of food aside with an amplified sigh, her stern expression softening as she looked at Jetti. "You need a bath, my lady," she said lovingly. "It's been far too long."

Jetti didn't argue. She simply stared at the far corner of the room, with desolate surrender. Anka left without another word, summoning the staff to begin the slow process of filling the tub. One by one, they carried in overflowing basins of scalding water, the rising steam spreading through the room like a balm against its chill. The deep puncheon barrel slowly filled.

When it was almost ready, Anka returned, carrying the last basin of water with a steady grip, her expression a mixture of duty and unwavering compassion. She stood before Jetti, her movements deft but unhurried, each gesture imbued with care. The faint scent of a fresh bar of milled soap rose from the water, but it did little to soothe the somber atmosphere of the room.

Anka's hands moved with practiced precision, unfastening the buttons of Jetti's gown one by one. The fabric, once elegant and perfectly tailored, now fraying, hung loosely on Jetti's frame, as if even it had given up trying to hold her together. When the last button came undone, Anka helped her stand. The motion was slow and awkward. Jetti's body stiffened as though every joint protested the simple act of rising. The gown slipped from her shoulders, cascading to the floor, revealing the extent of her fragility.

Jetti's skin, once vibrant with health and flushed was now pallid, stretched thin over the delicate bones of her shoulders and ribs. An angry, raw patch of skin marred her lower back, a bed sore that burned with every feeble movement. The edges were darkened, the center a raw red, and Anka's breath hitched briefly at the sight. It was the result of too many days spent lying in bed, her grief pinning her to the mattress as effectively as a ballast stone.

Every step Jetti took was slow and mechanical, her movements devoid of vitality, as though she were a marionette pulled along by Anka's steady strings. Her feet shuffled on the cold floor, the muscles in her legs trembling with the effort. Each tug of her body against the air sent a fresh wave of pain radiating from the sore on her back, making her wince with every subtle shift.

Anka's touch was tender, yet Jetti flinched as though it hurt all the same. She bit her lip, her breath shallow, a stark reminder of how much her body had betrayed her. Grief had drained her not just emotionally but physically, leaving behind a shell that barely seemed capable of holding her upright. Anka, ever patient, adjusted her hold, her hands steady yet careful, as though holding onto something as delicate as spun glass.

Every motion felt like an ordeal, every stretch of her skin a fresh reminder of how deeply sorrow had seeped into her very being.

With a tenacious grip, Anka helped her into the water. The heat enveloped Jetti's frail body, and for a moment, she tensed, as though the sensation was too foreign to comprehend. Her thin frame sank into the tub, and Anka's heart ached at how much weight she had lost. It was as though grief had not only aged her but stolen something essential.

Anka picked up the bar of soap and a freshly laundered cloth, and worked it into a lather. It was the same soap Joel had favored, and its aroma stirred something in Jetti, a reminder of an evening filled with passion and laughter, the night before he vanished. The ache in her chest tightened, but it was different now, less sharp, more like a hot ember, glowing deeply in the shadowed recesses of her heart.

The cloth moved over her skin, the intensity shocking after days spent wrapped in cold neglect. Jetti closed her eyes, allowing herself to feel it, the small comfort of being cared for, of being reminded that she was still here, still alive.

Anka worked diligently, her hands steady as they washed away the grime and despair. With each careful stroke, it was as though she were peeling away a layer of sorrow, revealing something fragile but unbroken beneath. When she was done, she wrapped Jetti in a thick linen robe, its fabric downy against her newly cleansed skin.

Sitting Jetti before the mirror, Anka combed through her fine, tangled hair. The knots resisted at first, stubborn as the turmoil Jetti carried inside her, but Anka persisted. Her fingers worked with steady determination, weaving the strands into smooth, shining order. When the last tangle was gone, she braided Jetti's hair, the pattern simple but elegant, a statement of care.

As Anka tied the end of the braid with an aqua ribbon, she looked at Jetti's reflection in the mirror. For the first time in weeks, there was a hint of life in her eyes, faded but unmistakable. "There now," Anka said, her voice filled with abundance. "You'll feel better tomorrow, my lady. You'll see. One day at a time."

Anka carefully selected a fresh gown from the armoire, her fingers grazing the silky, lightweight fabric. It was a pale cornflower blue, simple but elegant, chosen as much for its gentleness against Jetti's skin as for its beauty. She unfurled the gown with care, the material flowing like water over her hands. With practiced movements, Anka eased it over Jetti's head, ensuring it didn't tug or press against the tender, angry sore on her back. The fabric of the gown settled over her frail frame, clinging to her body, its touch as unobstructed as a whisper, and though it couldn't erase the emotional pain, it offered a semblance of comfort.

Satisfied that she had done all she could for now, Anka guided Jetti to a chair by the window. The winter luminescence spilled through the frosted panes, pale and soothing, casting parallel patterns on the floor.

Beyond the glass, the gardens stretched out, stark and frozen under winter's unyielding grip. The hedges and fountains, once vibrant with life, were buried beneath a pristine blanket of snow. Even in its stillness, the landscape held a quiet beauty, a reminder of the seasons' rhythm.

"Look," Anka said, tranquil as though speaking too loudly might shatter the fragile moment. "The world is out there, waiting for you." Her hand gripping Jetti's shoulder for a moment before she moved to retrieve a small book from a nearby shelf.

She placed the leather volume in Jetti's lap, its edges worn by years of use. "Poems," Anka explained. "Read, if you can. Or just hold it. Sometimes, even the smallest bit of imagination can help."

Jetti didn't open the book. Instead, her fingers moved absently over the embossed lettering on its cover, tracing the grooves with a listless precision. The density of it was both grounding and oppressive, a tether to a world she wasn't sure she could reenter. Her view fell to her hands, thin and pale against the dark leather, as if they belonged to someone else.

Anka knelt beside her, smoothing the folds of Jetti's gown with practiced care. The gesture was as much an act of comfort as practicality, a reassurance that she wasn't alone. "You're stronger than you believe, miss," Anka said, her voice steady but laced with uneasy conviction. "But you have to take that first step Jetti, for yourself, if for no one else."

The words hung in the air as the firelight danced on her face, illuminating the sheen of tears welling in her eyes. The ache in her chest remained, vast and unbearable, an emptiness she had never known before. Yet, as Anka's steady hands rested over her own, something stirred within her.

It wasn't confidence, but a whisper of something close, a fragile thread of possibility. And in the unrelenting comfort of Anka's presence, Jetti felt the first shift of optimism, however small, that perhaps one day she might take that step forward.

Chapter Twelve:
Whispers of Chai

The New Year loomed just days away, brimming with anticipation and promise. For many in Romania, it was a symbol of renewal, a fresh chapter waiting to be written after years of despair. The Czernowitz streets, once somber under the weight of fear, now hummed with whispers, a subdued undercurrent of speculation and longing. Could it be true? Could the Great War, which had stolen so much and so many, truly be drawing to a close? The rumors rippled like the first notes of a forgotten melody, fragile yet irresistible, carrying with them the possibility of life resuming its rightful course.

For the Jewish community, 1918 carried an even deeper resonance. The year's numerical symbolism, tied to 'Chai', the Hebrew word for the number eighteen and the word for life, held profound meaning. 'Chai' wasn't just a word; it was a prayer, a declaration of the future, a belief in survival against all odds. To a people who had endured so much, the connection was both a comfort and a challenge, a reminder that life could endure even in the face of unimaginable hardship. For many, this sacred connection infused the coming year with anticipation that went beyond mere optimism; it was a lifeline, a sacred promise of reinvention and freedom.

And yet, the air in Czernowitz remained uncertain, caught between the past and the future. The scars of war were fresh, many families fractured, lives lost, dreams shattered. Even as whispers of peace grew louder, they were met with equal measures of skepticism. The city held its breath, not yet daring to believe that such a monumental shift could be within reach. The New Year stood on the horizon like a question mark, its promises tantalizing but untested, its possibilities both exhilarating and terrifying.

Yet within the mansion, the atmosphere was starkly different. Silence hung in the air, broken only by the melodies of the grand hall clock, each chime a merciless reminder of time slipping away. The usual bustle of preparation for the New Year's feast had dulled to a distant murmur with the muted clatter of pots, the clanging of maids polishing silver. These were sounds that once brought comfort, but now felt futile, swallowed by the authority of Jetti's despair. The house, typically alive with inspiration and movement, mirrored her grief. Shadows clung stubbornly to the corners, stretching across the walls like ghostly sentinels to her sorrow. Even the flames in the hearth flickered weakly, dim and uncertain, as if they, too, had grown weary of fighting her suffocating gloom.

Jetti sat by the window, her thin figure draped in a shawl that hung loosely over her shoulders. The frosted glass reflected her gaunt face, pale as the snow that coated the gardens outside. Beyond the windowpanes, the world was a pristine expanse of white, the kind of winter landscape that should inspire poetry or emotion in the heart. But to Jetti, it was a cruel mockery, a blank canvas that offered no comfort. The snow seemed endless, a cold abyss that mirrored the void within her. Where others might see the promise of spring lying dormant beneath winter's frost, Jetti saw only lifelessness.

The number 18 was the promise of 'Chai', of life itself, that felt like a taunt. What did life mean when the person who had been her future and her love, had vanished without a trace? The year ahead stretched out before her like a barren road, its milestones meaningless without Joel by her side. She thought of the festive table that would soon be set in the dining room, her brothers and sisters gathering with their husbands and wives to toast the year to come. Jetti could already picture their smiling faces, the clink of glasses filled with wine, the laughter that would carry through the halls. She imagined their well-meaning attempts to coax her into the celebration, their promising eyes urging her to join in the cheer.

And yet, something seemed to urge her forward, its walls whispering of past New Year's celebrations. She thought of joyful gatherings, music spilling from the piano in the drawing room, and the clatter of carriages arriving at the grand entrance. The feelings of those memories was distant but not entirely unreachable, as if the mansion itself refused to let despair have the final word. As the clock struck another hour, Jetti remained in her suite, her heart caught between her grief and the faint, elusive promise of 'Chai'.

From the rooms below, cheerful sounds of activity floated up to Jetti's suite. The bursts of laughter and lively chatter as the staff went about their preparations, their voices carrying shared jokes and stories. It was as though they had made a pact to infuse the mansion with energy and joy, refusing to let sorrow claim every corner.

At the center of it all was Anka, her sharp eyes and attention to details orchestrating the household like a maestro guiding a symphony. She moved with brisk precision, her commands efficient yet laced with compassion, inspiring the staff to carry on despite her age.

She oversaw every detail, ensuring the silver gleamed like moonlight and the fine linens were pressed to perfection before being draped over the dining table with care. The centerpiece, a simple yet elegant arrangement of evergreen boughs and crimson winter berries, was placed with deliberate precision, its vibrant hues a bold contrast to the muted atmosphere. In the kitchen, the cook worked tirelessly, the comforting aromas of freshly baked sweets and savory dishes wafting lovingly through the halls, offering a small semblance of normalcy.

And yet, despite her determination, Anka's eyes often drew toward the staircase leading to Jetti's suite, her thoughts clouded with worry. The reticence from above was deafening, a sound louder than any clamor she had ever known. She pressed on, her movements purposeful, as though willing the house to hold its breath and wait for Jetti to rejoin the world below.

Chapter Thirteen:
Shadow of Hope

Upstairs, Jetti had drifted further into her solitude as the day wore on. She remained curled up in the oversized chair by the window, a ghostly figure dwarfed by the high back and plush arms. Her body, fragile and worn, seemed to fold in on itself as if retreating from the world. The book of poems Anka had placed in her lap days ago remained closed, its leather cover uncreased and barely touched. The braided strands of her straw-toned hair, carefully woven by Anka's skilled hands, fell loosely over her shoulders, a strange juxtaposition to the stark hollows of her cheeks and the sunken void of her eyes.

The pain that clung to Jetti was tangible, an oppressive force that filled the room like a dense fog. The pungent odor from her neglected linens embracing the cold sharp air that crept through the chinks in the old windows. The world outside sparkled with fresh snow beneath the pale sun, a picture of vitality, while inside, Jetti seemed a woman frozen in time.

Anka continued to try to stir some semblance of life into her mistress. The thought of leaving Jetti to waste away, untouched by the symbolism of the year to come, was unbearable.

After stoking the fire to chase away the chill in the room, Anka approached Jetti's chair, her tone rich with affection.

"My lady," she began, kneeling beside Jetti and clasping her hands, "you cannot let this New Year pass as if it means nothing. You must come downstairs, if only for an hour. Your family is waiting for you. "Chai' that is what this year is meant to bring. You cannot ignore it."

Jetti turned her head slowly, her eyes glassy and unfocused. Anka pressed on, her voice gaining determination. "Your brothers and sisters, they need you. We all do. You are right here, my lady. There is life in you yet, though you may not feel it now."

The words hung in the air, a delicate balance of plea and challenge. Jetti's lips parted a little bit, as if she might respond, but no sound emerged. Her fingers tightened around Anka's for a fleeting moment before falling slack again, her disposition drifting past her maid to the window. Outside, sunlight struck the snow, turning it into a shimmering expanse of glistening crystal, each facet catching the flakes like a million tiny reminders of the life that continued beyond the confines of her grief.

Something stirred in Jetti's chest, not quite hope, but the smallest bit of awareness. It was fragile and fleeting, an acknowledgment that the world outside, however broken, continued to move. The symbolism of the New Year brushed against her sorrow like a tentative hand, pressing at the edges of her despair, waiting for her to decide if she would let it in.

Her will shifted back to Anka, their eyes meeting for the briefest moment. Jetti's lips parted again, but the words she sought remained elusive. Instead, a single tear slid down her cheek like a bead of glass before falling into the folds of her gown.

Anka knelt before her, her hands enveloped Jetti's own. Her voice trembled with quiet intensity. "You've endured more than anyone should ever have to," she said, her eyes glistening. "But you are here, Jetti." She reminded her again. "Life hasn't let go of you, even if you can't feel its hold just yet."

The mention of life had sparked something fragile within Jetti, like the barest ember struggling against an overwhelming tide of ash. It began with a flashback, one she hadn't dared to let surface in the haze of her sorrow. She thought of her parents, their laughter intertwined as they danced in the drawing room after dinner, her father twirling her mother with a joy so vivid it seemed impossible that such love could have been destroyed so young. Their love, radiant and enduring, had shaped her world, grounding her siblings in a home filled with devotion and tradition.

Her mind drifted further, to the image of her grandmother, her hands aged but steady as she lit the Shabbat candles each Friday evening. The flames had always mesmerized Jetti as a child, their flickers casting a sacred shimmer across the room. Her grandmother's voice reciting the blessings, echoed quietly in her ears. Those very candlesticks now sat in her dowry chest, untouched and waiting, relics of a heritage that seemed impossibly distant but undeniably hers.

Another image arose, unbidden but insistent: a holiday meal from years ago. The dining table was crowded with family, its surface laden with platters of fragrant dishes, the air alive with laughter and conversation. And Joel... she remembered Joel. He sat across from her, his dark blue eyes crinkling with amusement as he teased her about a story she had shared. The way he smiled at her then, kind and unguarded, had made her heart flutter. She could almost hear his laughter again, feel the brief touch of his hand brushing hers as he passed her a glass of wine.

The memories brought more tears, hot and unrelenting, but they carried with them something other than pain. They reminded her that she was tethered to this world, to this family, to these people. She was bound by threads of love and memory that reached back through generations, threads that refused to fray even in the face of her despair.

Anka continued. "Come to the table, if only for a moment. Sit with your family. Eat something, even if it's just a piece of bread. Let this year begin with a breath of newness."

Jetti hesitated, her hands gripping the arms of the chair as though they were her only anchor. Slowly, painfully, she nodded. It wasn't much, but it was a step; a small, trembling acknowledgment that she could not let herself vanish completely, not yet.

And as the Finkelthals prepared to mark the arrival of 1918, with its promise of life and renewal, the shadow of optimism began to take root in Jetti's heart, fragile and uncertain, but present nonetheless.

Chapter Fourteen:
New Years Eve

Jetti stood before the mirror in her suite, the dimming of late afternoon casting a paleness on her reflection. Anka fussed around her, carefully adjusting the lace collar of the gown they had chosen together. The deep sapphire fabric shimmered subtly as Jetti moved, its rich color chosen to bring out the brightness of her sea blue eyes... eyes that had been dulled by weeks of tears. Jetti smoothed the gown with trembling hands, her fingers brushing the intricate beadwork that adorned the loose fitting bodice. She felt a small surge of excitement, though it was accompanied by an undercurrent of trepidation.

"You look beautiful, my lady," Anka said, stepping back to admire her work. The maid had braided Jetti's freshly cleaned hair with care, weaving a thin strand of pearls through the plaits before pinning it into a loose bun on the back of her head. The effect was simple yet elegant, a perfect complement to the gown. Jetti gave a small nod, unable to find her voice, and turned toward the door.

As they stepped into the hallway, Jetti paused, looking over at the narrow, wooden back staircase she had so often relied on. Its worn steps had always been a covert refuge, a familiar path that offered comfort and discretion. But tonight was different. Tonight, she turned her eyes toward the grand marble staircase, its gleaming surface reflecting the brilliant crystal of the chandeliers. The choice felt substantial, almost symbolic, as though taking those steps meant acknowledging her place in the world once more, a decision both daunting and monumental.

The sound of her heels against the polished floor click-clacked in the hallway as she made her way toward the front of the mansion. The staircase loomed before her, its sweeping curves and gleaming banisters a testament to the wealth and institution of her family. Anka gave her an encouraging smile, stepping back as Jetti placed a tentative hand on the rail. She drew a deep breath and began her descent.

Each step felt like an act of courage, the rustle of her gown accompanying her like a whispered anthem. The chandelier above sparkled, its crystal prisms refracting across the marble, and for a moment, Jetti felt almost regal. She knew her family was waiting in the dining room below, their laughter and voices carrying distinctly through the cavernous halls. Excitement and trepidation battled within her as she reached the final step, pausing to steady herself before crossing the threshold.

The dining room was a spectacle of celebration and festivity, the candlelight casting an amber sheen over the polished silver and fine lace tablecloth with matching napkins. The air was filled with the mingling aromas of roasted meats and spiced pastries, a feast prepared with care by the staff under Anka's watchful eye. Jetti stepped into the room, and for a moment, the chatter paused as heads turned toward her, she could tell they were surprised to see her.

"Jetti," her eldest brother Aaron said, rising from his seat with a wide smile. "You've joined us." His voice carried a mixture of surprise and relief, and soon the others followed his lead, welcoming her with kind words and happy smiles. Jetti nodded, murmuring greetings as she took her seat next to him and his wife, Esther.

Aaron, ever the family's anchor, was in his element, regaling the table with stories from his work as a banker and loan merchant. His sharp features softened when he spoke of the future, of rebuilding and thriving, speculating the war's end. Esther sat beside him, her calm presence a steadying force as she laughed to herself behind her delicate hands at his anecdotes.

Jetti, however, struggled to feel at ease. She clasped her hands tightly in her lap, watching over the table as her siblings talked and laughed around her. Nurit and Joseph, her husband, shared a playful exchange, their words drawing laughter from Nina and her neighbor-turned-husband, Henry. Across the table, Abraham, who everyone called Avi, and Ruth sat close, their riveting conversation punctuated by joyous smiles.

Though surrounded by family, Jetti felt the ache of Joel's absence more keenly than ever. The candlelight and metallic clinking of silverware seemed distant, muted by the storm of emotions within her. She forced a smile when her brother Avi caught her eye, but the effort felt insincere. The dining room, with all its stimulation and love, was a stark contrast to the emptiness she felt inside.

Aaron raised his glass, his voice powerful and steady as he toasted to the New Year. "To life," he declared, his words resonating deeply with the family's shared anticipation for the days to come. The glasses clanged in a harmonious chorus, their sound ringing out like a benediction. But for Jetti, the toast felt like a cruel irony.

As the evening wore on, Jetti sat still, her hands trembling as she listened to the conversations swirling around her. The joy and camaderie of her family exuded happiness, yet it only deepened her sense of inadequacy. She wondered if she could ever find her place among them again, if the new year would bring her anything more than the ghosts of what could have been.

Across the table, her sister Nurit beamed, her hand resting on Joseph's arm. Joseph, a lawyer with an air of authority, listened intently to Aaron's tales, occasionally interjecting with his own insights.

Next to Aaron and Esther, Nina, Jetti's other sister, was seated beside her husband Henry Singer. The Singer family owned the mansion next door, and their arranged marriage solidified the connection between their families. Henry's booming laugh filled the room, a contrast to Nina's serious demeanor.

Her other brothers sat together at the far end of the table, their camaraderie a bright, unfiltered energy that contrasted with the subdued conversations of their older siblings. Benjamin, a clockmaker, had always been meticulous and sharp-minded, traits inherited from a great-uncle who had once been renowned throughout Czernowitz for his exquisite craftsmanship. With a flourishing business now under his care, Benjamin often carried an air of quiet focus, but tonight, his eyes sparkled with rare levity. He regaled the two brothers, Alan and Milton, each only a year apart, with a story about a peculiar customer who had insisted on a clock that chimed in the exact cadence of her favorite waltz. His impersonation of the woman's imperious tone sent his brothers into fits of laughter.

Alan, who managed the family's long-standing haberdashery and textile plant, leaned back in his chair, shaking his head with mock exasperation. His wiry frame and perpetually ink-stained fingers marked him as a man of industry, someone who had spent countless hours poring over fabric samples and ledgers. Yet tonight, his usual stoicism was replaced by a boyish grin. "And did you tell her that the waltz clock would cost her double?" he quipped, earning a round of chuckles from the table.

Milton, the most creative of the three, had a certain flair that set him apart. As a goldsmith and lapidarist, he was the artist of the family, the creator of intricate designs that adorned the necks, fingers and wrists of Czernowitz's elite. Tonight, he wore one of his own creations; a tiepin shaped like a starburst, its delicate gold filigree, and brilliant stones catching the candlelight. "Forget the waltz," Milton chimed in, his voice carrying a playful lilt."What we need is a clock that belts out opera...maybe then, Alan will actually wake up on time for his morning deliveries, instead of snoozing through the rooster's entire shift!"

Their laughter spilled across the table an unrestrained sound that obscured the edges of the evening. The years of hardship, the ongoing war, the uncertainty seemed, for a moment, to fade into the background. Benjamin reached for his wine glass, his fingers delicately holding on the stem as he surveyed his brothers with a grin. "You know," he said, his voice subdued, "we've come a long way. Sometimes I think of the workshop, the way it smelled of varnish and metal shavings when we were boys, and I can hardly believe we're here now."

Alan nodded, his expression turning thoughtful. "And the looms in the back of the textile plant," he added. "Papa used to let us watch the weavers for hours, though he always warned us not to touch the warp threads."

Milton raised his glass with a dramatic flourish, a mischievous smile playing on his lips. "To Father's patience… and to us, for not ruining the family businesses despite our best efforts as children!"

Their toast, though lighthearted, carried an undercurrent of gratitude that resonated deeply. Jetti watched them from her seat, a fake smile touching her lips despite herself thinking about her parents. Their laughter, their teasing, their shared memories, were a testament to autonomy, to the bonds that had held their family together through war, loss, and change.

And yet, as Jetti listened, her heart ached with a bittersweet longing. Her brothers, so vibrant and full of life, seemed untouched by the depression she carried. Their world was one of possibility, of futures unburdened by the past. She envied their lightness, even as she cherished their presence. For tonight, she allowed their joy to wash over her, a small reprieve from the darkness that was consistently at the edges of her mind.

The room around her seemed distant, her mind, however, was consumed by the image of their youngest brother, Yosef who would turn fourteen this year. The memory of his innocent smile, the gleam of excitement in his eyes, felt like a lifetime ago. Aaron had sent him away to Bucharest, at nine years old, to the prestigious *Iulia Hasdeu National College*, a decision that had both torn her heart and filled her with a bittersweet sense of resignation. It was the best and the worst of choices. At the time, the school had been the pinnacle of academic excellence in Romania, a place where the brightest minds were molded for greatness. Aaron had believed it was the opportunity Yosef needed to secure a future beyond the confines of their small bustling town, a future where ambition could soar without limits. Yet, in her heart, Jetti couldn't shake the gnawing feeling that by sending him away, they had severed something precious, something too deep for words. The world outside was changing rapidly, and she feared for what might become of Yosef, alone in the heart of the city. What if he was lost to them, to this new world they could barely comprehend? The candlelight flickered again, casting long shadows on the walls, and for a moment, Jetti almost wished she could return to those simpler days when they had all been together, before the world started to fracture into pieces they couldn't fit back together.

The laughter and chatter of her brothers and sisters broke her thought, and swirled around her, but it felt as though she were listening from a great distance, separated by an invisible wall. They tried so hard, her family—her beloved siblings who meant well. They spoke in bright voices, lifting their glasses, sharing memories of past years, but Jetti could not find her place among them. She was caught in the ring of a life that had once been full of promises, now faded out by grief.

Her concentration drifted absently to an imaginary empty chair beside her, the place where Joel should have been sitting. His absence, to her, was like a gaping wound in the evening's festivities. She imagined it filled with him, with his pleasant smile, his masculine voice calling her name, his hand resting gently on her shoulder. Instead, the space was empty and cold, a stark reminder of what was lost. She tried not to let it consume her, but the reality of it all seemed to grow with every passing moment. She could almost hear the possibility that had once surrounded their future, their love, a plan that seemed so clear just weeks ago.

She knew her family meant well. Before Joel came back they had spoken of him with fondness and potential, their voices full of encouragement, envisioning a life for Joel and her that was intertwined with theirs. They had spoken of weddings, of children, of dreams fulfilled. His return was met with open arms, their excitement genuine, as though he had always belonged to their world. Jetti had been swept up in it, carried away by their belief in a bright future ahead. But now, as she sat at the table, their expectations pressed heavily on her chest. She had wanted so much to share in their joy, to laugh along with them, to take part in the celebration. Yet she couldn't shake the deep ache and embarrassment that settled in her heart.

Her mind wandered, and she found herself wondering where Joel was now, on this New Year's Eve. Was he far away? Was he even thinking of her as she sat here, trying to hold herself together? The thought of him... wherever he might be... only added to the gnawing emptiness. Had he found peace in his absence, or was he just as lost as she was? Her heart clenched at the thought that he might be out there, somewhere, and she would never know what had become of him.

She looked around at her brothers and sisters, their laughter exurberant with the clink of glasses and the excitement of voices. They were here. And as much as she felt lost, they were willing to carry her, to bring her back into the fold. She realized, with a sudden clarity, that their love was not just a reminder of what had been, but also a lifeline, a thread that might one day pull her from this darkness. The pain was real, yes, but perhaps it would pass with time. Perhaps, in the years to come, they would make new memories and experience new joy, even if it never erased the past.

Chapter Fifteen:
Family

A small breath of relief washed over her as she took in the scene before her; the camaderie, the familiar faces, and the laughter that filled the space. Jetti allowed herself to feel something other than her grief. The year ahead, the year of 1918, was uncertain, but for the first time in weeks, she could almost believe that it might bring something other than loss. It might bring healing. It might bring a chance to live again.

The thought was fragile, like a delicate bloom pushing through the cold soil after a long, harsh winter. But in that fleeting moment, Jetti allowed herself to feel hopeful, just a little. She didn't know where Joel was, or what the future held, but maybe, just maybe, she was ready to step into her life again.

Aaron leaned toward her. "Jetti, eat something. You look like a ghost," he said, his tone laced with concern. Esther nodded in agreement, reaching over and placing a piece of schmaltzed challah on her plate.

Jetti forced a small smile and broke off a piece of the bread, placing it in her mouth. The taste was almost nonexistent, as though her grief had dulled her senses.

As the meal progressed, she felt her emotions pressing down on her like an unseen hand. The laughter and engaging conversation around the table, the clink of silverware, the rustle of linens, all seemed to swirl around her, distant and muffled. It was her sister Nurit, seated just across from her, who steathily reached under the table, her fingers brushing against Jetti's knee in a simple yet profound gesture of solidarity. The touch was loving, a lifeline extended without words. Jetti could feel the warmth of her sister's hand, an intentional reassurance that someone was there supporting her.

"You're not alone, sister," Nurit whispered, her voice so low it was almost swallowed by the chatter of conversation. But the sincerity in her words was unmistakable. Jetti met her sister's eyes, the understanding between them as clear as the air around them. Nurit's grey eyes held a significant wisdom, a depth of empathy that only the closest of bonds could foster. Jetti nodded in response. The gesture, however small, was a reminder of the unwavering love of her family, even if she couldn't fully embrace it yet.

Nurit had always been a presence of calm grace, her name itself an embodiment of the qualities she exuded. Nurit, Hebrew for 'flower,' a fitting reflection of her character; elegant, radiant, and always present. It was a name that carried with it a sense of beauty, not just in the way she looked but in the way she moved through the world. She had an inner peace that could brighten up the room, and an innate ability to soothe even the most troubled hearts. Her charm, the way she made others feel at ease, was a mastered kind of magic that many admired.

Often associated with the Persian buttercup, Nurit carried a significance that resonated deeply with Jetti, especially on a night like this. The Persian buttercup, a delicate flower native to Jerusalem, was also known as the 'Flower of David.' It thrived in the harshest conditions, its vibrant beauty defying even the most unforgiving environments. Known as the 'resurrection plant,' it could endure long stretches of drought, blooming anew with even the smallest droplet of water.

Nurit, like the flower she was named after, possessed an extraordinary resilience—a kind of strength that allowed her to endure hardship and loss while finding ways to rise again. Jetti remembered it vividly: after their parents' death, it was Nurit who had taken care of her, guiding her through the depths of their shared sorrow and helping her find her way again. On this night, the memory of her sister's unwavering support brought comfort to Jetti's broken heart.

She had always admired her sister for that readiness, that knowing determination. Even now, in the midst of her own grief, Nurit remained a steady presence. Her hand on Jetti's was more than just a gesture of support, it was a promise, an assurance that even in the darkest of times, there was possibility. The touch reminded Jetti that life, like the flower, could bloom again, even after a long, painful winter.

Nurit had always been her anchor, the one constant through storms both distant and near. Jetti didn't know what the future held or whether the ache of this loss would ever truly fade. But in that moment, she understood something vital… she didn't have to carry it alone. And that sometimes, survival began with the earnest closeness of someone who refused to let go.

Aaron rose gracefully from his seat at the head of the table, his movements composed and deliberate. There was an assertive elegance to him, a confidence that came not from dominance but from years of thoughtful leadership and care for his family's future. His hands, smooth and steady, reflected his nature, hands that had penned agreements, offered warmth in a handshake, and guided others with calm assurance. Though they were untouched by hard labor, they carried the imprint of decisions made with diligence and heart. As he stood, glass in hand, the room gradually fell silent, the stoicism of his presence and the ability to endure, drawing the family's attention with ease.

Lifting his glass high, Aaron's deep voice rang out with clarity and conviction, steady as ever. "This year, 1918, is the year of 'Chai'" he began, the Hebrew word rich with meaning, carrying centuries old tradition. "A year that beckons us toward renewal, toward peace. A year that asks us to carry forward, despite all that has been lost." His words settled into the air, loaded with significance, as he scanned the room, ensuring they felt his promise.

"This year," Aaron continued, his voice steady and filled with conviction, "we must remember that the hardships we've faced— though painful and daunting—are not the end of our story. We have endured, and we will continue to endure. In every challenge, in every loss, there is something to be learned. Our strength comes not from avoiding hardship, but from facing it head-on, and rising stronger for it."

He looked at his siblings, his concern resting a moment longer on Jetti. His expression lulled as if to remind her, without words, that she, too, was not alone in her grief. "We are more than what has happened to us. We are more than the sum of our struggles. 'Chai' reminds us that there is always the possibility of change. There is always the chance to begin again, to rebuild, to love."

Aaron raised his flute higher, the glassy chime of crystal ringing through the room, drawing all eyes to him. "To 'Chai'…to life," he said again, his voice rich with emotion. "May we honor it by living fully, by loving deeply, and by standing together. For in this family, there is nothing we cannot overcome."

The conviction of his words hung in the air like a promise.

The family raised their glasses in unison, the delicate ring of crystal catching the joy in the air. It was more than a toast, it was a vow, a promise that they would face the future together, as a family.

The room sparkled with the delicate chime of champagne toasts, voices and laughter of her brothers and sisters rising together in a chorus of possibility and new beginnings. The air was thick with savory roasted meats and freshly baked bread, the delicate perfume of pine boughs that had been carefully arranged on the grand table. It was a feast for the senses—a celebration of the promise that the New Year might bring. The sound of laughter and engaging conversation filled the space, as if attempting to push the shadows of Jetti's grief and loss into the corners of the room. Yet, for Jetti, the toast felt like a suffocating reminder of the uncertainty churning inside her. Her hand trembled as she reached for her glass, the crystal smooth and cool, lifting it with justified hesitation.

As the evening wore on and the celebration continued around her, Jetti sat unobtrusively in her chair, her eyes observing her family. She watched them embrace, their faces flushed with the fanfare of camaraderie, the sound of their easy laughter wrapping around her like a familiar blanket. They were so full of life, so effortlessly resilient, as if the hardships they had endured were mere stepping stones to greater joys. The bond between them, unbroken by the years of grief, war, and suffering, was a testament to their commitment and unity.

Unexpectedly, a small, fragile thought began to form in the back of her mind. Could it be possible? Could 'Chai'—the sacred symbol of life, ever hold meaning for her again? Could she ever heal from the pain that had consumed her, or was she destined to remain trapped in this endless cycle of grief? The question hovered in her mind, like a delicate butterfly just out of reach, she allowed herself to wonder if the answer might one day come.

Since Joel left, Jetti had moved through her days like a shadow of herself, completely numb, and hollow, surviving only because she felt like she had no other choice.

And then, as she looked around the room. She felt it clearly: the grief she had been carrying didn't belong to her alone. Joel had walked away. *He* had chosen distance. And she… she had let his absence define her world.

The ache remained, but a new kind of ache joined it, one born of truth. She had more to give. More to feel. If she waited for him to return in order to feel whole again, she would be waiting forever. And in that moment, something inside her shifted.

She realized she could no longer afford to stay buried in the space he left behind. If there was to be a future, it would have to be one she carved out herself. She wasn't healed. But she was awake… Finally. She realized at that moment, she wanted to live.

Chapter Sixteen:
Fragments of Purpose

The morning after the New Year's celebration was dazzlingly bright, the winter sun gleaming off the pristine snow fall that blanketed the gardens outside. The rays streamed through the frosted windows casting shimmering patterns on the walls of Jetti's bedroom. It was as though the universe itself was extending an olive branch, beckoning her to step into its embrace, and not let the sorrow consume her anymore. Today, she would make an effort to live again.

Jetti called for Anka, her voice carrying through the hallway. When the young woman entered, her expression was a mixture of concern and curiosity. Jetti stood by the window, her hands clasped in front of her.

"Anka," Jetti began, her voice steady, "let's take the dowry chest out of this room."

Anka blinked, momentarily caught off guard. Her body shifted to the small chest, sitting like a solemn sentinel in the corner of the room. "Your dowry chest, miss?" she asked, her voice tinged with hesitation.

Jetti nodded, her fingers tightening as she turned to fully face Anka. "Yes," she said. "It belongs in the vault. That's where it should be."

For a moment, Anka didn't move, her brows knitting together as she studied Jetti's face. "Are you sure?" she asked, her voice laced with both caution and care. "It has been here so long... and..."

"I'm sure," Jetti interrupted but with a conviction that surprised them both. "It's time."

Anka hesitated, her fingers brushing the edge of her apron as though searching for a pocket. Finally, she nodded. "As you wish, my lady," she said. Crossing the room, she ran her hand over the polished surface, her movements careful and deliberate. "I'll have someone help me carry it."

"No." Jetti's response was swift, and Anka paused, glancing back at her. "We'll do it ourselves, just you and me."

Anka's lips parted slightly, her surprise evident, but she offered no protest. "Very well," she said after a beat. "We can manage."

Together, they maneuvered the small chest across the room. As they moved, Jetti's thoughts drifted unbidden to the day the family vault had been constructed. It was 1904, she was only ten years old, but the memory remained vivid.

"I remember when the vault was built," Jetti said suddenly, her voice steady as they carried the chest. Anka glanced at her, surprised by the unprompted words, but kept her mouth shut, letting her speak. "My father oversaw every detail himself. He said it was to protect the things that mattered most to us."

Anka tilted her head as she replied, "He must have been a very thoughtful man, your father."

"He was," Jetti agreed, a sad frown tugging at her lips. "He cared deeply about what the future might hold… about ensuring we were ready for it."

As they finally reached the doorway, Anka stopped; she looked at Jetti, a question apparent in her eyes. "And you? Are you ready for what comes next?"

Jetti glanced at her, and though the question hung heavily between them, she didn't look away. "I don't know," she admitted after a moment. "But this… this feels like a good step."

Anka nodded, her own expression reflecting a loyal understanding. Together, they carried the chest out of the room, the sound of their footsteps fading as they moved away from the suite.

As Jetti and Anka carried the dowry chest down the corridor to the basement, Jetti's thoughts were deep in the memory of the vault's construction. The rhythmic creak of the chest in their hands seemed to remind her of the clanking and churning of the giant digging machines she had watched as a child.

"My father was so particular about every detail of the vault," Jetti began, her voice steady despite the strain of carrying the chest. "I can still hear the machines breaking the grounds of the estate… the shouts of the workers as they directed the equipment."

Anka glanced over, waiting for her to continue.

"They tore the earth apart," Jetti said. "Right outside near the drawing room. All the children stood at the window, wide-eyed, watching the chaos. The machines, the shouting, it felt like we were witnessing the creation of something extraordinary, something powerful."

Anka smiled. "It must have seemed almost magical to you then."

Jetti nodded, her grip tightening on the chest. "It did. The way the soil gave way to foundations of reinforced cement. My father was adamant about its stability. 'Nothing will move it,' he said. And when the walls were lined with metal, each piece fitted and hammered into place… it was like watching an artist at work."

"Your father sounds like a man who valued permanence," Anka observed, her tone thoughtful.

"He did," Jetti replied. "He said the vault would protect our family legacy. It wasn't just about security, it was about preserving what we cherished, holding onto the history that made us who we are."

They paused at the top of the stairs to adjust their grip. Anka took the moment to catch her breath and then asked, "And the door? Did it look like something from inside a bank?"

A small smile appeared on Jetti's lips, and for the first time in days, there was a lightness in her voice. "Oh, the door! It arrived on a cart pulled by the strongest horses I'd ever seen. Polished steel, intricate mechanisms. It gleamed like silver in the sunlight. My father called it a masterpiece, and I believed him. It wasn't just a door, it was a statement, like a piece of art."

Anka tilted her head, the chest momentarily forgotten. "Did you ever see inside of the vault door, before it was finished?"

"Only once, just before they died..." Jetti admitted, her tone quieter now. "The locksmiths worked for days on the mechanism. When it was finally ready, my father called us all to watch before they closed it up. The way it opened, the way the gears moved, it was mesmerizing."

She went on, "Before they died my mother used to tell us stories about how the vault should be like a library, but for treasures. She told us to imagine the inside having walls lined with shelves, ready to hold the heirlooms of our family."

Anka's grip on the chest steadied as they began descending the east-wing stairway. "Your parents must have been so proud of what they created."

"They were," Jetti said, her voice laced with bittersweet emotion. "But they never got to see it finished. They died before it was completed. The vault ended up holding more than just our treasures, it became a resting place for their legacy."

They reached the landing, and Anka set her end of the chest down for a moment, wiping her brow. "And now?" she asked gently. "Do you feel the same way about it?"

Jetti hesitated, looking down the hallway toward the door that led to the vault. "I think," she began slowly, "that it's time for me to make the dowry chest a part of that legacy. It doesn't belong in my room anymore. It belongs with everything my parents built to protect."

Anka studied her for a moment, then nodded.

As they continued toward the vault, the chest between them, the heaviness of it, seemed less oppressive. The assurance in Jetti's voice and the steady rhythm of their footsteps signaled something small but significant.

They continued carrying the chest taking breaks on the way through the winding halls and stairways of the mansion, Anka's voice, tentative yet curious. "You hardly ever talk about your parents, Jetti." Hesitating to ask, but did anyway. "How did they... how did they die?"

Jetti paused mid-step, the chest suddenly feeling heavier in her hands. She let out a breath she hadn't realized she was holding, and they set the chest down. "It's not a story I tell often," she admitted, her voice tinged with both reluctance and pain. "It's... peculiar, tragic, and cruel. Sometimes I wonder if sharing it makes it feel more real."

Anka didn't look away. "If you want to talk about it," she said, "I'll listen."

Jetti nodded as if the memory were playing out in front of her. "It was the summer of 1904, the same year they started building the vault. They had gone to Vienna, a trip meant to be a celebration. My father had dreamed of buying a grand piano, a Bösendorfer, one of the finest instruments ever crafted. He said it was to be something that would fill our home with music and grace for generations."

Anka's brows furrowed. "A piano? That doesn't sound... dangerous."

"No," Jetti said with a bitter smile. "It wasn't the piano itself. It was what happened during its transport." She paused, gripping the chest more tightly as they continued their careful descent down the stairs. "My father chose it himself. He wanted the best for my mother. Its dark wood gleamed like a mirror, and my mother spent hours in the showroom, running her fingers over the keys, playing the melodies it would bring to our lives. It was a symbol of everything they wanted to teach us, an instrument of beauty and elegance, just for our family." Jetti stopped to wipe a tear from her cheek. "My parents always wanted the best for us."

Anka's footsteps slowed. "What happened?" she asked.

"They arranged for the piano to be transported by train," Jetti explained, her voice thick. "They were meticulous, paying extra to ensure it would arrive in perfect condition. But at the station, as it was being loaded onto the freight car, something went wrong. The pulley system they were using to lift it… failed."

Anka's eyes widened, and she stopped altogether, the chest momentarily forgotten between them. "Failed?"

Jetti nodded, her throat tightening. "The piano was massive, and packed in a large wooden crate. It was much heavier than they'd accounted for. When the pulley system gave way, it swung wildly, out of control. The workers shouted, scrambling to stabilize it, but it was too late. The crate with the Bösendorfer inside slipped from its restraints and fell."

She swallowed hard, her voice dropping. "My parents were standing nearby. They had just stepped closer to watch the crate begin to be lowered onto the train car. The crate… it…" She trailed off, her words faltering. "It crashed down onto the platform with them beneath it. I can only imagine the sound being deafening, like thunder and smashing piano keys, and splintering wood. In an instant, they were gone."

Anka gasped, her hand flying to her mouth. "Oh, Jetti," she whispered. "That's… that's horrible."

Jetti's lips pressed into a thin line as she forced herself to continue. "The news traveled quickly home, shocking everyone who heard it. For my siblings and me, it was… surreal. They had left the house so full of life, eager to bring back a gift of music. And instead…" She exhaled shakily. "Instead, they were gone. The Bösendorfer gone with them—this magnificent thing meant to symbolize our family's enduring love for music—became the very thing that shattered it."

Anka shook her head, her voice trembling with emotion as they picked up the chest and continued. "And the piano? What happened to it?"

"It was completely destroyed, crushed beyond repair. The work crew removed it and the broken crate from the station, splintered and useless," Jetti said. "I never saw it, but I can imagine hearing the sound of it breaking, the cries of the workers, and the devastation that followed. Even though I wasn't there that sound haunts me more than anything."

They reached the bottom of the stairs and carefully set the chest down, Anka setting her side down first, her expression full of sorrow. "You've held this for so long," she said. "No wonder it's hard to talk about. It's not just grief—it's... cruelty. A twist of fate no one could prepare for."

Jetti gave a slight nod, glancing at the chest between them. "After their deaths, the house seemed abandoned. Even the construction of the vault, which my father had overseen with such pride, felt like a hollow victory. It was finished soon after, but without them to see it completed... it wasn't the same."

Anka hesitated, then placed a hand firmly on Jetti's arm. "You said the vault was meant to preserve everything that mattered most to your parents. Maybe putting this chest there isn't just about moving it out of your room. Maybe it's a way to honor them."

Jetti felt something softening in her expression. "Maybe," she said. "It feels like the right place for it now. A step toward letting the past rest."

With that, they picked up the chest again and continued toward the vault. The hallway ahead was cool and damp, but Jetti's mind was more clear now, filled not only with the sorrow of loss but with a great sense of purpose—mirroring her father's dream and her mother's love for preserving what mattered most.

Jetti blinked, took in a deep breath, and returned to the present. She looked at Anka and helped her lower the dowry chest into the depths of the vault surrounded by family treasures. Together, they stepped back out and watched as the metal door swung closed with a deep thud. In that moment, Jetti felt a lightness, as if something had finally been let go. The chest, once a constant reminder of her life with Joel, was now sealed away, no longer part of her everyday world. She wouldn't have to see it again, or carry its sorrow with her.

Chapter Seventeen:
Moving Forward

The wind carried a new freshness, as if the air itself sensed a turning point. Several days had passed since Jetti and Anka had locked the chest away in the vault, but the moment settled in Jetti's bones like a dismal reckoning. She stood at the window, bathed in morning light, her silhouette defined and deliberate. Then, with a voice that cut through the hush of the house—clear, steady, and resolute—she called out, "Anka." When Anka stepped into the room, Jetti turned from the glass, her posture taller, more determined than it had been in days. There was no need for words; the look in her eyes said everything—something had shifted, and there would be no turning back.

"I want to change the look of my suite," Jetti said. "It needs to feel different. It needs to reflect me… I want something new."

Anka's eyes lit up with surprise and encouragement. "A fresh start," she said, nodding eagerly. "That's a wonderful idea, Jetti. We can start in the attics—there's so much up there we could use to transform your space."

Anka's voice spurred Jetti onward. "Yes," Jetti agreed, as determination gave way to anticipation. "Let's go see what we can find."

The two women ventured up to the attics, an expansive space that seemed to stretch endlessly above the main part of the sprawling building. As they opened the creaking wooden door, a rush of cold, dry air greeted them, carrying with it the musk of aged wood, and floral attar from sachets long forgotten. Dust motes danced lazily in the sunlight streaming through the narrow windows, creating opulent beams that illuminated the forgotten artifacts stored within.

"This place feels like a museum," Anka said with a laugh, brushing cobwebs away from a tall gilded mirror leaning against the wall.

Jetti smiled faintly, running her hand over the smooth, cool surface of a marble table with ornate twisted legs that looked like grape vines. "It holds so much history," she murmured. "Every piece here belonged to someone, meant something to those who lived here before me."

As they explored, their footsteps tapped in the space, in unison with the squeaky creaks of the floorboards. Jetti's hands lingered on an intricately carved vanity table with an inlaid mother-of-pearl design that caught the radiance like tiny stars. "This one," she said, her voice steady. "This will replace the one Joel admired."

Anka nodded approvingly, brushing dust from the tabletop. "It's beautiful. It'll fit perfectly in your suite."

They continued their search, their conversation flowing easily as Anka pulled back protective linens from various pieces. A pair of upholstered chairs in velvety teal fabric caught Jetti's attention. She ran her fingers over the fabric, smiling at the subtle texture. "These... these will go by the window," she said. "For a reading nook."

Anka clapped her hands together. "Perfect! They're inviting and elegant. And the color will bring some brightness and life to the area."

As they moved deeper into the attic, Jetti found herself drawn to brighter options—softer fabrics, polished wood, and pieces with intricate but understated designs. Anka suggested swapping the somber drapes in Jetti's room for cream silk ones, delicately embroidered with subtle floral patterns. "These will let in more light," Anka said, holding the fabric up to a window. "They'll make the room feel airy and alive."

Jetti nodded, her smile widening just slightly. "Yes. That's exactly what it needs."

Piece by piece, they curated a selection of items, each one chosen for its ability to transform her living quarters. It was no longer about preserving the room as it had been, a shared space filled with memories of Joel. Instead, it became a reflection of Jetti herself—her steadiness, and independence.

By the time they descended the attic stairs with their chosen items noted and a plan forming, Jetti felt something inside her heart. A spark of excitement glimmered faintly—a feeling she hadn't believed herself capable of anymore… Change.

The next evening, Jetti's suite began its transformation, shedding its oppressive atmosphere like a snake discarding its old skin. The first change was the removal of the massive canopy bed that had dominated the room, its dark wood and drapery casting shadows even on the brightest day. In its place, she chose a simple single bed with a carved wooden frame. The new bed, set against the far wall, opened up the room dramatically, creating a sense of grandeur through space itself. The floor, now more visible, became a canvas for Jetti's vision. She selected several rugs, and placed them carefully, layering one atop the other in mismatched patterns and textures thus creating a unique look that added depth and character.

Despite all the changes, Jetti decided to keep the puncheon tub, a luxury she couldn't bear to part with. Its deep, sturdy design had long been her sanctuary, and she imagined the comfort it would bring after cold winter days. Its presence remained a testament to her love for small indulgences.

By the hearth, she added an ornate metal fireplace screen, an intricate work of art with tall herons woven delicately into the wire patterns. The screen's fine craftsmanship caught the firelight, the herons seeming almost alive as the flames swayed behind them. It was a piece she had discovered in the attic and claimed immediately, its uniqueness resonating with her desire to craft a space that felt truly her own.

The cream silk drapes now framed the tall windows, their delicate embroidery catching the evening dusk. Late sunbeams spilled into the room unobstructed, illuminating the newly arranged furniture and brightening the shadows. The upholstered chairs, positioned by the window, created an inviting alcove where Jetti could sit and look over the gardens. As she settled into one of them, the chair's embrace cradled her, and for the first time in what felt like an eternity, the air inside the room felt as if it wouldn't strangle her.

Outside, the gardens remained stark and frozen, their beauty tinged with the winter sun as it began its slow descent. The snow shimmered with hues of amber and rose, painting the world in colors Jetti had almost forgotten could exist. She leaned back in the chair, allowing herself to imagine a future. A future where this room reflected not loss but renewal. A future where life, fragile and uncertain as it was, might hold promise.

Just as the thought began to take root, a sound broke through... a knock at her door. It wasn't Anka; Jetti knew her knock by heart. This one was hesitant, unfamiliar. Her pulse quickened as she stood, the chair creaking maleficently beneath her. She hesitated, her hand hovering over the door handle.

When she finally opened it, she gasped at who she saw. Standing there, framed by the dim light of the hallway, was Henry Singer, her sister Nina's husband. In his hand, he held something small but unmistakable:

Joel's war medal.

The silver gleamed, its presence felt like a blow, sharp and cold. For a moment, the world seemed to tilt, the lines between memory and reality blurring as a tormenting quest gripped her heart. What could this mean? And why was Henry the one holding it?

Chapter Eighteen:
Shadow of Absence

Outside, the air carried the unmistakable earthiness of melting snow and the sweetness of budding floral blossoms. Spring was unfurling its arms across Czernowitz, brushing the gray pallor of winter aside in favor of fresh greens and vibrant hints of color. The transformation outside seemed to mirror the internal shift within Jetti. Two months had passed since she resolved to reclaim her life, to step out from the shadow of Joel's absence and create something entirely her own. The world was waking up, and Jetti felt as though she was, too. Purpose, fragile but growing stronger, took root in her heart like the first blooms of the season.

As part of that purpose, there had been one last trip to the vault. The recollection came back to her now, clear and oddly satisfying.

It burned as vividly as the fire had that evening, its flames crackling in the drawing room hearth. A week after New Year's Eve, Jetti sat stiffly across from Henry, her posture rigid, her eyes fixed on the war medal lying on the small table between them. The silver glint of its surface as the green and blue ribbon mocked her, a token of sentiment where words and answers should have been. Her fingers had brushed the edge of the ribbon, not with tenderness but with barely contained frustration. Why had Joel sent this? Why had Henry brought it? And why, in all of it, was she left to pick through the wreckage of her life while Joel simply walked away?

"It's been a month," she said, her voice steady but low. "I don't understand why he sent this."

Henry sighed, leaning forward, his elbows resting on his knees. "He didn't send it," he clarified. "He gave it to me when I saw him in Bucharest."

Her head snapped up, her eyes locking onto his. "You saw him."

Henry nodded. "I ran into him at the train station. I was on my way home from a meeting..." Henry hesitated, searching for the right words. "He looked like he was heading nowhere."

Jetti's brow furrowed. "What do you mean?"

Henry leaned back, running a hand through his hair. "He was... rough. Unkempt. Like he hadn't shaved or properly washed in weeks. I asked him why he left you."

Her fingers froze on the medal. She looked up with surprise and asked, "What did he say?"

Henry's voice calm. "He said the war had changed him. That he wasn't the same man anymore and didn't feel like he could be the husband you deserved. He... he said he needed to be with his family in New York, and mumbled something about letters."

Jetti's face hardened, but her trembling hands betrayed her. "His family?" she said bitterly. "And what am I?"

"You were everything to him, Jetti," Henry said. "That much was clear. He said there was no excuse for how he left, and he was sorry—deeply sorry. He just... he couldn't stay."

Her lips pressed into a thin line, and she looked away, her voice sharp. "So he ran."

Henry exhaled slowly. "Yes. He ran. He told me to tell you to move on. That he wasn't coming back."

The words hung in the air, oppressive and unrelenting. Jetti closed her eyes, willing herself to stay composed. "And the medal Henry, why did he give you the medal?"

"He thought you liked it," Henry said simply. "He wanted you to have it. I think... I think it was his way of leaving a piece of himself behind, even if he couldn't be here."

Jetti shook her head, letting out a bitter laugh. "A medal. As if that's supposed to make up for everything."

"It doesn't," Henry agreed. "But Jetti... I could see it in his eyes. He wasn't at peace with his decision. He was in pain, too. This wasn't easy for him."

She glanced back at the medal, her expression unreadable. "It's been four weeks, Henry," she said. "Four weeks, and I'm no closer to understanding why he had to do this."

Henry reached out, his hand resting on hers. "Maybe you don't have to understand it all at once. Maybe it's enough to know he cared. He just... didn't know how to stay."

Jetti's eyes remained fixed on the medal, its white shine catching the dim light of the room. Henry's words pressed, but another thought clawed its way to the surface, one she couldn't keep buried any longer.

"He didn't just leave me, Henry," she said, her voice tight. "He broke the contract. The one we stood under together, the one we signed, the one that tied us...me...to him in every way that matters."

Henry's brow furrowed, his hand resting on hers. "The ketubah," he said, understanding dawning in his eyes.

"Yes." Her voice wavered, but she pushed on. "When Joel walked away, he didn't just abandon me. He abandoned his responsibilities and our vows. And now..." She inhaled sharply, trying to steady herself. "Now I'm the one left with the pieces. The ketubah binds me, Henry. It means I can't just move on. I can't remarry. I can't even think about a future that doesn't have him in it, because legally, religiously, I'm still his wife."

Henry leaned back, his expression troubled. "Jetti, I..." he began, but she interrupted him.

"I don't think you understand." Her words came quickly now, a torrent she had held back for too long. "This isn't just about love, or heartbreak, or even what's fair. It's about my life. As long as Joel refuses to release me, I'm trapped. Do you know what it feels like to be bound to someone who doesn't want you? To carry a promise that means nothing to the person who made it?"

Henry's jaw tightened, but he said nothing, allowing her the space to continue.

"I thought the ketubah was a shield," she said bitterly, her voice unflinching. "Something to protect me, to ensure that we were equals in this marriage. Now it feels like a chain. One he's cast off, but continues to hold me." Her hands clenched around the edge of the medal, the ribbon crumpling under her grip. "And what's worse, he doesn't even realize it. Or… he doesn't care."

"Jetti…" Henry began again, his tone cautious, but she shook her head.

"I can't even divorce him without his permission. Do you know what that means?" Her eyes burned with welling tears as she finally looked at Henry's face. "It means I have no control. None. Over him, over this… over my own future. And Joel, in all his pain and guilt and whatever else he's carrying, didn't just leave me behind… he took away my ability to move forward."

Henry's shoulders sagged, the gravity of her words sinking in. "You're right," he admitted. "I don't understand what that feels like. But Jetti, I know you. You're stronger than this, I can see it in you; you are better than what he's left you with."

She gave him a bitter smile, the smallest trace of gratitude in her eyes. "I don't feel strong, Henry. I feel powerless. And the worst part is, I think Joel thought he was doing me a kindness by leaving this." She gestured sharply to the medal…"as if it could make up for the chains he's left me in."

Henry sat back, his face thoughtful and conflicted. "I don't have an answer, Jetti," he said quietly. "But I do know this: Joel might have broken his promises, but you… you're still here. And if anyone can find a way forward, even in this mess, it's you."

Jetti didn't respond immediately, her fingers loosening their grip on the medal. The unease stretched between them, but not entirely devoid of understanding. Finally, she looked at Henry, her voice resolute. "I don't know how to move forward, Henry."

He nodded, his expression stern. "Then let's figure it out, Jetti. One step at a time."

She didn't respond, judging the medal as the firelight danced across its surface. The room became noiseless, raw emotions filling the space between them.

The next morning, she and Anka had descended the cool, stone staircase, carrying Joel's war medal carefully wrapped in a linen cloth. It was Anka who had suggested putting it in the dowry chest. She'd said, to acknowledge Joel's part in her past without letting it haunt her future. Jetti thought that was a good idea, and had agreed, her steps growing surer as they moved through the dimly lit corridor toward the vault door.

Inside, the dowry chest waited like a patient sentinel. When Jetti opened the lid, she paused for a moment, her fingers brushing over the carefully arranged contents. The pearls, the candlesticks, the gemstones. She looked at them this time with positive determination; they were no longer symbols of failure but pieces of a life that had been hers to shape. With gallant deliberation, she placed the medal among them, its silver surface catching the lamplight. It felt like closing a chapter, one she had never thought she could.

"We all leave things behind," Anka had said, her voice steady in the shadows of the vault. "But it's what we carry forward that matters."

Jetti nodded, closing the chest with a finality that felt more liberating than sad.

Chapter Nineteen: Singers

Standing by the window in her suite and watching the first blush of spring spread across the gardens, Jetti thought about how she and Anka put away the medal in the dowry box and felt a small, steady spark of pride. She had taken a step toward peace, and with it, the beginnings of something new—a job at the Singer's Dress Shop. The offer had come unexpectedly, in Henry's calm and pragmatic way, as though it had been decided with her best interests in mind.

"You need something to focus on, Jetti, This might take your mind off of the past," he'd said one evening, the fervor in his tone emphasizing the practicality of his words. "Nina has been helping me in the office, and she's thriving there. But there's more to do than we can manage on our own. You're thoughtful, creative, and steady. You have qualities that would make you invaluable to the shop."

Jetti hesitated, uncertainty clouding her expression. "Henry, I've never worked in a place like that before. I wouldn't even know where to start."

Henry leaned forward, his hands resting on the table between them. "You'd start by being yourself," he said simply. "You have a natural understanding of people, Jetti, and an ability to bring order to chaos. You have known my mother Miriam for years, she would be there to show you the way. You would be working with fabrics, and helping guide the customers, you'd be more help than you realize."

The idea had felt daunting at first, but Henry's confidence in her was steady and unwavering, as though he already saw her thriving in the role. "Besides," he'd added with a small, knowing smile, "Nina would love having you there. You two work well together. Always have."

That had been the final nudge she needed. If her sister could find a place in this busy, industrious world, perhaps she could too.

As she turned from the window, the garden's vibrant greens and pinks in her mind, Jetti took a steadying breath. The days ahead were uncharted, but they carried the promise of something new. She felt a purpose, a sense of direction, and the comfort of working alongside her sister.

Jetti had thrown herself into work at the most esteemed gown shop in the city. Located on a bustling street corner, the shop was a treasure trove of fine fabrics and exquisite craftsmanship. Its windows showcased dazzling displays of dresses that seemed to float on air, drawing a steady stream of clientele who valued elegance and refinement. The Singer family had a reputation that extended far beyond Czernowitz, bolstered by their recent government contract to supply military uniforms. Their work was celebrated for its precision and quality, making them a household name during the war years.

Henry Singer, Nina's husband, was the eldest son of three, a charismatic man with a head for numbers and a flair for leadership. He managed the shop's day-to-day operations with the efficiency of a general, ensuring that every seam, stitch, and button met the family's exacting standards. His mother, Miriam, and her sisters, Esther and Golda, were the artistic soul of the business. They were skilled designers and seamstresses whose creations were both functional and beautiful. It was from them that Jetti and Nina were learning the art of dressmaking and alterations.

Jetti marveled at Miriam, a woman whose hands were as steady as her voice was commanding. She had an air of elegance about her, from the way she carried herself to the way she spoke of fabrics and patterns as though they were living things. Her sisters, Esther and Golda, were no less formidable, their fingers flying across fabric with the speed and precision of a master craftsman. Together, the Singer matriarchs had turned their business into an empire, and Jetti was in awe of their ability to blend artistry with practicality.

Jetti worked in the backroom alongside Nina, the two sisters surrounded by bolts of silk and wool, spools of thread, and the rhythmic repetitive whirring of sewing machines. Nina, vibrant and full of energy, had a knack for bringing joy to the room. She would whistle while they worked, her tunes blending with the chatter of the other seamstresses. "See, Jetti," she said one afternoon as she deftly pinned fabric onto a dress form, "this is what I love about this work. You take something raw and shapeless and give it form and purpose. It's like breathing life into fabric."

For Jetti, the work was cathartic. She found solace in the meticulousness of it, the precise measurements, the careful stitching, the satisfaction of seeing a garment transform under her hands. It required focus, leaving little room for thoughts of Joel or the ache of his absence. Her sorrow seemed to lift with each passing day, replaced by the steady rhythm of a new routine.

She almost couldn't believe how much her life had changed in such a short time. Working at the shop had given her not just a purpose, but a connection to a world she had long felt detached from. The shop was a hive of activity, filled with gossip and the occasional bursts of laughter. It was a stark contrast to the melancholy of her old life, and Jetti found herself thriving in the vibrant energy of it all.

Though she rarely thought of Joel now, the occasional kernel would surface, a shadow passing through her mind. On these rare occasions, she would pause, needle poised in her hand, and wonder where he was, if he was alive, if he ever thought of her. But the moments were fleeting, and she would push them aside, reminding herself of the new life she was building. Spring was a season of rejuvenation, the snow melted, the city came alive with the sound of birdsong, and budding flowers. This was her season, her chance to bloom anew.

Chapter Twenty:
New Life

Miriam Singer had an eye for detail and an intuition sharpened by years of motherhood and sisterhood. A mother of three grown sons and the eldest of three sisters herself, she had spent her life observing and understanding people, often noticing things long before they were spoken aloud. It was no different with Nina. Though her daughter-in-law had said nothing, Miriam had noticed the signs, an absentminded touch to her abdomen, a newfound weariness in her steps that she had seen many times before. Miriam smiled to herself; Nina was expecting.

She shared her observation with Jetti one morning as they arranged bolts of fabric in the workshop. Miriam's tone was gentle but tinged with amusement as she leaned closer, her voice low to ensure no one else overheard. "Your sister hasn't said a word yet, but mark my words, Jetti…Nina is with child."

Jetti paused, her hands on a roll of taffeta. "Are you certain?" she whispered, her eyes widening.

"Certain as the sun rises," Miriam replied with a knowing smile. "I've had three of my own, remember? And I've seen enough nieces, nephews, and friends to know the signs. She may not even realize it herself yet, but soon enough, she'll have no choice but to tell Henry."

Jetti smiled, a mix of excitement and wonder filling her soul. "Nina will be thrilled," she said. "And Henry, he'll make a wonderful father."

Miriam nodded, her face brightening at the thought. "Of course he will. And as for us, we have work to do. Nina will need new clothes, and she won't want everyone to know right away. We'll make something beautiful for her, something that grows with her but doesn't give anything away until she's ready."

As Miriam spoke, her thoughts wandered briefly to her younger sons, Michael and David, who were twins and had just turned twenty. Unlike Henry, who was already settled with a wife and now likely a child on the way, the twins remained unwed. The Singer family, wealthy and well-respected, had yet to find suitable matches for them, though Miriam knew it was only a matter of time. Arranged marriages were common in their community, and while Michael and David were young, the search for wives was becoming a topic of increasing importance.

"Michael and David might have to wait a bit longer," Miriam remarked, more to herself than to Jetti. "But Henry's child will be the first of a new generation. Such a blessing."

Jetti looked at Miriam, admiration in her eyes. "You've built something wonderful here," she said. "Your family, your shop, everything."

Miriam reached out to tuck a loose strand of hair behind Jetti's ear. "And you're part of it now, Jetti. Never forget that."

Their bond deepened in that moment, rooted in shared secrets and mutual respect. Together, they began planning a dress that would celebrate new life, not just for Nina, but for all of them.

The Singer workshop was bathed in the pastels of late afternoon, its subdued rays catching on the rows of fabric bolts and spools of thread that lined the shelves. Jetti stood beside Miriam at a large cutting table, her hands smoothing the delicate azure blue fabric that would soon become a dress for Nina. Miriam's practiced fingers moved with the precision of a surgeon, pinning the fabric into place with a speed and confidence that left Jetti in awe.

"You see, Jetti," Miriam said, her voice fervent yet instructive, "the key to a good maternity dress is not just its beauty but its adaptability. We'll add discreet panels here at the seams" she gestured to the side of the bodice "with stitching that can be let out as Nina grows. No one will notice the alterations, and she'll feel elegant, and most of all comfortable."

Jetti leaned in closer, studying Miriam's technique as the older woman folded a small pleat into the fabric. "It's incredible," Jetti said, her voice tinged with admiration. "I would never have thought of adding fabric this way. It's like a secret built into the dress."

She chuckled, her eyes crinkling at the corners. "Ah, secrets are the essence of a good design. And a woman always needs a few secrets, don't you think?" She winked before continuing, "This will save her from needing an entirely new wardrobe, and after the baby comes, we can adjust it back. Nina will thank us."

They worked in companionable silence for a while, the only sounds the snip of scissors and the occasional vibrating shuttle of the sewing machine. The dress began to take shape: a clear sky blue creation with elegant teal accents and sleeves that tied at the shoulders. Miriam's ingenuity shone through in every detail, from the hidden panels of taffeta designed to disguise a growing belly to the convertible sleeves that made the dress suitable for both summery days and cooler evenings.

"What do you think about pockets?" Miriam asked, holding up one of the skirt panels with a sly smile.

"Pockets!" Jetti exclaimed, her eyes lighting up. "I love them! It's such a clever idea. Imagine having a place to carry a little notepad or some coins. It feels like another secret."

Miriam smiled. "Every dress should have a touch of practicality. Women need more than just beauty Jetti, we need function too."

Over the course of the week, Jetti tried on the dress several times to ensure the fit was perfect. Standing before the mirror, she admired how the taffeta fell gracefully over her waist, the clever design leaving no hint of the hidden panels or the pockets. "It's lovely," she said, running her hand over the fabric. "It is absolutely beautiful."

"It definitely is," Miriam agreed, her voice carrying a note of maternal pride. "But don't think I haven't noticed, Jetti, you and Nina, you're so much alike. If I didn't know better, I'd think you and she were twins."

Jetti's heart swelled at Miriam's words, her throat tightening with emotion. It had been fourteen years since she lost her mother, and in Miriam, she found comfort and guidance that felt achingly familiar. "Thank you, Miriam," she said, her voice barely above a whisper. "That means so much to me."

Miriam reached out and placed a hand on Jetti's cheek. "You're a talented young woman, Jetti. And you have a good heart. Nina's lucky to have you as her sister, and I'm lucky to have you both in my workshop."

As they resumed their work, Jetti couldn't help but feel a sense of belonging that had eluded her for so long. The Singer family's world of bustling creativity and determination was becoming her refuge, and with Miriam's guidance, she felt encouraged for the future, a future she was slowly learning to craft with her own two hands.

That morning, Jetti and Miriam worked diligently side by side in the shop, where shadows stretched across the work table and fabrics.

Nina was scheduled to arrive later that afternoon, and the task before them required both precision and secrecy. Every stitch, every fold of fabric, had to be perfect, and above all, the dress had to be kept hidden. Nina's favorite hues of deep sky blue and teal were unmistakable, as was the delicate taffeta that shimmered like a spring morning. If Nina so much as glimpsed them, she'd be curious. Too curious.

Jetti bit her lip in concentration as she stitched a delicate seam that would later be let out as the pregnancy progressed. Miriam's instructions had been meticulous, and Jetti found herself in awe of the older woman's skill. "Like this?" Jetti asked, holding up the panel for Miriam's inspection.

"Exactly," Miriam replied with a nod, her own hands deftly sewing ties onto the detachable sleeves. "You're a quick learner,

Jetti. Keep your stitches small and close. They'll hold until she needs them to change."

The two women worked in harmony, their movements synchronized like a well-rehearsed dance. Miriam began to sing a Yiddish lullaby, a tune that Jetti found soothing. Without realizing it, she joined in, her voice weaving with Miriam's in a musical harmony. The melody filled the room, wrapping around them like a thread binding their shared purpose.

"Do you think she suspects anything?" Jetti asked after a while, glancing up at Miriam.

Miriam chuckled. "Nina? She's sharp, but she's also busy with the accounts and running the shop with Henry. I doubt she's noticed a thing. But we mustn't underestimate her. That's why we're being careful."

After two focused hours, Miriam set down her needle with a sigh of satisfaction. "That's enough for now," she said, brushing her hands together. "Let's pack this away before Nina arrives."

Jetti carefully folded the pieces of the dress, her fingers holding the virgin fabric. The blue bodice shimmered like water, its teal accents catching the lines of the design. It was a beautiful dress, one that Nina would surely adore, but only when the time was right. They placed the delicate pieces into a special storage box lined with cedar to keep moths at bay. Miriam tucked a sprig of lavender inside for an extra touch of care, its fragrance a reminder of new beginnings.

Next, they gathered the fabric scraps and loose threads, sweeping them into a small bag that Miriam tied securely. "These need to go straight to the bin out back," she said. "If Nina sees even a hint of these colors, she'll know we're up to something."

Jetti nodded, her expression serious as she helped tidy the workbench. They wiped away any traces of their work, returning the shop to its usual state. By the time they finished, the room showed no sign of their secret project. It was as if the morning's work had never happened.

They stepped back to admire their efforts, Miriam placed a hand on Jetti's shoulder. "Good work today," she said proudly. "When the time comes, Nina will be so grateful. And you'll have played a big part in making her something truly special."

Jetti smiled, her heart swelling with a mix of pride and anticipation. She felt a sense of purpose, a connection to something greater than herself. With a final glance at the now-hidden dress, the two women set about preparing for Nina's arrival, their shared secret tucked safely away.

Chapter Twenty-one:
Busy Hands

As Jetti prepared for bed later that evening, her thoughts swirled with anticipation for the following day. She couldn't wait to return to the shop, not just to work on Nina's dress but to pepper Miriam with the questions that had been methodically forming in her mind. The dress was a marvel of ingenuity and beauty, a project that made her heart swell with pride, but it was Miriam's calm knowing demeanor, as they worked that intrigued Jetti even more.

Miriam carried herself with the majestic confidence of a woman who had experienced life in all its joys and trials. Her hands, deft and skilled with needle and thread, spoke of years of creating and mending, of nurturing not only garments but also a family. Jetti marveled at how seamlessly Miriam managed her responsibilities as a wife, a mother, and a businesswoman, all while carrying an aura of maternal acumen that reminded Jetti of her own mother. The questions bubbling inside her weren't about sewing techniques or fabric choices; they were about something much deeper, about life, creation, and the mysteries of motherhood.

Jetti's curiosity about pregnancy wasn't born out of ignorance. Even though her mother had passed away when she was ten, her education had been thorough, thanks to Aaron's insistence. Her eldest brother had always been pragmatic, ensuring his younger sisters knew enough about their bodies to avoid scandal or unplanned pregnancies.

But what she knew was factual and clinical, gleaned from books and carefully chosen conversations. What she longed for now was insight, an emotional understanding of the journey. What did it feel like to carry life within you? What did the stages of pregnancy truly entail, beyond the scientific explanations she'd read as a child?

As she lay in bed, staring at the ceiling, Jetti imagined the questions she would ask Miriam. "What does it feel like when you first know? Is it a flutter, a certainty, or an unclear suspicion?" she wondered aloud to the stillness of her room. She thought about Miriam's three sons. Henry, the steady eldest, and the lively twins, Michael and David. Miriam had been through this journey two times, each one no doubt unique, and Jetti knew there was wisdom in Miriam's experiences that no book could capture and she couldn't help but wonder what it was like for Nina, with the mystery of her first pregnancy still so new.

The following morning, the excitement to return to the shop made Jetti spring out of bed earlier than usual. The air was crisp with the promise of spring, and sunshine filtered through her bedroom window, casting patches on the floor. As she dressed, she mentally rehearsed how she would broach the topic with Miriam. She didn't want to seem intrusive or too eager, but she was certain that Miriam, with her maternal intuition and kind demeanor, would understand her curiosity.

When Jetti arrived at the gown shop, Miriam was already there, her hands busy arranging bolts of fabric on the shelves. The shop smelled noticeably of flowers and cedar, a scent that forged with the early aroma of yeasty bread drifting in from the bakery next door. Miriam greeted her with a huge smile, her dark eyes sparkling as if she already sensed the questions Jetti was holding back.

"Good morning, Jetti," Miriam said, motioning toward the work table. "We have a lot to accomplish today. The dress is coming along beautifully, but there's much to be done."

Jetti nodded, her hands already reaching for the neatly folded fabric they'd tucked away the day before. "Good morning, Miriam," she replied, her voice steady but tinged with the excitement she couldn't quite suppress. "I was hoping, as we work, I could ask you about something... personal."

Miriam paused, her hands resting on the edge of the table, and tilted her head in curiosity. "Of course, dear. What's on your mind?"

She hesitated for a moment, then smiled shyly. "It's about pregnancy. I know the basics...Aaron made sure of that... but I've always wondered... what is it really like? Not just the facts, but the feelings, the changes... the experience."

A knowing smile spread across her lips. She gestured for Jetti to sit beside her, threading a needle with practiced ease. "Ah, Jetti," she said, her voice patient. "Pregnancy is as much a journey of the heart as it is of the body. Let's work on the dress, and I'll tell you everything you wish to know."

Miriam picked up a piece of the fabric, running her fingers along its smooth surface before positioning it on the table. "Pregnancy," she began, her voice steady, "is like sewing a dress. Each stage is a different stitch, a new piece of fabric coming together to create something extraordinary. At first, you don't see much, maybe just an idea, a possibility. But then you feel it in every part of yourself. It's subtle, almost like the first threads we lay down here."

Jetti looked up from her stitching, her fingers pausing over the needle. "When do you first know?" she asked, her voice eager. "Is it immediate, or does it take time to realize?"

Miriam chuckled, an amusing sound that filled the empty shop. "For some, it's immediate, a feeling deep in the pit of your being, like a whisper only you can hear. For others, it's slower, a realization that grows as surely as the life inside you does. With Henry, I knew right away. There was no doubt in my mind. With the twins..." She shook her head, a glimmer of amusement in her eyes. "Let's just say it took me a bit longer to understand why I was so tired all the time."

"The twins," Jetti repeated, grinning. "What was that like? Carrying two instead of one?"

"Oh, it was twice the trouble and twice the joy," Miriam said, her hands moving deftly as she demonstrated a new stitching technique on the fabric. "They moved constantly, always kicking, always reminding me they were there. By the time they arrived, I felt like I'd already been wrestling with them for months!" She laughed, and Jetti joined in, imagining the spirited boys as they must have been even before birth.

Jetti tilted her head, her expression thoughtful. "Does it hurt? Everyone always talks about the joy of having a baby, but they don't often talk about... well, everything else."

She reached across the table to pat Jetti's hand. "There's pain, yes, but it's a strange kind of pain. It's purposeful. Every ache, every discomfort, is a sign of progress, a step closer to meeting your child. And there's so much more than pain. There's wonder, joy, and sometimes fear, but above all, there's love. An overwhelming, consuming love that makes every hardship worth it."

Jetti nodded, her eyes wide with fascination. "Did you ever feel afraid? I mean, with the world as it is... wasn't it scary to bring a child into it?"

Miriam's expression grew serious for a moment, her hands pausing in their work. "Yes, of course. Especially during times of uncertainty. But that fear is what drives you to be tough, to protect and nurture. The world may be unpredictable, but children... they're our future, our chance to make things better."

Jetti leaned forward, captivated. "What about Nina? Do you think she's ready for all of this?"

Miriam smiled knowingly. "Nina will be a wonderful mother, just as she is a wonderful sister and friend. But she doesn't know yet... truly know... how ready she is. That's something you discover along the way, just as I did, and just as you will when your time comes."

"My time?" Jetti asked, startled, her cheeks blushing. "I don't know if that will ever come."

Miriam looked at her kindly, her eyes twinkling. "Oh, Jetti, life has a way of surprising us. For now, focus on the present. Let's finish this dress, and tomorrow, we'll face whatever comes with open hearts and steady hands."

Chapter Twenty-two:
Threads of Motherhood

The Singer gown shop buzzed with its usual bustle of activity, but Miriam couldn't shake the unease that settled in her chest. Jetti hadn't come in that morning, a rare occurrence for someone so eager and dedicated. By mid-afternoon, she decided to act. After packing a basket with soup, fresh bread, and a corked glass bottle of cold chamomile tea, she paused, glancing at the beautiful box that held the finished dress. The familiar blue fabric and intricate stitching had been a labor of love, and she knew it would bring a little cheer to Jetti. She tucked it carefully under her arm and called for her maid, Inga, to accompany her.

The late spring air was breezy and fragrant with blooming flowers as Miriam made her way to Jetti's family home. Inga carried the basket, her steps short yet purposeful as they approached the grand estate. Miriam, ever composed, knocked on the door. To her surprise, it was Aaron who answered, his sharp features etched with worry.

"Miriam," Aaron said, his voice low. "Thank you for coming. She's upstairs, she hasn't been herself. I'm afraid she's taken quite ill."

Miriam placed a reassuring hand on his arm. "Don't worry, Aaron. These things often seem worse than they are. Let me see her." She gestured to Inga, who handed the basket to Aaron with a polite nod before retreating to wait in the kitchen.

Carrying the dress box herself, Miriam and Aaron climbed the grand marble staircase to Jetti's suite. With Aaron waiting outside, she paused for a moment at the door before entering. She looked at Aaron, her heart full with concern but her face calm and steady. When she stepped inside, she found Jetti lying in a small bed holding a bedpan full of vomit, propped up by pillows. Her complexion was pale, her hair neatly braided. But when Jetti saw Miriam, her lips curved into a big, grateful smile.

"Miriam," Jetti murmured, her voice weak. "You didn't have to come."

"Of course, I did," Miriam replied, setting the dress box down on a nearby chair. Aaron placed the basket of food on the bedside table leaving them alone.

"You're practically family now, Jetti. And I couldn't leave my best apprentice to suffer alone. How are you feeling, dear?"

Jetti sighed, her hand resting against her stomach. "Nauseous. Exhausted. I don't know what's wrong with me."

Miriam's sharp eyes relaxed as she perched on the edge of the bed. She reached out to take Jetti's hand in hers, her grip steady. "Sometimes the body has a way of telling us to slow down," she said, her tone soothing. "But you'll be all right. I brought you some food to help settle your stomach and..." She gestured toward the box. "A little surprise to lift your spirits."

Jetti's stared at the box, curiosity lighting her weary features. "What's in it?"

Miriam smiled. "Something you helped create. Your dress is finished, and it's more beautiful than I could have imagined. I thought you might like to see the fruits of your labor."

Jetti's expression turned to curiosity, a spark of interest and confusion breaking through her fatigue. "You brought it here... but why?"

For a moment, the mention of the dress seemed to distract Jetti from her discomfort. She sat up, her eyes on Miriam. "You didn't have to do that," she said, though there was a hint of gratitude in her tone.

"Nonsense," Miriam said with a wave of her hand. "I'm here to take care of you, Jetti. Now, tell me, when did all this start?"

"A few days ago… right before the sabbath," Jetti admitted, leaning back against the pillows. "I thought it was something I ate, but it hasn't gone away."

Miriam nodded, her expression thoughtful. She reached for the basket and poured Jetti a cup of the tea, handing it to her. "Drink this, it'll help settle your stomach. And don't worry yourself too much. We'll figure this out together."

As Jetti sipped the tea, Miriam sat back, watching her closely. The young woman's pale face reminded her of her own sisters when they were expecting, though she kept that thought to herself for now. Instead, she offered Jetti a comforting smile and reached for the dress box, opening it to reveal the azure fabric glinting in the afternoon daylight.

"See?" Miriam said, holding up the dress so Jetti could admire it. "You helped make this, Jetti. It's a masterpiece, and so are you."

Jetti's lips curved into a genuine smile as she admired the dress. For a brief moment, her weariness seemed to lift, replaced by the maternal comfort of Miriam's care and the beauty of their shared work.

Miriam sat beside Jetti's bed, her fingers smoothing the creases of the dress inside the box. Jetti had barely touched the food Miriam brought, but the tea had helped calm her nausea, and her cheeks had regained some color. Miriam knew the time had come… the time to speak plainly, to tell Jetti the truth she'd been avoiding.

She placed her hands on Jetti's, her eyes kind and knowing, and leaned closer. "Jetti, I think it's time we spoke honestly about what's happening. You've been ill for some days now, and I know you've been more tired than usual. But it's important you understand something."

Jetti blinked, a cloud of confusion hanging over her features. She shifted uncomfortably on the bed, unsure of what Miriam was implying. "I... I don't understand, Miriam. What do you mean?" Her voice was shaky, but she trusted Miriam, more than anyone else in the world right now.

Miriam hesitated for a moment, as if deciding how to begin. Then, with a happy sigh, she spoke. "Jetti, I helped you make this dress for you... I've known for a while. I could see it in the way you've been feeling, the way you've been carrying yourself." She placed a hand over Jetti's, her touch warm. "You're pregnant, my dear."

The words hit Jetti like a blow to the chest. Her breath caught, her heart thundering. She stared at Miriam, her lips parted, but no words came out. It was as though the world had stopped turning, the very air in the room chilled in an instant. She had known for a while something was wrong, but pregnancy? It seemed so impossible, so unimaginable.

"Miriam..." Jetti whispered, her voice small and unsteady, as if testing the words. "But... how did you know? How could you be sure?" Her eyes searched Miriam's face, her mind trying to make sense of it all. "I didn't know... I don't understand. How is this even possible?"

Miriam's eyes softened with tenderness and understanding. "I'm a mother, Jetti. I've carried children, and I've raised them. It's in the way your body changes, the way you speak, the way you look at life." She paused, her voice filled with empathy. "I saw the signs. And I've seen many women in your situation, in the same place you are now. I could feel it in my heart."

Jetti let Miriam's words sink in, her eyes beginning to brim with tears. Until now, the truth had hovered at the edge of her awareness. She hadn't allowed herself to believe it... not fully... not until she heard it spoken aloud. And now, the reality struck with a force that stole her breath. Joy, fear, disbelief, and something even deeper surged through her, crashing like a tide she couldn't control. Her hands trembled, as they often did when anxiety crept in—a habit she was painfully aware of. A new life was growing inside her... and everything had just changed.

"Joel…" she whispered, the name slipping from her lips like a prayer, a plea. "Joel… I never thought… I never imagined it would be like this." Her voice cracked, and she turned her face into the pillow, trying to stifle the sobs that rose within her.

Miriam's heart broke for Jetti, but she didn't flinch. She stayed close, her presence unwavering as she comforted her. "Jetti," she said, "I know this is hard. It's not what you planned. It's not what you expected. But this child, this little one inside you, it's a gift. It's a part of you, and you will have the family support here in this home to raise a child." She squeezed Jetti's hand, offering reassurance, a steady force in the storm.

Jetti shook her head, tears streaking her cheeks. "How can I do this? How can I raise a child on my own? Joel left me, Miriam. He left me, and now I'm… I'm alone." The anger bubbled up in her chest, sharp and bitter. "How could he leave me like this? How could he not be here? He promised me he would stay. He promised me everything."

Miriam leaned forward, her voice calm but resolute. "You can do this, Jetti. You will do this. You have the support of your family. You will carry this child with love, and you will raise it with the same care and affection you've devoted to everything else in your life."

Jetti's tears fell freely now, her shoulders trembling as a surge of emotions overwhelmed her. Fear rose first, followed by anger, then loss. But beneath it all was something else, buried deep inside, difficult to name. She knew Miriam was right. As impossible as it seemed, she would survive. She would not let fear or the absence of Joel define the course of her life.

After a long moment, Jetti wiped her eyes, taking a deep, shaky breath. Her voice was steady now. "I'll raise this baby, Miriam. I'll give it everything it needs. I'll make sure it has a future, and I'll make sure it knows love, and kindness, and consistency. I'll teach it, and I'll love it like nothing else. I won't let it grow up like I did, without a mother who couldn't care for me properly." Her eyes locked with Miriam's, with a spark of determination in her eyes. "I'll give this child everything. Everything."

Miriam smiled, tears glistening in her own eyes. "That's the spirit, Jetti. You'll be a wonderful mother. You may not have the answers yet, but you'll find them as you go. And I'll be here for you. Your family will be here for you. You will never be alone."

Jetti took a deep breath, wiping her tears away, and nodded. "Thank you, Miriam. I can't say that enough. Thank you for being here. Thank you for helping me see this through."

"You don't need to thank me, Jetti," Miriam replied with a tender smile. "It's what family does. And you're part of my family now, always."

With that, Jetti stood up slowly, her decision settling around her like a cloak. She was ready. She was ready to face whatever came next. And no matter what, she would protect this child.

Chapter Twenty-three:
Expectations

The weeks following Jetti's discovery of her pregnancy unfolded in a blur of activity, anticipation, and shared moments with her family. Working at the dress shop had become a sanctuary for her, a place where her hands were busy, her mind focused, and her heart lightened by the companionship of Miriam and the others. Each stitch she made seemed to reinforce her determination to build a better future, not just for herself but for the little life growing inside her.

When Nina finally announced her pregnancy to the family a week later, the house erupted in joy. Miriam's suspicions had been confirmed, the delight in her voice as she congratulated her son Henry and his wife was contagious. Nina, blushing and animated, had embraced her pregnancy with an enthusiasm that made Jetti feel a sense of camaraderie she hadn't expected. They were now two sisters embarking on this journey together, their shared experience drawing them closer.

It wasn't long before Miriam and Jetti began work on another dress, this one for Nina. The practicality of Nina's daily life in the factory with Henry meant her clothing had to be functional as well as confortable. Jetti relished the opportunity to create something special for her sister, something that would both celebrate her growing family and accommodate her active lifestyle.

The fabric chosen was a fashionable, durable cotton in a bluish shade of sage green, perfect for the long summer days ahead. Miriam guided Jetti as they designed a dress with clever elements:

the front featured a row of sturdy buttons for ease of wear, and a smock-style apron could be attached or removed as needed. Pockets, of course, were an essential feature. Jetti had fallen in love with the pockets of her dress, and she knew Nina would appreciate having a place to tuck away small tools or a notepad as she moved between tasks at the warehouse.

"Do you think she'll like the smock idea?" Jetti asked, holding up the apron piece she'd just finished stitching.

Miriam smiled as she inspected the work. "She'll love it, Jetti. You've thought of everything—a balance of practicality and beauty. That's exactly what Nina needs right now."

Jetti felt a swell of pride. She had come a long way since the first time she picked up a needle under Miriam's guidance. Sewing wasn't just a skill; it had become a creative outlet and a way to connect with the women in her life.

As Jetti and Nina spent more time together, their conversations began to center around their shared experiences. They would sit on the veranda in the evenings, sipping tea, their laughter drifting with the summer breeze. Nina's stories of her work at the factory always made Jetti smile, though she couldn't help but marvel at her sister's energy.

"I don't know how you do it," Jetti admitted one evening. "I can barely keep up at the shop some days, and you're managing all that cumbersome work."

Nina laughed, resting a hand on her growing belly. "It's not easy, but it keeps me busy. And Henry's been extra careful about making sure I don't overdo it. Honestly, I think he worries more than I do."

Jetti grinned. "That sounds like Henry. Always the protector."

Nina's smile widened as she reached for Jetti's hand. "I'm glad we're going through this together. It's strange, isn't it? Our lives changing so much at the same time."

"It is," Jetti agreed, her voice tinged with both awe and trepidation. "But it's comforting, too. Knowing we have each other."

Though her moments with Nina were a source of comfort, Jetti often found herself lost in thought during her evenings alone. She would run her hand over her abdomen, marveling at the tiny fluttering movements within. The reality of her situation was both daunting and exhilarating. She was adjusting to the idea of raising this child without Joel, but her heart had never wavered.

Her baby would have everything. Jetti would make sure of it. And with the love and support of her family, Miriam's steady guidance, Aaron's fatherly instincts, and Nina's companionship, she knew she would find a way to make it work.

One evening, as she carefully folded the dress they had made for Nina into a gift box, Jetti whispered softly to her unborn child. "We're going to be okay, little one. I promise."

The next morning the air was still but fragrant, carrying the scent of blooming lilacs and freshly turned earth from the gardens that stretched between the Singer property and the massive estate where Jetti lived with her family. Clutching the gift-wrapped dress under her arm, Jetti walked briskly along the cobblestone path that meandered through the gardens, her excitement bubbling with every step. The Singer home was impressive in the gleaming rays of the early sun, the usual ruckus of activity replaced by the stillness of a Saturday's rest.

Jetti's steps quickened as she reached the grand veranda of the Singer home, a stately brick building with ivy climbing its walls, and windows draped in elegant lace. She paused to adjust her own dress, the teal and blue gown that she and Miriam had designed and sewed together. The dress had hidden pleats and a suitable empire waist that accommodated her growing belly without drawing attention to it. It was Jetti's favorite, and today, it felt perfect for the occasion.

She knocked briskly on the door, and it wasn't long before Nina appeared, her cheeks flushed with the bloom of pregnancy and her ever-present energy. "Jetti!" Nina gushed, her arms already outstretched for an embrace.

"I have something for you," Jetti announced, unable to hide the grin spreading across her face. "But we'll need somewhere to lay it out."

Nina's curiosity piqued, she led Jetti to the sitting room, a cozy space with plush chairs and a large oval table that caught the morning sunlight. As they settled in, Jetti placed the box carefully on the table and began untying the ribbon.

Recognizing the dress shop box she said, "I can't believe you've been working on something for me," Nina said, her hands resting on her belly. "You've already been doing so much."

Jetti smiled, her heart brimming with her sister's gratitude. "This is different, Nina. I wanted to make something special just for you, like Miriam did for me." With a flourish, she opened the box and carefully lifted out the dress.

It was a masterpiece of thoughtful design, a sage-green cotton gown that seemed to capture the essence of spring. The fabric was pliable yet sturdy, perfect for Nina's active days at the factory. The bodice featured delicate pintucks that added texture and style without being too formal, and a row of buttons that ran down the front, making it easy to put on and take off. The sleeves were puffed at the shoulder, tapering into a practical three-quarter length.

The skirt, cut generously, was the highlight of the dress. It included cleverly hidden pleats that could be let out as Nina's belly grew, ensuring the dress would fit comfortably throughout her pregnancy. The pockets were deep and seamlessly integrated, ideal for carrying tools or a notebook. Jetti had also added two detachable smocks, one in a coordinating plaid pattern, and the other in a floral, which buttoned neatly at the shoulders and waist, providing extra protection for the dress during work hours.

Nina gasped, her hands flying to her mouth. "Jetti, it's beautiful! How did you think of all this?"

Jetti beamed, smoothing her hand over the fabric. "Miriam and I worked on it together. We wanted it to be something you could wear every day, something functional but also lovely."

Nina reached out to touch the fabric, her fingers tracing the pintucks. "It's perfect. And these pleats...how do they work?"

Jetti demonstrated, pulling at the hidden seams to reveal the extra fabric. "As you grow, you can let these out. It's easy to sew them back in after the baby comes if you want to use a dress again."

"And the smocks?" Nina asked, holding up the detachable piece.

"For your work at the factory," Jetti explained. "They button on, so you can remove them when you aren't working. There are two patterns so the dress won't ever get boring. And these pockets, look how deep they are!"

Nina laughed, slipping her hands into the pockets. "I love the pockets! You've thought of everything, Jetti. Thank you."

She sat down beside Nina, smoothing the fabric of her own dress. "Miriam made this one for me before I knew I was pregnant," she said, gesturing to the gown she wore. "It works the same way. See the pleats here? And the empire waist? It's been such a relief to have something that fits and looks nice."

Nina studied Jetti's dress with admiration. "It's beautiful. And so clever. You're really learning so much, Jetti."

She blushed at the praise, her hands resting protectively over her belly. "I just want to be prepared. For everything."

Nina reached over and squeezed her sister's hand. "We'll get through this together, Jetti. You and me. And these little ones." She patted her own belly with a smile.

Jetti felt a surge of emotion, unconditional love for herself strengthening once again. "Yes, we will," she said. "We'll make sure of it."

As Jetti walked back home, the sun hung mid-sky, casting afternoon shadows over the gardens she passed. It was a Saturday that felt like a gift, a rare day when the world seemed to stop, allowing her a reprieve from the chaos of work and hidden worries.

The dress for Nina had been a triumph, and seeing her sister's delight had warmed a part of Jetti's heart she hadn't realized had gone cold. Yet now, as she meandered down the cobblestone path, a familiar sense of solitude settled over her. She traced the edges of the ribbon in her pocket, the one that had tied the box closed, as if anchoring herself to the moment.

Entering the house through the back door into the kitchen, she exchanged pleasantries with the cook, who handed her a plate of soft cheese, fresh bread, and a few pickled vegetables. Jetti thanked her, retreating to her suite with her modest meal. Bathed in the newness of spring air, the space felt like an intimate sanctuary. The teal chairs by the open window beckoned, and she sank into one with a sigh, balancing the plate carefully on her lap.

The breeze filtered through the curtains, carrying the essence of lilacs and the delicate rustle of leaves. It was a perfect day for reading, and Jetti reached for the novel on her bedside table, a well-worn copy of *Jane Eyre*. She found herself drawn to Jane's strength, her independence, her resolve to carry on despite heartbreak. It felt oddly comforting to lose herself in another's struggles, as if the story whispered to her that she too could endure.

Chapter Twenty-four:
Knell of the Bell

Five months had passed since Joel had walked out of her life, the lack of any parting words reverberating blindly in her mind. At first, she had been consumed by the pain of his absence, her days a blur of longing and disbelief. But now, Joel was little more than a shadow at the edge of her thoughts. Occasionally, she wondered if he might write, if a post card might arrive one day with his familiar scrawl, but those moments were fleeting. She remembered that he had only written three times in the years he was away at war, so she wouldn't get her hopes up.

Her focus had shifted. The work at the Singer shop, the joy of crafting garments that were tangible and beautiful, had grounded her. Her pregnancy, though daunting, had become a source of reflection. She would not dwell on what could have been; instead, she would build something new.

The flutter was subtle as she rested her hand on the front of her gown, but the fullness beneath her palm was unmistakable. She couldn't help but wonder who this little life would grow to be. Would they have Joel's dark eyes or her sharp wit? Would they grow to love the same stories she cherished or find their own path entirely?

Jetti chuckled outloud, brushing away the thought. There was so much unknown, so much to prepare for, but she was determined. This child would have a life full of love and learning. She would see to it personally.

A knock at her door startled her from her thoughts. "Come in," she called. It was her sister, Nurit, peeking her head in.

"Are you busy?" She asked, stepping into the room without waiting for an answer.

"Not at all," Jetti replied, closing her book. "What's on your mind?"

Nurit perched on the arm of the other teal chair, her eyes sparkling with curiosity. "I heard you went to see Nina. Did she love the dress?"

"She did," Jetti said with a chuckle. "She couldn't stop talking about the pockets."

Nurit grinned. "Pockets are revolutionary, you know. It's the first thing I'll demand when I have a dress made."

Jetti laughed, a sound that felt foreign yet freeing. She felt a sense of contentment creeping in, a glimmer of the life she was building for herself; one stitch, one step, one day at a time.

Nurit leaned back in the chair, folding her legs beneath her as if settling in for a proper chat. "So," she began, her voice teasing, "have you thought about names yet? For the baby?"

Jetti blinked, a little caught off guard. "Names?" she repeated, the question lingering in the air. "I... haven't thought much about it yet."

Nurit tilted her head, her expression keen and encouraging. "Well, you've got time, but it's fun to imagine, isn't it? If it's a boy, maybe something traditional, like David or Samuel. And if it's a girl... oh, how about Rivka or Tova? Something elegant."

Jetti smiled, the idea of choosing a name suddenly feeling less daunting. "I've always liked the name Aaron for a boy," she admitted, her thoughts drifting to her eldest brother and his steadfast guidance. "It feels... honorable. And for a girl, maybe something modern, like Sylvia or Charlotte. Names that carry vitality, but also grace."

Nurit nodded, her enthusiasm growing. "Aaron is perfect, especially with how much you look up to him. And Charlotte... oh,

I adore that! It's so elegant and timeless. Like a queen from one of those storybooks Mama used to read us, the ones with enchanted castles and magical kingdoms."

Jetti's smile faltered at the mention of their mother, but she quickly recovered. "I wonder if the baby will come early, like you did, Nurit. Or perhaps it'll be a September baby, just as expected. I suppose we'll see."

Nurit leaned forward conspiratorially. "I was early because I couldn't wait to see the world," she said with a playful grin. "Maybe your baby will take after me and surprise us all."

They both laughed out loud before Nurit's expression turned more serious. "Have you been keeping up with the news? It's strange, isn't it? Everything happening here, and yet the world feels like it's on fire."

Jetti nodded, focusing on the open window where the breeze carried with it a morose sense of unease. "Yes, the papers have been full of it. The war seems endless, and I hear people whispering about what will happen to our city if things shift further."

Nurit bit her lip. "Joseph said Austria-Hungary is starting to crumble from the inside. The Germans are holding on, but it feels fragile, doesn't it? And with the Russians and Germans pushing closer, I wonder how long Czernowitz will feel like home."

Nurit leaned back in the chair, adjusting her skirts as she settled in more comfortably. "So," she said after a pause, "have you been hearing much about this flu that everyone keeps whispering about? It's all Miriam Singer could talk about when I visited her last week."

Jetti tilted her head, her brows knitting together. "The flu?" she repeated. "Miriam hasn't said anything about it at work. I've heard snippets, something about it being bad in Vienna, but we haven't paid much attention. Should I be worried?"

Nurit nodded solemnly, her voice dropping to a near whisper as if speaking the words aloud might invite trouble. "They're calling it an epidemic, Jetti. Some say it's worse than anything they've seen before. It's spreading fast, and people are scared."

Jetti's hand instinctively went to her belly, a protective gesture she didn't even notice. "How bad is it here? Has anyone in Czernowitz fallen ill?"

Nurit shrugged, a sense of unease crossing her face. "Not that I know of, but the papers say it's only a matter of time. There's talk of people traveling less, trying to avoid crowds. Aaron said the warehouses might cut back production hours if things get bad, and people get sick."

Jetti frowned, her mind already racing. "What can we do? I mean, what should I do? Being pregnant..." Her words trailed off, and she looked down.

Nurit reached out, placing her hand over Jetti's. "You're doing everything right, Jetti. Resting when you need to, eating well, staying close to family. Miriam said something about wearing scarves over your mouth in crowded places. It sounds strange, but maybe it helps."

Jetti nodded slowly, trying to absorb it all. "I'll do whatever it takes to keep this baby safe, Nurit. Whatever it takes."

She smiled, her tone lightening. "Of course you will. You're already an incredible mother, even if you don't realize it yet. And besides, we'll all help you; me, Joseph, Aaron, Nina, Miriam, everyone."

Jetti's lips curved up, though the worry didn't completely leave her eyes. "Thank you, Nurit. I don't know what I'd do without you. Or without all of you. Family is everything, isn't it?"

"It is," she agreed. "And don't forget it. Whatever happens, whether it's this flu or the war or anything else ,we'll face it together. Just like we always have."

Jetti sighed, her fingers brushing over the delicate embroidery on the cushion beside her. "It's hard to imagine what the future will hold, for us, for this city. But I do know one thing; no matter what happens, we'll endure. Just like always."

The sisters sat for a moment, the breeze drifting in through the open window. The world outside might have been filled with uncertainty, but in that room, surrounded by the credibility of their bond, Jetti felt just a little bit more at peace.

Then, the distant but unmistakable knell of bells tolled; sharp, somber, and persistent. Nurit stiffened, her hand tightening around Jetti's. "That's not the hour bell," she whispered, her voice barely audible.

Jetti turned toward the window, her heartbeat quickening. The bells carried an ominous weight, their rhythm slow and deliberate, echoing across the city like a warning. A shadow passed over Nurit's face as she leaned closer, lowering her voice to a hush.

"Do you think… it's already here…the flu?"

A shiver slipped down Jetti's spine despite the warmth of the sun-drenched room. Her fingers drifted down, her palm instinctively finding the rise of the little promise growing within her. "I don't know," she whispered, her voice trembling. "But I think we're about to find out."

The air between them thickened with love, dread, and the shared understanding that the world around them was shifting in ways they weren't ready to face.

Chapter Twenty-five:
Spanish Flu

Monday morning arrived with a crisp breeze and the fresh smell of rain in the air. Jetti, clutching a drawing tube under her arm, stepped briskly along the cobblestone path to the Singer dress shop. Her heart fluttered with excitement as she thought about the sketches she'd spent the weekend perfecting. This time it was an innovative nurse's gown, designed with serviceability and adaptability in mind. The gown featured hidden pockets, interchangeable buttoned smocks, and durable fabric ideal for long shifts, similar to the one she had designed and made for Nina but more practical. Jetti couldn't wait to share the designs with Miriam.

As she approached the shop, her excitement turned to confusion. The usual scurry of activity was absent. No workers passed by carrying bolts of fabric, and the front door hung ajar, the shop silent inside. Pushing the door open, Jetti's steps clicked on the polished wood floors. The dust from chalk and something metallic lingered, but no voices called out to greet her.

"Miriam?" she called, setting her drawing tube on the counter. "Nina? Henry?"

No answer. Jetti felt a pang of unease creep into her chest. She turned toward the warehouse entrance at the back of the shop, where the workers usually bustled around machines and cutting tables. As she entered the large, airy space, the sight that greeted her made her stop in her tracks. Only half the workers were there, Even Ester and Goldie weren't there, their usual lively banter replaced by the murmur of sewing machines. The air felt charged with an unbreakable tension.

Suddenly, a rough cough broke the silence behind her. Jetti whirled around to see Ralph, the foreman, standing there, his face pale and lined with exhaustion. His thick canvas apron hung loosely over his frame, and he clutched a rag in one hand. He coughed again, the sound harsh and wet, making Jetti instinctively take a step back.

"Ralph," she said cautiously, "where is everyone? Why is it so quiet today?"

He sniffled and wiped his nose with the back of his hand before speaking. "They're all sick," he rasped, his voice thick with congestion. "Half the workers, maybe more. Miriam, Henry, Nina… they didn't come in today either. Same story. Everyone's getting this blasted flu."

Jetti felt a jolt of panic as his words sank in. "The flu?" Her voice barely above a whisper.

Ralph nodded grimly, stifling another cough. "It's bad, Jetti. Real bad. Spreading like wildfire. I tried to tell the boss we should close the warehouse for a few days, but you know how it is, business doesn't stop."

"But you're sick too," Jetti pointed out, her eyes widening as she stepped back further. "You shouldn't even be here!"

He shrugged, a bitter smile tugging at his cracked lips. "Someone's gotta keep this place running. Workers need wages, and orders have deadlines. What else can we do?"

Jetti stared at him, her mind racing. Ralph sneezed abruptly, turning his head but barely managing to cover his mouth with the rag. Horror washed over her as she realized how close she was standing to him. Nurit's words from the weekend came rushing back to her 'cover your mouth, avoid crowds.' She hadn't expected to face this reality so soon.

"I… I… I need to go," Jetti stammered, taking another step back. "I'll come back when things are… better."

Ralph nodded absently, his attention already turning back to the warehouse floor. Jetti spun on her heel and rushed back into the shop. Her hands shook as she gathered fabric scraps, quickly stitching together a makeshift mask using three layers of fabric and the ribbon she kept in her pocket. The needle moved in quick, frantic jerks, her usually steady hands trembling with urgency.

Once the mask was done, she tied it securely over her mouth and nose, feeling absolutely ridiculous but determined. She hurried to the front of the shop, flipped the **OPEN** sign to **CLOSED**, and locked the door. With her makeshift mask in place, she darted down the cobblestone streets toward home.

The townsfolk turned to stare as she passed, their eyes narrowing in suspicion or curiosity at the sight of her covered face. She ignored them, her focus fixed on one goal, getting home safely. Her heart pounded as she climbed the steps to the front door, fear paralyzing her with its grip.

As she removed the mask and sank into her favorite teal chair, she closed her eyes for a moment, willing herself to stay calm. The world outside felt more uncertain than ever, but inside her, life was growing. For the baby's sake, she reminded herself, she would stay healthy, no matter what.

Jetti sat, staring out the window as the breeze stirred the curtains. Her mind raced with everything she'd just witnessed at the shop. The foreman's harsh cough continued to replay in her ears, and the sight of the nearly empty workspace haunted her. This flu was no longer a distant worry whispered about in town; it was here, in her community, affecting her friends and family. A faint quiver stirred inside her, subtle yet undeniable, like a whisper beneath her skin. She had to act, and quickly.

First, she decided she couldn't take any chances with her health or the baby's. Rising from the chair, she went to her desk, pulled a piece of paper and a pencil, and began jotting down a plan. She'd need to gather supplies: food and basic medicines to last at least a few weeks. She would avoid crowded places at all costs, only venturing out when absolutely necessary. Jetti's heart ached at the thought of isolating herself, but survival for her and the baby was the priority now.

She also realized she had to warn her family. Grabbing her

shawl, she headed to her brother Aaron's office. The streets were quieter than usual, the air overcast with unease. She pulled the mask back over her face, ignoring the sideways glances from a few passersby. Finally reaching Aaron's building, she knocked at his office door, quickly, urgency tightening her chest.

Aaron opened the door, his face breaking into a big smile that quickly faded when he saw the mask. "Jetti? What's going on, why are you wearing fabric over your face?"

She stepped inside and removed it. "Aaron, it's the flu. It's worse than I thought. Half the workers at the Singer shop are sick, and Miriam, Nina, and Henry didn't come in today. I'm scared, Aaron. We have to be careful."

He frowned, rubbing his chin as he listened. "I've heard about it spreading, but I didn't think it would hit us this fast. You're right to be cautious. We need to protect you and the baby."

She nodded, grateful for his support. "I'm going to stock up on supplies and stay home as much as possible. Will you help me with a list? I don't want to forget anything."

Aaron agreed, and together they brainstormed essentials; dried goods, canned food, fresh produce, and herbs for remedies. He promised to send one of his assistants to fetch the items so she wouldn't have to risk exposure at the market.

Once back home, she began setting up a system to sanitize anything that came into the house. She had the cook boil water, adding vinegar for cleaning surfaces and utensils. She also asked Anka to scour the pantry shelves, rearranging them to make room for the incoming supplies. Her movements were swift and deliberate, driven by the maternal instinct to protect her child.

But as night fell, isolation began to settle on her. She sat by the fire, the warmth doing little to ease the chill of loneliness creeping into her heart. She thought of Miriam and Nina, wondering how they were faring. The baby in her womb gave another flutter, a reminder of her purpose, and she placed her hand over the growing life.

"I'll keep us safe," she whispered. "I promise."

Chapter Twenty-six:
Stolen Future

The next morning, Jetti woke with a renewed sense of determination. She decided to continue working on her sketches for the nursing gowns, believing that her designs would make a difference. Setting up her drawing materials in the sunlight by the window, she worked tirelessly, refining every detail; the buttoned smock, the hidden pockets, the durable but breathable fabric. Her sketches became a way to channel her fear into something productive and meaningful.

By mid-afternoon, she had an entire collection of designs ready. Jetti decided she would write a letter to Miriam, explaining her ideas and ask for feedback. If Miriam and the Singers could find a way to produce these gowns, they might help the nurses caring for the sick and provide much-needed income for the workers once they returned.

The thought lifted her spirits. As she sealed the letter and slid it into the drawing tube, she made arrangements to have Anka deliver it. She'd done her best to adapt to the circumstances, finding satisfaction in her creativity and her love for the unborn child. Though the road ahead was uncertain, Jetti felt like moving forward was her only option.

That evening, she lit a candle by her window and said the *Mi Shebeirach* prayer for her family, her community, and the world beyond. The floral air whispered through the curtains, carrying with it a fragile sense of peace. Whatever came next, she would face it with courage and bravery.

Jetti was carefully stitching the edge of a simple cotton scarf when a sudden knock at the door startled her. Setting down her needle, she walked to the door, already sensing that something was wrong. When she opened it, Anka stood at the threshold, her face pale and a scarf tied tightly over her nose and mouth. Her eyes were wide, full of worry.

"Anka?" Jetti asked, concern knotting her stomach. "What's happened?"

Anka hesitated, her voice trembling as she finally spoke. "It's the Singers. They're all sick, Jetti. This flu… it's everywhere, and I'm scared."

The news hit Jetti like a blow. "All of them? Miriam, Nina, everyone?"

Anka nodded gravely. "It started with Michael and David. They were in Vienna on business, picking up fabric. They must have gotten sick there and brought it back. They fell ill almost as soon as they returned. Fever, chills, coughing that doesn't stop. Miriam says they've barely been able to drink water for days."

Jetti clasped a hand over her mouth, her thoughts racing. "And the others?"

"It spread so quickly," Anka said, her voice breaking. "Haiam is bedridden now, his fever is not breaking. Henry caught it too, but he's holding on better. And Nina… oh, Jetti, she's so weak. With the baby…" Anka shook her head, unable to finish the sentence.

Jetti stepped back, leaning against the wall for support. She felt like the world was collapsing around her. "What about Miriam?"

"She's up and moving," Anka replied, "but just barely. She's trying to care for everyone, but it's taking a toll. I spoke to her from the balcony. She wouldn't let me get close, not even to pass her the Kichlach I made for them. She told me to place them into a basket she lowered down with a rope."

Jetti closed her eyes, picturing Miriam standing on the grand balcony, her matronly figure now weighed down by worry and exhaustion. "What did she say to you?"

"She told me not to come back," Anka admitted. "She doesn't want anyone else exposed. She said the house feels like a prison now. Every cough echoes through the halls, every fevered cry reminds her how close they are to losing someone."

Jetti's knees buckled, and she grabbed the back of a chair for support. "And Nina?" she whispered, her heart breaking.

Anka hesitated, then said, "She's the worst, Jetti. The fever has drained her completely. Miriam said she can barely eat or even open her eyes. The baby... Miriam's worried that if Nina doesn't recover soon..."

Jetti didn't let her finish. "No," she said firmly, tears burning her eyes. "Nina will get through this. She has to. She's strong, Anka. She's always been strong."

Anka wiped at her eyes with the corner of her sleeve. "I hope you're right. I left the drawings for the nurse's gowns by the side kitchen door, but I don't think anyone will see them. No one's coming or going from the house, and I didn't see any of the staff. I'm so scared, Jetti. I don't want to get sick either."

She looked at Anka, understanding the fear etched on her face. "You were right to stay away from them. You've done enough, just by going there and helping how you could."

Anka nodded, with guilt clearly in her eyes. "I don't know if I've done enough. I wish I could do more."

Jetti placed a comforting hand on her shoulder. "You've done what you can. Now we just have to hope and pray. For Miriam, for Nina, for all of them. You should stay home now; please don't go anywhere, as you know Aaron has made arrangements for food and supplies to be brought to the mansion for everyone."

Anka stayed for a moment longer before finally retreating to her own room in the staff wing. Jetti closed the door and leaned her head against it, her thoughts swirling. She was terrified for Nina and the baby, for Miriam and the boys. But she also knew she couldn't give in to despair. She had to stay well, for herself, for her own child.

Taking a deep breath, she returned to her sewing table, focusing on finishing a quilted baby blanket. Every stitch felt like a prayer, a plea for the health and safety of her loved ones.

The week passed in a haze of grief, fear, and emptiness. Jetti remained in her room, the curtains drawn against the cruel sun that seemed indifferent to the sorrow that had overtaken her world. She sat on the edge of her bed, clutching a piece of fabric, a remnant from the dress she and Miriam had sewn together for Nina. The bright green flower pattern felt mocking now, a painful reminder of lives lost and futures stolen.

When Anka came in, always masked and carrying a tray of food, Jetti would barely acknowledge her. Her meals were left untouched more often than not, the smell of even the simplest broth turning her stomach. Anka would carefully tidy the room, folding the pile of unused linens or straightening Jetti's discarded sketches, and then retreat without pressing her to talk.

The news had come gradually, each blow heavier than the last. First, it was Michael and David, their young bodies unable to fight off the relentless fever. Haiam, Ester, and Goldie followed only two days later, and then Henry succumbed as well, leaving Jetti and Anka to cling to fragile hope that Nina and Miriam might pull through.

But they didn't.

Nina, already so weak and carrying her unborn child, slipped away in the early hours of the morning. Her death shattered whatever strength Miriam had left. She passed the next day, her body exhausted from caring for everyone else while neglecting her own health.

The Singers were gone.

The once-bustling estate was lifeless now, the windows shuttered, the halls empty. No laughter, no music, no chatter of business deals or sewing machines clicking and buzzing in the shop. Just silence, broken only by the distant sounds of birdsong or the occasional passing cart in the street.

Anka sat on the edge of Jetti's bed one evening, her own face pale and drawn from worry. "Jetti, even though you are staying locked away like this, you have to eat, do it for the baby" she said, her voice muffled behind the mask she was wearing. "It's not good for you, or for the baby. You need to eat. You need to walk, and maybe go breathe fresh air."

Jetti turned her face toward the window, though her thoughts remained unfocused. "They're all gone, Anka," she whispered, her voice hollow. "How can the world go on when they're all dead?"

Anka reached out and took Jetti's hand. "The world does go on. It has to. For your baby, if nothing else. That child needs you to be healthy. You're the only one who can give it a chance to live, to thrive."

Tears welled in her eyes, but she didn't wipe them away. "Nina's baby never even had a chance... What if..." Her voice broke, and she couldn't finish the thought.

"You're not alone," Anka said. "You have me, and the rest of the family. We'll help you. But you have to help yourself too Jetti, please don't let this destroy you, like when Joel left. You have to stay alive for the baby."

Jetti finally looked at her, grief etched deeply into her face. "I don't know how to start again, Anka. Everything feels so... empty."

Anka squeezed her hand. "You start small. One step at a time. You eat a little, you walk a little, and then maybe, one day, you sew again. Nina would want that for you. Miriam would too."

The mention of their names brought a fresh wave of tears, but Jetti nodded. "I'll try," she said, though her voice lacked conviction.

Anka stood, smoothing her apron as she prepared to leave. "Good. I'll bring something special tomorrow. Maybe a little Sarmale from the kitchen and some Poppy Babka. You'll eat it, even if I have to sit here and watch you."

Jetti managed a weak smile, the first in days. "All right," she whispered.

As Anka left, Jetti sat in shock, a piece of fabric clutched in her hand. She thought of Nina, of the joy they'd shared over their pregnancies, of the plans they'd made. She thought of Miriam's wisdom, Haiam's booming laughter, and the brothers' endless teasing.

Their memories surrounded her like a fragile cocoon. And though her heart felt shattered, a tiny ember surged deep within her. For her child, for her family's legacy, she would survive. She would learn to live again, step by step, stitch by stitch.

Chapter Twenty-seven: Grief is Cruel

The sound of coughing outside her room jolted Jetti from her thoughts. It was rough and persistent, wretching ominously in the empty hallway. Her chest tightened as she recognized who's voice she heard. It was her brother Ben.

She stood abruptly, the fabric in her hand falling to the floor, forgotten. Her pulse quickened as she quickly opened the door and saw him leaning against the wall across the hallway, his face pale and his forehead glistening with sweat.

"Ben!" she exclaimed. "What's wrong? Are you sick?"

He waved a hand weakly, trying to dismiss her concern. "It's nothing, Jetti. Just a little cough, that's all."

But she wasn't convinced. She placed a hand on his arm, guiding him toward a chair in the hallway. "Sit down. You look terrible."

He resisted for a moment before relenting, lowering himself onto the chair near a window. His breathing was labored, and his shoulders sagged as though carrying an invisible pack on his back.

Jetti quickly thought about the makeshift mask she had been wearing the week earlier and ran back to her room to get it, she tied the mask over her mouth and nose and went out to where Ben was now bent over holding his head in his hands.

"How long have you been feeling like this?" she asked, her voice sharper than she intended.

"A day or two," he admitted reluctantly. "I didn't want to worry anyone."

"Not worry anyone?" Jetti's voice rose. "After everything that's happened to the Singers? You should have told us immediately!"

Ben coughed again, the sound tearing through the hall like a warning bell. He winced and looked at her with weary eyes. "I didn't want to scare you, Jetti. You've been through enough."

Her anger melted into concern as she knelt beside him, taking his hand. "Ben, we can't take chances. Not with this flu. You need rest, and you need to stay away from everyone else until we know what we're dealing with."

He nodded, too tired to argue. "I'll go to my room. Just... don't tell Aaron yet. He'll only worry more."

She hesitated. Aaron had already been so overwhelmed by the constant stream of bad news and loss. But this wasn't something they could afford to keep from him.

"I'll think about it," she said finally. "But you promise me, no more hiding how you feel. If it gets worse, I'll send for a doctor immediately."

Ben gave a weak smile. "You're starting to sound like Anka."

"Good," Jetti replied. "Maybe you'll listen."

As he stood to leave, she handed him a clean scarf from her dresser. "Wrap this around your face. If you're sick, we can't risk anyone else catching it."

Ben took it without argument, his hands trembling. He paused at the door, looking back at her. "Jetti, I'll be fine. You focus on you and the baby, all right?"

She swallowed hard, forcing a nod. "I will. But you focus on getting better."

After he left, Jetti closed the door and leaned against it, her heart pounding. The fear that had ebbed slightly in the past few days came rushing back, suffocating her. She pressed her hands to her abdomen, as if shielding the child inside from the chaos around her. Then immediately splashed the vinegary water from her wash basin on her hands then her face.

She dried them with a piece of linen and muttered to herself, "Please," as she looked out into the universe. "Please let him be all right. Let us all be all right."

Chapter Twenty-eight: Decimation

The house felt heavier than ever, the shadow of illness stretching its long fingers toward them once more. It was cloaked in silence… the kind of silence that crushed the spirit and settled deep into bones. Everyone was sequestered to their own suites. No one was to move about the house except a few of the staff including Anka and the cook, who were sworn to remain inside and not venture out.

Jetti sat by the window in her room, wishing she could hear the incessant coughing, which was unnatural to think about because it only meant that they were still alive. With her hands folded over her lap, her eyes unfocused as she stared into the empty garden below in complete and utter reticence. Lavender had started to bloom, their delicate purple blossoms swaying like sentinels in the spring breeze, but their beauty felt like a cruel mockery of the devastation inside the Finkelthal mansion.

Ben died first, just days after Jetti's frantic insistence that he stay in his room and rest. His cough had worsened, turning into a fever that ravaged his body and left him delirious. When the end came, it was mercilessly quick, leaving Jetti stunned and reeling.

Alan followed soon after, collapsing in the middle of his shop. The workers at the textile mill carried him home, their faces pale and drawn as they placed his fevered body in his bed. Despite the care and the prayers offered up in whispered desperation, the illness consumed him within days.

Milton fought valiantly against the fever that overtook him. He had been full of dreams and plans, often sharing his sketches for intricate jewelry designs with anyone who would look. But even his youthful stamina wasn't enough to fend off the relentless grip of the flu.

Now, Jetti sat alone, her grief pressing down like a leaden shroud. Anka had been the one to break the news each time, her face increasingly lined with sorrow as the family grew smaller with each passing day. Each death felt like a new wound, cutting deeper into Jetti's already broken heart.

When Anka entered her room this time, her eyes were somber, her usual composure slipping. She held a tray with a bowl of plain soup and some day-old bread, setting it down on the small table by the window.

"Jetti," she began, her voice trembling, "I've spoken with the rabbi. He says we must prepare for the mourning rituals. The family has been... has been decimated."

Jetti turned, her face void of emotion. "Decimated," she repeated, the word tasting bitter on her tongue. "It's more than that, Anka. It feels like we've been erased."

Anka knelt beside her, taking her hands. "Not erased, Jetti. Not while you and the baby are still here. You carry their memory, their legacy. Aaron and Esther are also here and haven't gotten sick, thanks to your warnings and planning."

A single tear slid down Jetti's cheek, and she brushed it away angrily. "I don't want this burden. I wanted them here. All of them."

"I know," Anka said. "But you endure, Jetti. You always have. And now, you must find even more within yourself, for the baby, for your brothers who remain, for the name your family still carries."

Jetti closed her eyes, her thoughts drifting instantly to Yosef at the **Iulia Hasdeu National College** in Bucharest. A wave of fear swept over her, her hands trembling at the thought. Had Aaron remembered to send him a letter, to check on him and ensure he was safe? She made a mental note to write to Yosef herself, her chest tightening at the burden the letter would carry. She would have to tell him about his brothers deaths. This news would shatter the fragile illusion of safety she so desperately wanted to preserve for him.

Her hands unconsciously moved to her abdomen. The child growing inside her was the only spark of optimism in an otherwise desolate world. She thought of the names her brothers and sisters had suggested, of the stories they'd shared, and the dreams they'd had for the future.

"I'll do it," she whispered, her voice barely audible. "I'll endure. I'll make sure this baby knows who they were, what they meant to me."

Anka nodded, her expression resolute. "That's all anyone can do, Jetti. Carry on and honor the ones we've lost."

As Jetti lay in her bed that night, the demise of the house stretching endlessly around her. Grief pressed down, heavy and relentless, filling every corner of the room. Her fingers curled around the fabric of her handmade dress, the one Miriam had sewn just a month ago, its soft folds grounding her in the present. She closed her eyes, her lips forming a whispered prayer... not for herself, but for the tiny life she carried. In the stillness, it was the one fragile thread of certainty she could hold onto, a glimmer of life against the vast shadow of loss.

PART II

PART II

Chapter Twenty-nine:
Anticipation

The cool breeze of September evenings swept freely through the partially opened windows of the Finkelthal mansion, carrying with it the earthiness of autumn. Days were warm, their amber hue softer now, and the promise of change in the air. Inside the grand estate, the surviving members of the family moved quietly, their grief heavy but their will steadfast. Life had to go on, even amidst the devastation of the flu.

The graves of their siblings lay fresh in the family plot, a stark and painful reminder of the toll the flu had taken. Aaron, Avi, and Nurit, the only siblings who had contracted the illness and survived, wore visible signs of their ordeal. Their faces were gaunt, shadows of their former vitality, and though they moved with a cautious fragility, they were alive, a delicate blessing that none of them took for granted. Jetti often reflected on how narrowly they had escaped an even greater loss and felt certain that her insistence on precautions of covering their faces, washing with vinegar water, avoiding outsiders, and maintaining strict isolation had been their saving grace.

Esther, Ruth, and Joseph, by some fortune, had never fallen ill. When the flu swept through their family, they retreated deep into the mansion, avoiding contact with those who had been infected. Their absence from the sickrooms spared them the worst of the physical toll, but the atmosphere of sickness and grief hung over them like a shroud. Jetti often thought of their forbearance, a small source of comfort amid the overwhelming sorrow. While they were spared the

165

illness, they carried losses just as deeply, their survival bound to the death of the somber halls.

The quarantine was strict. No staff left or entered the home; even the family moved cautiously around one another. Aaron had taken charge of arranging food and supplies, managing everything with the precision of a man who understood the fragility of their existence. Fresh produce and dry goods arrived at the back door each week, delivered by Aaron's assistant, who remained masked, and gloved. The deliveries were immediately sanitized, boiled, or baked, a ritual the family clung to as a shield against the invisible threat that had already claimed too much.

Jetti never got sick, staying mostly in her room. She found comfort in solitude, though it was a loneliness that sometimes felt suffocating. The ivory curtains fluttered in the breeze, and the teal chairs near the window became her sanctuary. She read out loud for hours on end, devouring novels, poetry, and essays that carried her far from the confines of the mansion. When her eyes became tired of words, her hands found solace in sewing or embroidery.

She had given up on her fashion sketches. Without the Singers, without Alan's mill, there seemed little point in dreaming of designs no one would be able to manufacture. The emptiness left by the loss of Miriam and Nina felt too raw, and Jetti couldn't bring herself to imagine a future in that world without them. Instead, she turned her needle and thread toward more practical endeavors: baby clothes.

The little garments were simple but sturdy, made of scraps of fabrics she'd scavenged from the remnants of their family stores. She stitched tiny shirts, gowns, and blankets, sticking to neutral tones; creams, grays, and whites, because she didn't know if she carried a boy or a girl. Each stitch felt like a small act of defiance, a swift declaration that life would go on, even in the shadow of so much death.

On one particular morning, Jetti sat by the window embroidering a delicate floral design onto the corner of a baby blanket. The act of creating something beautiful, no matter how small, gave her a sense of purpose. She'd taught herself the art from an old instructional book Anka found in the library, practicing with scraps until her fingers grew dexterous. She found peace in the slow rhythm of the needle, the way the thread could transform plain fabric into something meaningful.

Occasionally, her siblings would stop by her door, their conversations muffled through the wood. Nurit often brought news from the household, though it was usually mundane; updates about food deliveries, notes on the condition of their farm animals, or read the occasional letter from Yosef in Bucharest. Jetti rarely joined them for meals, preferring the solitude of her room, but she appreciated their efforts to include her.

One evening, after the sun slipped below the horizon and a bluish haze settled over the mansion, Aaron, now fully recovered, knocked on the door.

"Jetti, may I come in?" he asked, his voice hoarse but steady.

"Yes," she replied, setting down her sewing.

Aaron stepped inside, his once broad shoulders now stooped from weeks of illness and loss. He carried a small parcel wrapped in brown paper.

"I found this among Alan's things," he said, placing it on her desk. "It's not much, but I thought you might want it."

Jetti unwrapped the parcel carefully, revealing a bundle of fabric swatches and a small notebook. It was Alan's sample book, filled with tiny squares of fine textiles and notes on their origins. Her throat tightened as she ran her fingers over the familiar handwriting.

"Thank you," she whispered, tears pricking her eyes.

Aaron sat down across from her, his expression somber but kind. "I know you've been keeping to yourself the last few weeks, Jetti, but I want you to know how much we need you. You may not know it but you have always been the stalwart one, the one who holds us all together."

She smiled, her fingers brushing against the embroidery in her lap. "I don't feel that way," she admitted. "I feel... lost."

Aaron nodded. "We all do. But you're creating something, Jetti. You're bringing life into this family, both with your baby and with the work you do. That's wonderful."

His words stayed with her long after he left, resonating as she noticed the deepening twilight. She allowed herself to imagine a future, not just for herself, but for the child she carried and the family that remained. And as the stars began to dot the sky, she picked up her needle once more, ready to keep stitching compassion into the fabric of their lives.

Chapter Thirty:
Bright One

It was late in the afternoon on September 19, 1918, when Jetti felt the first sharp twinge in her abdomen. She had been sitting by the window, watching the sun slowly go lower in the sky, embroidering a final touch onto one of the tiny baby gowns she'd made, when a sudden gush of heat spread through her lap. For a moment, she sat stunned, her heart pounding as the realization dawned: her water had broken. The baby was coming.

Panic and excitement swirled inside her as she stood up, her knees trembling. She clutched the arm of the teal chair for balance, calling out into the tranquil house, her voice breaking the stillness that had settled over the mansion in recent weeks.

"Anka! Nurit! Esther! Ruth!"

The urgency of her voice carried through the halls, and soon, the sound of hurried footsteps followed. Anka, ever the steady presence, was the first to arrive, her face calm but her eyes brimming with determination.

"Jetti," she said, placing a supportive hand on her arm. "It's time, isn't it?"

She nodded, her breathing shallow and fast. "The baby... it's coming."

One by one, the women gathered in her room. Esther, with her sharp mind and efficient demeanor, immediately began organizing supplies. Ruth, now several months pregnant herself, clung to Jetti's hand, her eyes wide with a mixture of fear and awe. Nurit exuded her quiet strength, with tender words soothing Jetti's frayed nerves.

Anka took charge, "We need hot water, clean linens, and plenty of light," she instructed. "Nurit, go stoke the fire and boil water. Esther, fetch every clean towel and sheet you can find. Ruth, stay with Jetti. She'll need you by her side."

The house, usually so somber in its mourning, became a hive of activity. The remaining men, Aaron, Joseph, and Avi, were sent to the far end of the mansion to the smoking room with a bottle of brandy, their presence deemed unnecessary. Someone would get them later once the baby had arrived.

In the midst of the chaos, Jetti focused on her breathing, clinging to Ruth's hand as waves of pain began to roll through her body. She looked at her sister-in-law, who now shared the same sacred connection of motherhood.

"Ruth," she whispered between contractions, her voice trembling, "I'm scared. What if I can't do this?"

Ruth squeezed her hand tightly, her own eyes glistening with tears. "You can, Jetti. You're the strongest person I know. And soon, you'll be holding your baby, and everything will be worth it."

Anka's voice cut through the room like a steady drumbeat. "Jetti, focus. Look at me. Breathe deeply. You can do this."

The hours crept by, each moment dragging into what felt like an eternity. Outside, the day dissolved into twilight, the women worked with expected urgency. The air was thick with the humidity of boiling water, lavender oil that had carefully been dabbed on Jetti's temples by Ruth, and the copper tang of blood. Jetti's labored breaths filled the space, punctuated by occasional gasps and groans that emphasized the rising intensity of her contractions.

Anka, steady and resolute, was an unyielding presence by Jetti's side. Her hands moved with practiced precision, dabbing Jetti's brow with a damp cloth, adjusting pillows, and guiding her through the relentless waves of labor. Esther hovered nearby, a calming influence in the chaos, her hands ready with fresh towels and her voice offering hushed reassurances. Nurit darted in and out like a shadow, her arms full of supplies; fresh linens, basins of scalding water, and the clean cloths that seemed to disappear as quickly as they arrived.

The grandfather clock in the hall chimed six, then seven, its musical notes marking the slow passage of time. By then, the room had grown darker, the candles casting shadows on the walls. Jetti's cries grew louder, her power waning as exhaustion set in. Her fingers gripped the edge of the bed tightly, her knuckles white, and her sweat-soaked hair clung to her face in damp tendrils.

"Almost there," Anka encouraged, her voice cheered. "Just a little more, Jetti. You're doing beautifully."

Time seemed to blur into a haze of pain and determination. The clock struck eight, its deep chimes reverberating through the house, and Jetti, summoning every ounce of strength she had left, bore down with one final, desperate push. A primal cry tore from her throat, raw and unfiltered, and then the room fell into a stillness so profound it was as though the mansion itself held its breath.

This lasted only a heartbeat before it was broken by a piercing, sweet wail that filled the room, cutting through the tension like sunlight breaking through a storm. Anka let out an audible laugh, tears glistening in her eyes as she lifted the wriggling, crying newborn for Jetti to see.

"It's a girl," Anka announced, her voice trembling with joy and relief. The baby's cries blared in the room, a sound so full of life it sent a ripple of emotion through everyone present. Esther clapped a hand over her mouth, her eyes brimming with tears, while Nurit stopped in her tracks, frozen with awe.

Jetti, drenched in sweat and utterly spent, let her head fall back against the pillows, her chest heaving as she caught her breath. But when she opened her eyes, her attention fixed immediately on the tiny, squirming bundle Anka held.

Her tears flowed freely as she reached out for her daughter, carefully placing her tiny body against her chest. "A girl," she murmured, her voice thick with emotion. "My beautiful girl."

Ruth knelt beside her, tears streaming down her own face. "She's perfect, Jetti. Absolutely perfect."

Anka busied herself cleaning and swaddling the baby while Nurit and Esther tidied the room, their faces glowing with triumph. Jetti leaned back against the pillows, her daughter nestled against her heart, and for the first time in months, she felt a sense of peace.

"What will you name her?" Ruth asked, stroking the baby's downy head.

Jetti looked down at her daughter. The baby's delicate fingers curled instinctively around Jetti's thumb, a gesture so small yet so powerful that it seemed to anchor her entire world. Her daughter's face, flushed pink from the effort of her arrival, was delicate and serene, with a tuft of fine, blonde hair crowning her head. As Jetti traced the curve of the infant's cheek with her finger, she felt a deep, unshakable connection take root, a bond that would define her life from this moment forward.

The room was stirring with the rustle of fabric and the baby's lulling, rhythmic breaths. The other women watched in hushed anticipation, their expressions a mixture of joy and awe waiting for Jetti to answer. Ruth knelt beside the bed, her hand resting on Jetti's shoulder, while Anka stood near the foot, her capable hands now resting idly at her sides.

"I haven't decided yet," Jetti said, her voice steady despite the tears that glistened in her eyes. She glanced up at the women surrounding her, drawing wisdom from their support. "But I want her name to mean something. A reminder to live my best life for her. To give her everything I can."

Ruth leaned closer, brushing a damp strand of hair from Jetti's face. "Whatever name you choose, it will be perfect. Just like her," she whispered.

Jetti smiled purposefully, attending to the baby in her arms. Her daughter stirred, her mouth opening with a tiny yawn, and Jetti's heart swelled with a fierce and protective love. The memory of a name surfaced in her mind, a name she had read once in one of her many books. Berta. It was a Germanic name, rooted in the Old High German word 'berhta', meaning 'bright one.'

"Bright one," Jetti murmured, the thought taking hold. "Bright and full of promise." She looked up at Anka, her decision final. "I'll name her Berta. It feels right."

"Berta," Anka repeated, a smile creasing her face. "A beautiful name for a beautiful child."

Everyone in the room was elated. The baby, Berta, nestled closer to her mother, as if acknowledging her new name. Jetti felt a sense of calm wash over her, a rare and welcome reprieve after the storm of grief and loss that had consumed her life over the past year.

She thought of all the challenges that lay ahead, the hard work it would take to rebuild her life and provide for her daughter. Yet, in that moment, she felt capable of it all. Her daughter's name, "Berta - bright one," was more than a reflection of the baby's charm, it was a beacon, a reminder that light could pierce even the darkest of times.

The women in the room began to move again, tidying up and tending to the aftermath of the birth, but Jetti remained lost in the wonder of her daughter's face. Ruth sat beside her, speaking about the days ahead, the care the baby would need, and the support they would all give Jetti as she adjusted to motherhood.

Jetti listened, nodding occasionally, but her thoughts kept drifting back to the journey that had brought her here. The losses she had endured, the strength she had discovered within herself, and the new baby she now held in her arms. Naming her daughter Berta felt like closing one chapter and opening another, a chapter filled with the promise of love, growth, and capability.

As dusk settled and shadows deepened, the candlelight and the low crackle of the fire became the room's only illumination. In the pleasant setting, Jetti leaned down and pressed a tender kiss to the top of Berta's head. "Welcome to the world, my bright one, little Berta," she whispered. "We have so much to do, you and I. And we'll do it together."

Anka and the sisters continued tidying up the room. The linens were stripped and replaced with fresh ones, the puncheon emptied and refilled with clean water, and the floor swept meticulously, sachets of dried flowers were put in the corners of the room to freshen the air. Despite the exhaustion of the night, their spirits were buoyant as they worked together, pausing now and then to coo at the tiny baby resting contentedly in Jetti's arms.

"We need to make this perfect," Anka said, adjusting the drapes to let in fresh cool air. "The men will want to see Berta, but they'll also want to celebrate you, Jetti. This is your moment too."

She reclined with Berta nestled against her chest, nursing fiercely, offering a smile of satisfaction. "I can't imagine what they'd want to celebrate about me. This little one is the bright star of the day."

"That's where you're wrong," Ruth interjected, smoothing the bedcover. Her cheeks rosy with excitement, both from the joy of Berta's arrival and the anticipation of her own child. "You're the reason she's here. You've been through so much and shown us all what perseverence looks like. They're coming to honor you."

Chapter Thirty-one:
Brotherly Love

The room had been thoughtfully prepared, every detail touched with the love that binds a family through generations. By the open window, a small table held a vase of daisies Anka had gathered that morning, their sunlit petals now fading in the candlelight. A pleasant scent with the sweetness of steeped tea and the comforting aroma of freshly baked biscuits rested on a tray nearby. The fireplace glowed low in the hearth, casting a tawny hue across the room, and from the hallway, the grandfather clock chimed the hour... ten o'clock... its familiar toll wrapping the house in reverie. It was a room waiting not just for visitors, but for something deeper: a moment of connection, of family. Soon the brothers would arrive to meet the baby girl born just hours before, and celebrate Jetti.

The sound of footsteps on the grand staircase announced the arrival of the men. Aaron, Avi, and Joseph entered the room cautiously, their faces alight with happiness and pride. They each carried something in their hands, gifts chosen with thought and care.

Aaron, ever practical and forward-thinking, stepped ahead first. "For you, Jetti," he said, placing a wooden box on the table beside her. Inside, nestled in a bed of velvet, was a Vest Pocket Kodak camera. "I thought you might like this. You've always had an eye for beauty, whether in fabric or design. This way, you can capture the moments that matter."

Jetti's eyes widened as she examined the sleek device, its craftsmanship impeccable. "Aaron, this is incredible," she said, her voice thick with emotion. "I don't even know how to use it."

"You'll learn," Aaron said with a grin. "And when you do, I expect to see pictures of Berta and all the wonders
you'll create in your life."

Next came Avi, who approached with a small leather-bound book in his hands. He passed it to Jetti with a sheepish smile. "It's a journal," he explained. "I thought… maybe you'd want a place to write. To reflect, to dream, or just to keep track of the little things that make each day special."

Jetti ran her fingers over the glossy leather cover, feeling the raised embossing of her initials. "Avi, it's beautiful," she whispered. "Thank you. This means so much."

Joseph, her brother-in-law was last. He carried a wrapped bundle, which he unfolded to reveal a small but intricately carved jewelry box. "For your keepsakes," he said simply. "Something to hold the pieces of your journeys with Berta, so you never forget where you've been and what you've overcome."

Jetti opened the box, marveling at the delicate woodwork and the bold notes of cedar. Inside, the compartments were lined with plush purple velvet. "It's perfect," she said, tears welling up again. "All of it. All of you. I don't know how to thank you."

"You don't have to," Aaron said, sitting beside her on the bed. "You've already given us so much by being the incredible woman you are. And now you've given us Berta."

The mansion had settled, the gardens outside bathed in moonlight. A cool breeze drifted through the open window, carrying the sour must of decaying leaves and the pin-light of stars overhead. The fire in the hearth crackled. Berta slept peacefully in Jetti's arms, her tiny chest rising and falling in perfect rhythm, a reminder of the life they were all so eager to nurture and protect.

Jetti glanced around at her brothers, their thoughtful gifts arrayed on the small table. Aaron leaned back in a chair, his eyes half-closed but his smile content. Avi was leafing through a book he'd pulled from a shelf, while Joseph sipped his tea. The comfort of their presence settled over her like a blanket, a peaceful reassurance that she was not alone.

As the clock struck eleven, the clanging chimes ringing through the house, Aaron stood, stretching and yawning. "It's late," he said, his voice low. "We should let you rest."

Jetti nodded, her voice barely above a whisper. "Thank you. For everything. For being here."

Aaron gave her shoulder a compassionate squeeze. "Always, Jetti. That's what family is for."

As everyone left the room one by one, their footsteps drifted away into the winding hallways of the mansion, lost in its dim recesses, while Jetti stayed where she was, cradling Berta close. The firelight danced in her eyes as she looked at the gifts her brothers had brought; the camera, the journal, the jewelry box, all symbols of a future they believed in for her, and one she was beginning to believe in for herself.

She grinned, her gaze drifting to the window where the moon hung low in the night sky. The world outside was vast and uncertain, but here, in this moment, surrounded by tenderness and possibility, Jetti felt something she hadn't in a long time: the rare, unshakable certainty of being wholly loved. And with it, a whisper of excitement, as if the night itself carried the promise of something new on the horizon.

Chapter Thirty-two:
Heart of Czernowitz

By 1920, Czernowitz, affectionately called "Little Vienna," stood as a beacon of cultural sophistication and regrowth. Among its cobblestone streets and lively marketplaces, the Finkelthal family, once renowned for their diverse businesses, redefined their role in the city's thriving Jewish community. Each shop and venture embodied not only their entrepreneurial spirit but also their deeply rooted commitment to family and community.

The city's multicultural society provided an eclectic customer base, and the Finkelthals skillfully adapted their offerings to cater to the diverse population. The family's once-thriving network of businesses had been pared down, reflecting a household forever changed by the tragedies of the previous decade. The loss of their siblings; Ben, Alan, Milton, and Nina, had left more than just empty seats at the family table, it had torn a hole in the fabric of their daily lives. Each one of them had brought a unique energy and skill to the family, and their absence was a constant ache, felt in the stillness of the once-boisterous home and the quelled corners of their shuttered shops.

Ben, the clockmaker, had been a sharp-witted genius, his workshop filled with the cacophonous ticking of dozens of timepieces he lovingly assembled and repaired. His precise nature and dedication to his craft had made him a trusted figure in Czernowitz, and customers had come to rely on his ability to breathe new life into their heirlooms. Without Ben, the rhythmic sound of clocks marking time seemed to enhance their grief, and his workshop now stood abandoned, a poignant reminder of his meticulous hands and thoughtful presence.

Alan, ran the family textile mill and haberdashery, he was a force of creativity and commerce. Known for his sharp eye for fabrics and a knack for predicting fashion trends, he had built a reputation for quality and innovation. The vibrant patterns and rich textures of the fabrics he once curated seemed to pale in memory without his charismatic leadership. His loss left not just an emotional void but also a significant gap in the family's business awareness of forcing Aaron to make the painful decision to close the mill and hat shop, consolidating resources for the future.

Milton, the goldsmith and lapidarist, had been a beacon of artistry and charm. His shop had gleamed with the brilliance of his handcrafted stones and jewelry designs that adorned brides, mothers, sisters, and marked milestones in the lives of many families in the community. Milton's constant smile and quick wit had drawn people into his shop as much as his exquisite acumen to design. His absence was keenly felt not only by the family but also by a community that had trusted him with their most precious moments. Without Milton, the sparkle of the family's enterprises seemed a little dimmer.

Nina's death was the hardest to bear. She had been pregnant with her husband Henry Singer's child, their future shimmering with promise despite the challenges of the time. But the flu spared no mercy. Both Nina, pregnant with their first child, and Henry succumbed within days of each other, leaving an unfillable void. Their lives ended not in the safety of the Finkelthal home, but next door at the Singer's residence. The house now stood empty, a hollow shell of its former community and vitality.

The loss reverberated far beyond the personal grief of the family. The Singers, once a cornerstone of the community, were now a memory. The family business, once thriving in the bustling city center, had also fallen victim to the ripple effects of war and illness. What had once been a symbol of their industrious spirit now stood vacant, its windows dark, its doors closed.

And yet, the Singer family's legacy refused to vanish entirely. Before the war began, they had sent cousins to America, branching out in the hopes of securing a future away from the turmoil of Europe. It was there, across the ocean, that the family's name endured, carrying with it the legacy and ambition that had defined their lineage for generations.

Chapter Thirty-three:
Mercantile

Aaron, as the head of the household, carried the weight of these losses on his shoulders. Each decision he made was shadowed by the deaths of his brothers and sister, with the knowledge that the responsibility for the family's survival now rested squarely with him.

The Great War's end brought relief to the world, but the economic shifts that followed presented new challenges. Aaron, with his characteristic pragmatism, chose to consolidate the family's remaining businesses, focusing on fewer but more sustainable ventures. This strategy, though necessary, was a constant reminder of what they had lost, both in the tangible sense, and the intangible vitality the brothers had brought to the family.

Through the lens of the newly redesigned businesses, the city of Czernowitz came alive. The mercantile's bustling aisles, the dry goods store's vibrant textiles, the bakery's inviting aromas, and the photography studio's gleaming portraits painted a vivid picture of a community in motion. For the Finkelthals, their work was not just about commerce; it was about sustaining the traditions and spirit of a people who, even amidst loss and change, remained at the heart of Czernowitz's identity.

The family faced the shifting economic landscape of postwar Bucovina with pragmatism and determination. Inflation and new Romanian laws challenged their enterprises, but Aaron's leadership ensured the family adapted for success. His decision to consolidate resources into fewer businesses allowed the family to focus on what mattered most, providing for the community while preserving their legacy.

The mansion itself seemed subdued now, the laughter and debates that had once charged through its halls replaced by the melancholic rhythm of survival, and crying babies. The remaining family members leaned on one another, finding solace in their shared memories and the enduring legacy of the family they had lost. In every decision Aaron made, in every shop they maintained, and in every interaction with their community, the presence of Ben, Alan, and Milton was missed dearly, but still remained a solid testament to the unbreakable bond of family and the enduring impact of their lives.

The mercantile, strategically located on a prominent corner near Czernowitz's bustling city center, was more than just a store, it was a community keystone. Townsfolk flocked to its wide aisles, drawn by the promise of finding everything from sturdy farming tools to essential household wares. Shelves were meticulously organized with cast-iron pots, polished wooden buckets, and neatly labeled jars of preserves that gleamed in the light. The smells of freshly oiled wood combined with the tang of burlap sacks brimming with grains, creating an earthy, welcoming atmosphere. Customers often lingered, their voices rising in animated conversation as they bartered prices or caught up on the latest news.

Aaron decided that this business would be the perfect fit for Nurit and Jetti to run, this decision earned him respect among patrons, the sisters sharp acumen for faces, names, and even family histories made every customer feel valued. Many locals maintained running accounts at the shop, a testament to the deep trust the Finkelthals extended to their neighbors. The family's approach was as much about sustaining the community as it was about conducting business, ensuring that everyone who walked through the doors felt part of something larger.

The mercantile became a second home for the sisters, a place not only to work but to nurture the next generation. Nurit, practically bursting with the excitement of her own pregnancy, brought an infectious sense of happiness to the store. Her expanding family symbolized a brighter future, and her joy was evident in the way she carried herself as she moved through the bustling shop.

Little Berta and her cousin Rivka, only months apart in age, were constant fixtures in the lively space. Each morning, Ruth and Avi would arrive at the bakery with Rivka bundled in her pram, her chubby cheeks rosy from the fresh morning air. Ruth would walk her over to the mercantile, settling her into a child's pen beside Berta. The girls greeted each other with delighted squeals, their bond growing closer with each passing day.

Tucked safely into the sturdy enclosure behind the counter, nestled between crates of goods and rolls of fabric, the two children brought a palpable joy to the store. Their cheerful coos and infectious giggles were a magnet for patrons, who often paused to wave or offer small treats. Their innocent joy brought a brightness to the mercantile, an almost magical contrast to the shadows of loss that hung over the family. Nurit, with her vibrant energy and anticipation for her own child, often leaned over to tickle the girls or hum lullabies to them as she worked.

The sight of Berta and Rivka playing together, and the anticipation of another little one on the way, infused the store with an atmosphere of promise. It was a daily reminder that even amidst life's hardships, the future was brimming with possibilities. Together, Jetti and Nurit found camaderie in their shared roles as businesswomen and mothers. Their days filled with the rhythm of work, laughter of children, and the excitement of anticipation of what was yet to come.

For Jetti and Nurit, the presence of the childeren together offered a sense of purpose and healing. In Berta and Rivka's shared laughter and wide-eyed wonder, they experienced not just the future of their family but the enduring spirit of certainty. The store, once merely a place of business, now pulsed with life, enthusiasm, and the promise of new beginnings.

The patrons adored the sight of the two bright-eyed toddlers. Their innocent charm brought a touch of lightness to the active shop.

Regulars often paused mid-conversation to make silly faces and were rewarded with gurgling laughter or a toothy grin. "They're good luck, those little ones," an older customer declared one day, slipping a sweet into the children's play area as a gift. Another patron, a seamstress, gifted small hand-stitched dolls, which the girls clutched with tiny, curious fingers.

The children's presence also deepened the bond between Jetti and Nurit. While one managed the front of the store, discussing orders or cutting fabric, the other kept an eye on the children, their teamwork seamless and natural. Together, they struck a balance that allowed the store to flourish and encourage the children to thrive in an environment filled with compassion and love.

The space behind the counter became a symbol of the commitment to family and business, a reminder that even amid hard work, there was room for love, joy, and aspiration for the future. It wasn't uncommon for patrons to leave the store with more than just goods. They often carried away stories of the little ones and the resilient family behind them, who turned every moment into one of connection and care.

Chapter Thirty-four:
Chaos of Commerce

Across the avenue, the family's bakery and open-air market thrived. In the early hours of the morning, the deserted streets would stir to life as farmers arrived, their carts laden with crates of fresh produce, jugs of creamy milk, and baskets of speckled eggs. The rhythmic clatter of hooves and the low murmur of greetings elevated the earthy aroma of soil and dew.

Inside the bakery, the shelves gleamed with golden loaves of braided challah, their glossy tops shining, alongside trays of flaky pastries dusted with powdered sugar and rows of hearty, crusty bread. Yeast, honey, and cinnamon created an inviting smell that wafted out onto the streets, drawing in customers like moths to a flame.

The market stalls buzzed with vibrant energy as the morning unfolded. Voices rose and fell in the spirited cadence of haggling, punctuated by bursts of laughter and the clink of coins exchanging hands. Aaron, the ever-attentive overseer, made his rounds with practiced ease, greeting familiar faces and ensuring every detail was just so. His presence was a steady anchor, the calm amidst the chaos of commerce.

Each day, Ruth and Avi, gifted bakers in the family, brought their creativity and love for tradition to the bakery's offerings. They balanced the comforting familiarity of Jewish staples with inventive flavors inspired by the wider world. A touch of orange zest in a honey cake, a sprinkling of exotic spices in a savory loaf. These subtle innovations breathed new life into the market's fare while remaining rooted in the culinary heritage that defined them.

Once the bakery's doors were unlocked and the first customers welcomed inside, Ruth would walk Rivka over to the mercantile, where her cousin Berta waited.

One of the most surprising and innovative additions to the business portfolio was a chic photography studio, nestled beside a stylish beauty salon. This modern venture was the brainchild of Joseph, Nurit's husband, whose foresight and business acumen had long been an asset to the family. A lawyer by trade, Joseph understood the tides of change sweeping through society and encouraged them to embrace emerging trends. He predicted the growing middle class's appetite for portraiture and saw an opportunity to expand the family's influence beyond the traditional businesses of baking and mercantile.

The photography studio quickly became a favorite among locals, offering a chance to capture life's milestones in a way that felt both accessible and luxurious. Its walls were adorned with examples of their work; wedding portraits, family gatherings, and even candid shots turned into timeless keepsakes. The studio's ability to transform ordinary moments into cherished memories was unmatched, and word of its artistry spread quickly.

Beside the studio, the beauty salon added another layer of sophistication to the enterprise. Managed with skill and grace by Esther, Aaron's wife, the salon became a hub for elegance and transformation. Esther's nimble fingers worked magic, crafting intricate hairstyles inspired by the latest Viennese and Parisian trends. Her calm demeanor and meticulous artistry drew a loyal clientele, women who left not only with stunning new looks but also with a renewed sense of confidence.

The two businesses operated in perfect harmony, each enhancing the other's appeal. A visit to the beauty salon often culminated in a session at the photography studio, where clients could immortalize their freshly styled hair in a glossy portrait. This synergy made the establishment a one-stop destination for those seeking to celebrate milestones or simply indulge in a touch of refinement.

Joseph's vision for the studio extended beyond photography. He recommended incorporating elegant backdrops and creative lighting techniques, transforming the modest space into a sophisticated atelier. He even suggested to Aaron to partner with local dressmakers and jewelers to provide clients with wardrobe options, ensuring that every portrait captured their best selves. The result was an experience that felt personal and glamorous, an offering that appealed to both the practical and the aspirational.

Meanwhile, Esther's salon mirrored the studio's attention to detail. Each station was impeccably maintained, the air delicately perfumed with rose and citrus oils. Mirrors framed in gilded wood reflected the artistry of her work and lively conversation filled the space. The salon wasn't just a place for hair and makeup; it was a social hub where women gathered to exchange news, share laughter, and feel a sense of belonging.

Together, the photography studio and beauty salon exemplified the family's adaptability and vision. They were more than businesses. They were spaces where creativity, community, and modernity converged, a testament to the family's commitment to evolving with the times while maintaining the service and excellence that had always defined them.

Despite the devastating losses that had carved an indelible void in their lives, they poured their grief into purpose. Each remaining family member found a role that honored the shared legacy of those they had lost, channeling their sorrow into the steady work of rebuilding. It wasn't easy because grief crept in, in the evenings, but their determination grew with each passing day.

The streets of Czernowitz, with its kaleidoscope of cultures and enduring traditions, became the perfect backdrop for the family's evolving story. Seasons painted the city in shifting hues; warm amber in autumn, sparkling white in winter, vibrant green in spring. And through it all, the enterprises pulsed with life.

But even as abundance bloomed within the family, shadows gathered quietly at the edges of their lives. When the laughter faded and the streets emptied, whispers began to reach them. Rumors of changes beyond their city, of unrest that threatened to spread. For now, the Finkelthals clung to the present, cherishing the fragile peace they had rebuilt.

As Jetti looked out at the city one evening, the faintest unease stirred in her heart, a question she couldn't yet name but felt she may one day have to face.

Chapter Thirty-five:
Young Berta

Jetti was precariously holding a cup of tea and a rhubarb scone, watching Berta from the kitchen doorway. She loved the way her daughter's loose curls bounced as she ran barefoot through the garden, laughing as she chased Rivka in circles.

"You should speak with Rabbi Cohen," Aaron said as he dried his hands on a linen cloth. "Joel left years ago. No word. No return. And now a child... a bright, beautiful child who carries his name but will never know him."

She didn't answer at first. "It wouldn't change anything," she murmured. "He's already gone... He's not coming back."

Aaron stepped closer, his tone gentler now. "But maybe it would change something for you. You deserve the chance to be free. To love again, if you choose. You shouldn't have to carry the shadow of a marriage he abandoned."

Jetti blinked, her throat tightening. "I never even got to tell him I was pregnant."

Aaron rested a hand on her shoulder. "Then let someone else tell you this: you've raised her for the last two years with more devotion and grace than most children will ever know. You built her life from love, not absence."

"Aaron, she doesn't even know the difference. She will never even know that Joel is her father... Look at her, she is so happy, I don't need a man to raise her. She has what is left of our family, that is enough." She responded.

He smirked, nodded and went back to his suite to get ready for his day.

Love shaped every corner of Berta's early years.

From the moment she could walk, she had explored the world around her with wide eyes and boundless curiosity. Jetti nurtured that with wonder and constancy. She sang lullabies to her in two languages, pointing out the names of wildflowers, kneading dough together on rainy mornings in the kitchen. She taught her daughter the rhythms of compassion and perseverance not through instruction but by example: every bedtime story, every wiped tear, every carefully stitched hem on a too-small dress told Berta that she mattered, that she was safe, and that her mother would always choose her.

By age two, Berta spoke in a melodic jumble of Romanian, German, and Yiddish, stringing together a confusion of words with earnest confidence. At three, she had memorized the routes through the market square and knew the names of every shopkeeper. By four, she was bright-eyed and clever, able to count inventory in both languages and recite nursery rhymes with dramatic flair, her voice carrying through the mercantile like a chime.

"She's like you," Nurit said once, watching Berta try to stack apples with clever determination. "But braver."

Jetti had smiled. "She doesn't have a choice."

Yet Berta's life was far from bleak. It was filled with abundance… morning walks in the garden, sticky fingers from honey pastries, the thrill of new ribbons in her hair. Her days were consumed with stories and songs, her nights wrapped in lullabies and the smell of her mother's favorite soap. She never felt the absence of a father; she had her Uncle Aaron, whose arms lifted her as high as the stars, whose voice told her stories of courage and kindness. To Berta, he was simply "Tata," and no one ever corrected her.

When the store had closed and Berta nestled into her lap with a blanket and a book, Jetti would breathe in the thick curls of her daughter's hair and feel both joy and a bone-deep ache. This love... this life... had come from sorrow, and yet it flourished.

Sometimes she would wonder what might have been if Joel had stayed. But the thought never remained. Because what she had made on her own, and the little girl she was raising was real. And every moment with Berta was a reminder that love, when fiercely tended, could grow roots deep enough to hold even the most broken heart steady.

The days turned into seasons, and Jetti didn't wait for answers from Joel anymore. She no longer imagined his return or replayed the last time she saw him. Instead, she focused on what was in front of her: the child she carried on her hip while balancing crates of dried goods, the child who cried in the middle of the night from bad dreams, and laughed hard enough to startle the shop cat out of its sleep.

By the time Berta turned four, she had become a fixture in the mercantile... just tall enough to peek over the counter, just bold enough to insist on trying to tye her own apron. She followed instructions better than most grown men, eager to help sort hardware or try to count bolts of fabric, her small hands quick and careful.

She was curious about everything. "Why do the nails smell like rain?" "Why does Rivka's belly button look different than mine?" "How do you know when someone is lying?" "When will I have a papa?" Jetti answered every question with as much honesty as she could manage, even when it scraped against old wounds.

Berta was bright—too bright sometimes. She picked up languages like they were songs. Romanian from the market women. German from the books Jetti read aloud at bedtime. Yiddish from the backroom banter between Aaron and the deliverymen. She soaked up rhythm, nuance, gesture, and mimicking accents and inventing stories of her own.

The mercantile became her second home. Customers often walked away with extra... an apple from Berta's hand, a drawing slipped into a parcel, a whispered joke that made them laugh harder than expected. She moved through the space like she belonged to it. Because she did.

She never asked about her father after that first time.

Aaron was constant. He brought her wooden puzzles and sang silly rhymes when she was sick. He carried her on his shoulders through the early morning fog to watch bread rise in the bakery ovens. He taught her how to spot a fair price, how to be generous without being a fool.

When someone new to town once asked if Berta was his daughter, Aaron had simply said, "No. She belongs to our family," and left it at that.

One night, after Berta had fallen asleep in the crook of Jetti's arm, sticky with sweat and jam, she sat in the reading nook in their suite, and stared out the window. The wind rattled the pane, like someone asking to be let in.

She whispered to the dark, "She's so happy. I'm doing this. Without him, without anyone."

And she was.

The road wasn't easy. There were days Jetti came home so exhausted her knees gave out when she pulled off her shoes. There were times when she stood in the pantry, crying over spilled flour or a broken jar. But there was always Berta's small hand reaching up to her cheek. There was always that steady, grounding voice in her ear…"Mama, I love you the most."

Jetti didn't need saving. She needed time. And she gave herself that, slowly and stubbornly, building a life not from what she had lost but from what she could still hold.

Chapter Thirty-six:
The Picnic

The sun warmed the cobbled courtyard behind the mansion, the air rich with rising dough drifted from the kitchen windows. It was early fall in Czernowitz, the kind of afternoon that blurred the lines between summer and fall. The sycamores along the driveway rustled with the first hints of change, their leaves whispering as a breeze carried through the hills.

Jetti stood near the delivery cart, her shawl tied snug across her chest, watching the new worker Aaron had hired help Avi carry sacks of flour into the bakery's cellar. His sleeves were rolled past his elbows, forearms dusted chalky white and sweat glistening at his temple. He hauled with intention, careful not to spill a grain, his movements efficient, practiced. He nodded when Avi spoke, but rarely added more than a few words.

"Aaron," Jetti murmured, as her brother approached with a wrapped bundle of rye tucked under one arm. "Who is that?"

Aaron glanced at Ripley before answering. "A good worker. He seems shy. Doesn't drink much. Pays attention to detail. I think he is a wanderer, maybe a war veteran with no home. I hired him a few days ago."

"Where's he from? He speaks High German like he studied at university. Ruth said he didn't even know how to light an oil lamp."

Aaron chuckled, brushing a fly from his lapel. "I'm not sure, I never asked. He's... different. Maybe a little strange. But he's kind, and he listens. That's more than I can say for half the men who came back from the war—if they came back at all."

Jetti narrowed her eyes. "Is he Jewish?"

"I don't know," Aaron admitted.

Jetti stiffened, but said nothing. Her daughter's laughter chimed from the Mercantile porch. Berta, now five years old, was playing with scraps of fabric and making believe she was sewing something together with imaginary needle and thread. Jetti exhaled slowly.

Aaron raised a brow. "Maybe you should get to know him a little better, you are both about the same age, and he doesn't have anyone here."

She trusted her brother, and it would be nice to have a companion. It had been years since Joel left, and she was ready for change; she was ready to find someone she could share her life with besides her family.

A few days had passed since her conversation with Aaron, and each evening at the close of his shift, Ripley wandered into the mercantile. He always bought the same thing—a single wrapped piece of hard candy, the kind children pressed against shop windows to admire. It was a small indulgence, one most working men couldn't justify. But Ripley was different. There was something in the way he carried himself—a confidence, a practiced restraint—that hinted at a life once touched by refinement.

Jetti had begun to notice his daily routine. From behind the register, she watched as he carefully unwrapped the waxed paper, folding it with delicate precision into the shape of an animal before handing it to little Berta. He never said much—just a polite nod, sometimes a "Good evening," before slipping back out into the deepening dusk.

There was a contradiction to him. His manners suggested a man who had once dined at proper tables and spoken comfortably in salons. Yet his coat was threadbare, his boots old and worn out by wear, and his posture wore the fatigue of someone used to traveling alone. There was a gentleness in the way he looked at the children, as if haunted by a memory too tender to name.

One night, after he left, Jetti found herself resting at the doorway long after the bell towers last chime had faded. Her eyes followed his silhouette as it disappeared beneath the poplars that lined the avenue, swallowed slowly by the night. Something about him remained in her mind—like a whiff of woodsmoke after a fire, faint but unforgettable.

She didn't know if his past was something to fear, or if his future was something to place hers in. But she felt it now—a subtle pull beneath her ribs. Not affection—at least not yet. It was something subtle, more curious. The beginning of a question she didn't yet know how to ask, let alone answer. But it tugged at her just the same.

Against her better judgment, Jetti decided to take Aaron's advice. To reach out to Ripley. It felt forward, unorthodox even. She wasn't in the habit of initiating anything with strange men—especially not those who carried the weight of untold stories on their shoulders. And yet, something told her that if she didn't, she might regret it.

The next day, Jetti stood beneath the ivy carved stone arch of the bakery with a picnic basket in hand. She wore a pale blue skirt and a clean blouse with the sleeves rolled past her elbows. Her braid was loose for once, blond locks curling around her face. Anka had prepared hard cheese, boiled eggs, pickled beets, a jar of apricot preserves, fresh challah dusted with poppy seeds, and a small tankard of cold beer.

This wasn't her idea. It was Aaron's, he was always poking in where he didn't belong. "He's new in town," he said. "You're alone. Maybe he's lonely too." She'd rolled her eyes at him, but he kept pressing until she gave in just to shut him up.

She had to admit, Ripley hadn't done anything to make her nervous. Not even when Berta toddled right up to him with sticky fingers and offered him a bit of stewed apple. He'd crouched down, careful and gentle, and said 'thank you' like it meant something. That counted for a lot.

Ripley appeared at the door of the bakery, hair damp from a rinse. He looked surprised to see Jetti.

"I hope you are hungry," she said, extending the basket for him to carry.

He blinked, caught off guard. "Is this... something people around here do?"

"I'm just asking you to carry the basket," she said quickly, brushing a loose strand of hair behind her ear as she stepped into the street.

"I have work to do for Avi before the Sabbath," he said as he reached for the basket.

She replied, "No you don't. I have been given permission to take you with me on an adventure, a small one, just some food and talk, a picnic if you like."

Ripley didn't resist, he was hungry, actually always hungry, so he placed the basket down on the bakery steps and quickly went inside to tell Avi and Ruth where he was going.

In unison they said, "Yes, we know... you should have a nice time with Jetti. Enjoy your day; we'll see you on Monday."

They walked east, past the edge of the neighborhood, where the clatter of carts gave way to chirping birds and the creak of distant oxcarts. The air smelled of tilled soil, drying hay, and early apples. Jetti led him along a well-worn path that cut through tall grass and sloped toward the forest.

"Berta is with Nurit and her son Kurti," she said after a few minutes. "Which means we can speak plainly."

Ripley nodded, then offered a small uncomfortable smile. "That's good."

They reached a shaded clearing nestled against the edge of the forest. Moss spread thick beneath their feet like velvet. The trees stood tall and still, except for the occasional flutter of birds in the branches. A brook murmured somewhere beyond the undergrowth, and the air now smelled like damp earth, pine resin, and fallen leaves.

Jetti spread the wool blanket over a flat section of loamy moss, smoothing the corners with flat palms. Ripley knelt beside her, setting the basket between them.

They ate slowly, savoring each bite. The cheese was creamy and pungent, the bread still a little warm in the center. Bees circled lazily, drawn to the sweet preserves, and the breeze carried linden and the scent of mushrooms from deeper in the woods.

Sunlight filtered through the canopy above, dappling the rind on the cheese and glinting off the jar of apricot preserves. Jetti plucked a poppy seed from her challah and flicked it into the grass, humming softly to herself.

Ripley took a sip from the small tankard of beer, his eyes darting around the clearing. He showed anxiety with his legs crossed stiffly, fingers toying with the swing top on the bottle.

"So," he said at last, his voice low but clear, "you don't need to do all this. I mean—whatever this is."

She grinned. "It was Aaron's idea. He thought you looked like you could use a friend."

Ripley nodded, not quite meeting her gaze. "Aaron's probably not wrong. But I'm not really from… here." He gestured vaguely toward the town. "Czernowitz, I mean. Just passing through, maybe."

"Where are you from, then?"

He hesitated. "Nowhere in particular." A pause. "Everywhere, I guess."

Jetti tilted her head, waiting, but Ripley only shrugged. "I don't plan on staying long."

The air between them grew stagnant. Even the forest seemed too quiet… no wind, no birdsong, just the natural creak of trees shifting against each other.

She looked down at the crust of her bread, unsure what to say... especially since she didn't even know why she was here in the first place.

"Joel... my husband... left me before Berta was born," Jetti said, breaking the silence. "He said he was going to find his family in New York; he just left and never came back. He doesn't even know he has a daughter."

Ripley said nothing, but the crease between his brows deepened.

"I never heard from him again," she continued. "Not a letter. Not a scrap. So I'm stuck because he never released me from our marriage with a *get*."

"A... get?" Ripley repeated, unfamiliar.

"In Jewish law, it's a divorce decree. Without it, a woman can't remarry. I've been raising Berta on my own ever since." She bit into an apple slice, swallowed, and stared at her hands. "Legally, I'm still his wife."

"I'm sorry," Ripley said, his voice low.

"You're not Jewish," she said, not as a question but a fact.

He hesitated. "No. I'm not religious. Not really anything."

She looked at him sideways. "That's unusual. For someone who speaks like a Berlin professor."

Ripley grinned. "I... had a friend. He taught me. High German, some history. We read books together. A lot of books."

She could tell he wasn't telling the truth... not all of it, anyway... but what stung more was how certain she was that Aaron had been wrong. There was nothing here, no connection, no spark of what Aaron thought she might feel. Just two strangers sitting in the woods, trying to fill the awkwardness. She wished it would end already, so she could stop pretending this had ever been a good idea.

They sat there for a while, letting the tension settle between them. Then Jetti stood and brushed crumbs from her skirt.

"Ruth mentioned that you know how to forage for mushrooms?"

He looked up, surprised. "Yes."

"Then prove it."

The forest welcomed them with dappled light. Leaves crunched underfoot. They moved slowly, Ripley scanning the base of trees, the shaded mounds where mushrooms love to hide.

"There," he said, crouching beside a patch of bright orange chanterelles. "Trumpet-shaped, they smell like apricots when they are fresh. Sweet and nutty when cooked."

Jetti knelt beside him, inspecting them. "Oooh, we can bring them back to the house and make a soup with them, I am sure everyone will like those."

Further along, near the stump of a fallen beech, they found a colony of oyster mushrooms, ivory and delicate.

"These are good too," Ripley said, plucking them carefully. "They are oyster mushrooms."

Jetti followed him as he stepped ahead toward a darker stretch of forest. The underbrush thickened, and the smell of decay grew richer. Peeking through the moss was a cluster of bluish-purple mushrooms.

"Bluets," Ripley said, crouching. "They're fine. Mild flavor. A bit floral."

Jetti squinted. "They don't look fine, they look weird Ripley. They are blue!"

"They're safe," he insisted. "I've eaten them before."

He placed a few into the basket, brushing dirt off the caps with his sleeve. They returned through the woods with their finds, the light growing darker with each step.

Back at the mansion, the kitchen was filled with preparations and clatter. Anka stood by the counter, shredding carrots into a bowl, her fingers tinged with orange.

"Chanterelles," she nodded approvingly. "Oysters, very good. But these…" She lifted one of the bluets and turned it over slowly. "We don't usually eat the purple ones."

Ripley waved a hand. "They're fine. I promise. I've definitely eaten these." And before anyone could object, he grabbed one from the pile and popped it into his mouth.

Anka raised her brow. "I don't trust mushrooms that make a man so quick to prove himself. When in doubt… throw it out, I say."

Jetti gave a weary smile but said nothing.

The lamps in the dining room flickered brightly as Anka placed a pot of steaming mushroom soup at the center of the table. The air smelled of herbs and roasted root vegetables, comforting and familiar. Plates were being set, laughter bubbled from the children in the next room, and footsteps pattered from the hall.

Ripley stood at the threshold between the kitchen and the dining room, one hand resting haphazardly on the doorframe. His face had lost some of its color, and his eyes, usually curious and bright, were shadowed with something harder to name.

"I think I need a bit of air," he said, trying to keep his voice casual. "A little too much sun this afternoon, maybe. I'm not feeling quite myself."

Anka looked up from the bread she was slicing, her brow furrowing. "Are you sure? Sit down for a moment. A bowl of soup, a cup of tea… it'll settle you."

Ripley offered an uncomfortable smile. "Thank you, Anka, but I think I just need some cool air."

Jetti turned from the sideboard where she'd been arranging cutlery. "Is it something more?" she asked, stepping toward him. Her voice was low, but steady. "You're pale."

He hesitated, and for a beat, something changed in his expression, kind of like a thread stretching taut between confession and retreat. "No, truly," he said. "Just tired… Your home is full of… love. It's beautiful. I think I need a moment to myself."

Jetti's eyes searched his. She sensed it…something off, or left unsaid, but she didn't press him. "All right," she said. "Don't go far. Dinner will be ready in a few minutes."

Anka crossed her arms, not hiding her skepticism. "You men," she muttered, though her tone lacked real bite. "Always vanishing just when things get interesting."

Ripley managed a chuckle, but it barely reached their ears. He stepped back toward the rear of the mansion, his hand gripped the kitchen doorframe for a moment, as if it would hold him up. "I'll be back soon."

And then he was gone, sensibly slipping through the back door like a shadow at dusk.

Jetti stood in his absence, staring at the empty space he left behind. The rich mustiness of cooked mushrooms, the clatter of bowls, the heat from the oven… all of it remained. But something had shifted. She didn't know how she knew. Only that she did.

Chapter Thirty-seven:
Wings on the Window

The smell of yeasty rising dough filled the bakery before the first rooster crowed. Ruth was already at the kneading table, sleeves rolled up, arms dusted in flour, braiding challah. Avi stoked the oven fire, a dull orange glow searing his face. The mundane rhythm of the morning pulsed forward—until Ruth looked up at the clock, it was almost eight.

"Where's Ripley?" she asked, brushing her hands against her apron.

Avi paused mid-swing of the ash shovel. "I guess he's not here yet."

"He's never late," Ruth said, frowning. "He's always down here before us. Go check."

Reluctantly, Avi wiped his hands on a rag and climbed the narrow stairs behind the oven, his boots thudding on each step. The small door to the upstairs room creaked open with the same groan it always had—but something was off.

Ripley's cot was unmade. The blanket was tucked sharp at the corners at the foot, but the top was in a tangled mess. The ceramic mug that usually sat on the small bedside crate was broken in pieces on the floor. His coat—always slung over the chair by the window —was gone.

Only one thing remained: a single folded paper bird resting on the windowsill. Its wings were angled upward, poised mid-flight. The blush of dawn filtered through the dust-coated glass behind it, casting the lightest shadow across the floorboards.

Avi stood for a long moment, then stepped forward and picked up the bird. It was delicate but confident—creased with care, rigid at the wings, its beak turned ever so slightly toward the open sky.

He went back down the stairs.

"He's gone," he said to Ruth.

"What do you mean, gone?"

"He's not up there, it looks like he left, all his stuff is gone. The only thing there was this." He held out the paper bird.

Ruth took it with flour-caked fingers, her lips tightening. "We have to tell Aaron."

Aaron stood hunched over a stack of papers in his dimly lit office at the bank, the scent of ink and dust thick in the air. The veil of morning hadn't yet reached this part of his office; he welcomed the typical Monday routine—the family finances on his mind.

But the sound of Ruth's footsteps broke his concentration. She appeared in the doorway, apron dusted in flour, her expression drawn.

"Aaron," she said, almost apologetically. "He's gone. No note. No word. Avi checked. He just… left."

She stepped forward and placed the paper bird onto his desk.

Aaron stared at it. "Who?"

Ruth practically shouted, "Ripley! He didn't show up for work this morning."

His fingers closed around the small, precise wings as if to crush them, but he didn't. Instead, he turned it slowly, examining the careful folds with growing dread.

He had seen men vanish before. After the war, it had become a kind of ritual—suitcases packed in the middle of the night, footsteps on gravel roads, no goodbyes. Some men just left everything behind. He thought of Joel, and what his abandonment had meant for Jetti. But this wasn't just any man. This was someone Aaron had brought into the fold. Someone he'd introduced to her.

His chest tightened.

He hadn't pushed hard, but he'd nudged. Encouraged. Suggested.

"She needs someone steady," he had told Ruth just days ago. *"Someone reliable. Kind to Berta. Ripley's been through something —maybe they'll understand each other."*

But now all Aaron could think of were Jetti's eyes when she spoke of Joel, the flatness in her voice when she said she'd long stopped expecting anything from men.

And now this.

She had begun to live again. To smile. To look forward.

And he had steered her toward someone unreachable. A man with no past, and clearly, no future here.

Aaron exhaled slowly, the paper bird suddenly unbearable in his hand.

"I'll go tell Jetti," he said, though the words felt thick in his throat. Not because he feared her anger—Jetti rarely wasted energy on anger—but because he feared her painful disappointment. He feared she might retreat again, the way she had during those long, dark months after Joel left. He remembered her grief—the kind that left deep shadows behind her eyes long after her tears had dried.

Because this time, it would be his fault.

Jetti stirred porridge at the stove, cinnamon wafting up in the steam. The kitchen was humid, drowsy with morning haze. A loaf of rye Anka had just baked rested on the cooling rack. Little Berta was in the parlor confidently singing to herself, arranging the paper menagerie Ripley had made her—two rabbits, a deer, and a frog. Jetti didn't have to be at the mercantile for another hour, and she cherished these relaxed moments with her daughter.

Aaron poked his head into the kitchen looking for Jetti. He didn't speak at first, shifting his weight between his feet like he had when they were children and he'd broken something of hers.

"Good morning, Jetti," he said hesitantly, holding the bird carefully in his hand.

She didn't turn from the stove. "Hello, Aaron. What are you doing here? Shouldn't you be at the bank?"

"He's gone, Jetti." He could barely say it.

She turned instantly, already knowing Aaron's answer but asked anyway, "Who's gone?"

"Ripley… He must have left in the night. No one saw him leave. But Ruth said that this morning he didn't show up for work at the bakery. When Avi went to check… Jetti… there was nothing left in his room but this."

He held the bird out to her. She turned slowly, eyes tracing the folds. It was different from the others… smaller, more intricate. She recognized the crease near the wing. He'd made one like it for Berta the first day they met. It had gotten wet and turned to paper pulp, so he had promised to make another for her over the weekend.

She took it from Aaron's hands and stared at it.

"I thought maybe…" he started, then stopped. "I thought maybe he was different…"

She nodded, looking at the bird. Her voice was even. "He was only here a couple of weeks, Aaron."

"I shouldn't have—"

She interrupted him with a small shake of her head. "Don't apologize. The war broke a lot of people. Some just… drift."

Aaron sat heavily at the kitchen table, hands laced. "Maybe he remembered something. Maybe he wasn't supposed to stay. Maybe…"

Jetti folded the bird, slid it into her apron pocket to give to Berta later, and turned back to the stove.

"It doesn't matter," she said. "Berta liked him while he was here. That's enough."

208

The porridge thickened, steam curling sweetly with nutmeg and cinnamon. She slowly stirred in some dried currants, carefully tapping the spoon on the sides of the pot in a pit-a-pat rhythm.

That night, as Jetti tucked Berta into bed, she gave her the little paper bird, and said "This is the last bird from Ripley, my baby." Her bright little girl looked up with wide, solemn eyes.

"Is Ripley gone?"

"Yes," Jetti said, smoothing the blanket across her chest.

"Will he come back?"

Jetti hesitated, brushing a curl from her daughter's forehead.

"I don't think so, my love."

Berta clutched the paper bird to her chest. "Do you think he will be okay?"

Outside, crickets sang in the garden, and the old cherry tree tapped against a glass window in one of the rooms below.

Jetti sat down beside her, leaned close, and kissed her cheek.

She didn't answer.

But she didn't say no.

Chapter Thirty-eight:
The Folded Goodbye

It was just after breakfast when Berta came toddling in from the parlor, clutching a bundle of her toys in both arms. The early autumn chill spilled through the kitchen windows, painting squares across the floor and glinting off the tin kettle on the stove. Jetti stood at the counter with a steamy cup of coffee in her hand, her hair still pinned from sleep.

"Mama!" Berta called, breathless and excited. "I rited you a letter!"

Jetti turned from the sink, drying her hands on the towel. "A letter? From you, my bright one?"

Berta nodded proudly and fished in her cloth pouch, where she kept Ripley's delicate paper creatures. One of them... the little bird... had come undone at the wing. She pulled it free and held it up.

She beamed, cheeks flushed. "Yah-huh! It's for you to read. I made it all myself."

She plopped the cloth pouch onto the table and tugged at the drawstring. It was faded red with tiny stitched flowers. It sat open as she pulled out, one by one, her most precious paper creatures. The rabbit with floppy ears. The deer with the bent hind leg. The two frogs, one who always looked like he was mid-jump. And then, finally, the little bird Avi had found in his apartment. The wings were both crumpled at the edge.

"This one," Berta said, holding up the bird like it was something holy. "The letter was hiding inside. But I found it!"

Jetti crouched beside her, pulling hair away from Berta's face. "You found it inside the bird?"

"Yes! But I didn't look at it. I folded it more. The frog helped."

"The frog helped you fold a letter?"

"Mmm-hmm," Berta said proudly, rocking on her heels. "He told me it was for you. I think Ripley told him before he flew away."

Jetti blinked. "Before Ripley flew away?"

"Yup." Berta was serious now, eyes wide. "He said goodbye to the frog. But not to us. So the frog said he would tell me when it was time. And today he said it."

Jetti's chest tightened. "You think Ripley gave the frog a message for you?"

"Nooo, Mama," Berta said loudly, as if Jetti had missed something obvious. "For you. But the frog kept it safe with the bird until I was ready."

Jetti smiled, masking the prick of unease behind her ribs. "And you didn't write it yourself?"

"Well..." Berta looked suddenly uncertain. "Maybe I helped a little? But it was already writed when I opened it."

She handed the crinkled bird to Jetti with both hands, beaming.

Jetti took it from her daughter's outstretched hand. It had once been folded with care, creased sharply and tucked into itself so neatly that, had Berta not tugged it apart by accident or curiosity, it might never have been found.

She half-expected a scribble of charcoal lines or a child's drawing of trees and stars. But as she unfolded the paper, her breath caught. The writing was small. It was so small she had to bring it to the window to see it better. Her heart tightened. The penmanship was too steady, too measured to be Berta's.

She realized she could have burned the paper bird to stoke the stove. She could have thrown it away, thinking it ruined. But here it was, cradled in her palm. Waiting.

It wasn't a note from Berta.

It was from Ripley.

She blinked, once, twice, trying to focus on the tiny words etched in narrow script:

Jetti,

I'm sorry I left so suddenly.

The truth is, I got sick from the mushrooms—stupid, I know. I made myself ill, and by the time I could stand again, I knew I had to go.

I didn't want to say goodbye badly. Or in front of Berta. Or you.

You were so kind to me. All of you. Kinder than I probably deserved.

Please tell Aaron thank you for everything. Ruth, Avi, Anka, all of them.

And you... thank you for the picnic, for trusting me, even just a little. You reminded me what it felt like to be seen.

Tell Berta I think of her laughter. That's what I'll carry with me.

But this isn't where I belong. I wish it were different. Be well.

—Ripley

Jetti stared at the letter, her thumb brushing over the signature, then up along the crease in the paper. The corners were worn, as if folded and unfolded several times before he had hidden it in plain sight.

She turned to Berta, who was now on her tiptoes at the edge of the table, trying to balance the frog on top of the rabbit.

"Sweetheart," Jetti said, crouching beside her again.

"When did you find this?"

Berta wrinkled her nose, thinking. "Umm… yesterday? No, today… after porridge. I was playing and the wing falled off, the frog jumped, and then I waited…the ritings, was inside."

"Okay, my little one…" Jetti was surprised Berta even knew what she had found.

"I thought it was magic," she whispered. "Like a spell. But frog said it was a 'pology. Is that what it is?"

Jetti reached for her daughter, pulled her close, and kissed her temple. "Yes," she whispered. "It's a kind of apology."

"From Ripley?"

"Yes."

"Is he coming back?"

Jetti hesitated, folding the note meticulously back into the shape of the bird.

"No, my love," she said at last. "I don't think he is."

Berta pressed her face into Jetti's shoulder, her little hands clutching the deer and frog. "I hope he's not too cold where he went."

She knelt and gathered her daughter into her arms, pressing her face into her hair. Berta smelled of floral soap and morning milk.

"You're magic, you know that?" Jetti whispered.

"I know," Berta said, grinning. "Like these animals that were paper."

Jetti held her a moment longer before rising and placing the bird carefully in the wooden box Joseph had given her the night Berta was born, near a box of matches, beside a spool of twine and a bunch of hair ribbons…where no wind could carry it away.

She didn't cry.

Not this time.

Instead, she tied on her work apron, buttoned the back of Berta's dress, and set about the day. Shelves had to be stocked, bolts of fabric would not cut themselves. Life, even with its little aches, had to go on. She wasn't surprised that he had left, but at least he had the decency to leave a note.

That night, after the oil lamp was dimmed and Berta was asleep beside her, one hand squishing the paper frog, Jetti opened the box again and touched the bird's folded body.

She whispered, "Goodbye, Ripley."

Then she closed it and left the letter where it was, carefully tucked between a child's imagination and the truth.

Chapter Thirty-nine:
Library School

The family library, a grand room lined with shelves of leather-bound books and lit by dawn's glow, had been transformed into a classroom. The big roll top desk now replaced with a wide oak table in the center covered with notebooks, pencils, and stacks of carefully selected texts for young children. The scent of ink and freshly sharpened pencils married with the rich aroma of food wafting from the nearby kitchen, creating an atmosphere both grounding and alive with possibility.

At the head of the table sat Mrs. Kohn, a retired schoolteacher and family friend, whose demeanor commanded respect from her young pupils. She had agreed to tutor the young children in the comfort of the Finkelthal home, a decision that delighted Jetti and her siblings. For Berta, Rivka, and Kurti, school wasn't just an obligation, it was an adventure they shared together.

Six-year-old Berta, with her fair skin, platinum blonde curls, and sparkling blue eyes, was the first to arrive each morning, her chubby hands clutching a slate board. She had an aura to her, an infectious joy that made even the most mundane tasks feel exciting. Beside her, Rivka, also six, with her chestnut waves framing a face of olive-toned skin, sat with practical intensity. Her dark eyes shone with curiosity, and she often took meticulous notes, earning her teacher's praise. Five-year-old Kurti, whose blonde hair and pale forget-me-not blue eyes mirrored Berta's, had a playful streak that sometimes drew giggles, and exasperated sighs, from the girls. He was a year younger and had a sharp mind just like his father Joseph.

Even though they were cousins they shared a bond that was more like siblings, their days spent side by side, learning and growing in an environment steeped in love.

"Can anyone tell me what the capital of Romania is?" Mrs. Kohn asked one morning.

Berta's hand shot up eagerly. "Bucharest!" she exclaimed, a triumphant grin spreading across her little face.

Rivka nodded in agreement, then added, "And it's where Papa goes for meetings sometimes." Her voice carried a hint of pride, reflecting her admiration for her father, Avi.

Kurti, not wanting to be left out, chimed in, "And they have fancy motorcars there!"

Mrs. Kohn chuckled, her stern expression softening. "Very good, all of you. It's wonderful to see how much you're paying attention."

Between lessons, the children's bond deepened through shared moments of discovery. They often huddled together in a sunny corner of the library, flipping through books with colorful illustrations or practicing writing their names. Berta's handwriting was bold and confident, Rivka's delicate and precise, while Kurti's letters sprawled across the page with a creative youthful exuberance.

Their days followed a steady rhythm: mornings spent in lessons, afternoons exploring the estate grounds and playing with the farm animals. The evenings filled with stories read aloud by Jetti, Nurit, or Ruth. The adults marveled at how quickly the children learned, their young minds eager to soak up knowledge.

"They're like little sponges," Ruth said one evening, watching Rivka and Berta work on writing letters in the cursive alphabet together. "It's a joy to see them thrive."

Avi nodded as he looked at Kurti, who was busily sketching what looked like a horse on the edge of his notebook. "They have each other, and that makes all the difference."

Though they occasionally bickered, as children do, their disagreements were fleeting, quickly replaced by laughter or a shared plan for the next day's adventures. The trio was inseparable, their connection rooted in a love that felt almost timeless.

On weekends, the children explored the mansion and created stories from each room which turned into a stage for their imaginations. They put on plays using costumes from old clothes and fabric stored in big trunks in the attic, Berta always eager to take the lead role, while Kurti designed the settings with his careful eye for detail. Rivka often volunteered as the narrator, her voice rising and falling dramatically as she brought their stories to life.

As the seasons changed, so too did the children's discoveries. With each new day, the entire estate became a living classroom, a place where curiosity was nurtured and imagination flourished. Afternoons often saw Berta, Rivka, and Kurti venturing outdoors, the sprawling estate their endless playground.

The garden, with its neatly tended rows of herbs and vegetables, became a wonderland. Rivka, ever observant, loved to point out the subtle differences between plants, her dark eyes lighting up as she explained which leaves were basil and which were mint. "Smell this, Berta," she said one sunny afternoon, holding a sprig of thyme under her cousin's nose. Berta wrinkled her nose at first but then broke into a giggle, declaring it smelled like "chicken soup!"

Kurti, meanwhile, had no patience for the finer details of gardening. He darted from flower to flower, chasing bees and butterflies, his pale curls catching the sunlight. "I'm a bee too!" he announced, buzzing loudly and making the girls laugh.

The barnyard was another favorite haunt, where the trio befriended a small flock of chickens and a curious goat named Greta, who had a habit of nibbling on anything left unattended, once stole Berta's straw hat. "Greta, no!" Berta shrieked, chasing the goat while Rivka and Kurti doubled over with laughter. It was moments like these that cemented their bond, shared hilarity, and adventure knitting them even closer together.

Evenings were reserved for family moments indoors. After dinner, the children would gather in the sitting room, or solarium, where Jetti, Ruth, or Nurit would read aloud from a worn book of fairy tales. The crackling fire warmed the room as the children listened with rapt attention. Rivka loved the stories of clever heroines, often sitting with her knees pulled to her chest, her eyes wide with wonder. Berta, on the other hand, preferred the tales of magical creatures, often interrupting with questions about where dragons and fairies might live. Kurti, the youngest, inevitably fell asleep halfway through, his head resting on his mother's lap.

On rainy days, the trio turned the mansion into their playhouse. The attic, with its forgotten trunks and dusty treasures, became their creative haven. "This will be the queen's robe!" Rivka declared, draping a piece of tattered velvet around Berta. Kurti held a broomstick like a scepter, narrating their impromptu play with dramatic flair.

"Bow before Queen Berta!" he announced, his voice booming as he pointed the scepter at an imaginary court.

Berta, always eager for the spotlight, rose to the occasion, tilting her chin and declaring, "I am the fairest queen in all the land!"

Their laughter echoed through the house, a sound that brought smiles to the adults. Aaron often paused his work to listen. "They're making memories they'll carry forever," he said one evening, sharing a look with Jetti, who nodded in agreement.

It was a childhood of simplicity and joy, woven with lessons, laughter, and love. Together, the cousins discovered not just the world around them, but the enduring kinship of family. It was a bond that would shape them in ways they couldn't yet understand, a foundation that would always bring them back to one another, no matter where life took them.

Chapter Forty:
Growing Passion

Three years later, the children had grown, not just in stature but in their interests and skills, each finding a unique path that delighted both their teacher and their families.

Berta, now nine years old, had blossomed into an eager linguist. Mrs. Kohn had recognized her knack for picking up languages early on, and lessons in German and Russian were added to her native Romanian studies. Berta's slate was often covered with elegant curling script, Hebrew and Cyrillic letters, her small hands carefully shaping each letter.

"Say it again, Mrs. Kohn," Berta would insist, her blue eyes bright with determination. "I want to get it just right."

Her enthusiasm for languages turned everyday conversations into little experiments. She would greet Rivka with a cheerful "Privet!" or mutter phrases under her breath while wandering the house. Her passion extended beyond lessons; she'd pore over books, asking questions about the roots of words and their meanings. "Did you know 'Bucharest' means 'city of joy'?" she'd say, her voice brimming with wonder.

Rivka, also nine, had developed a deep love for history. She absorbed every story Mrs. Kohn shared, from the legendary queens of old Europe to tales from the Jewish Bible. Her favorite pastime was retelling these stories, weaving them into intricate narratives that captivated her cousins.

"Imagine being Queen Esther," Rivka mused one afternoon, her dark curls bouncing as she animatedly acted out a scene. "So brave, standing before the king to save her people. I'd wear a gold crown, like this…" she grabbed a wreath of dried ivy to perch on her head, earning a giggle from Berta.

She also had a fascination with names and their origins, often pestering the adults with questions. "Uncle Aaron, where does my name come from? And yours?" she'd ask, her dark eyes filled with curiosity. Each answer was stored in her mind, adding to the tapestry of stories she was creating.

Kurti, barely eight years old, had turned into an artist with a sharp eye and a steady hand. Mrs. Kohn encouraged him to explore his gift, often assigning him creative tasks that intertwined art and exploration. One of his favorites was a game they dubbed "Kurti's Scavenger Hunt."

Each morning, he would surreptitiously retreat to a different room in the sprawling mansion, his sketchpad and pencils in hand. He would capture a specific detail of a room, maybe a vase of fresh flowers in the parlor, the ornate clock in the dining room, or the intricate molding above the library door. Once his drawing was complete, he'd hide it, and the others were tasked with finding the drawing, room, and the thing he had illustrated.

"Found it!" Berta squealed one afternoon, racing to the kitchen to point at the pitcher on a sideboard.

"You're getting too good at this," Kurti grumbled, though he was secretly pleased with her enthusiasm.

The scavenger hunts became a beloved tradition, blending Kurti's artistic flair with the shared joy of discovery. It wasn't unusual to hear Rivka and Berta arguing playfully over a particularly tricky drawing, their banter flowing through the halls.

As the children grew into their unique passions, Mrs. Kohn adjusted her lessons to nurture their individuality. The mornings were structured around reading, writing, and arithmetic, but the afternoons were more fluid, allowing each child to dive deeply into their favorite pursuits.

"They complement each other so well," Jetti remarked one evening as she watched the three of them comparing notes at the dining table. Berta teaching Rivka a German phrase, Rivka explaining the lineage of a medieval king, and Kurti sketching a castle based on her description.

Aaron nodded. "It's a joy to watch them grow together. They'll carry this bond with them for life."

The Finkelthal home thrived with the children's energy and creativity, each day an opportunity to learn, play, and create memories. They were growing into individuals with distinct talents and dreams, yet their shared adventures and love for one another remained the heart of their world.

Chapter Forty-one:
Clinging to Joy

The estate sprawled in wealth and vitality, its halls echoing with laughter and the ceaseless stir of family life, a fortress against time, while beyond its gates the world was beginning to shift.

By 1925, whispers of anti-Semitism had begun to curl like smoke into daily life in Romania. At first, it was subtle, a sudden increase in bureaucratic hurdles for Jewish shopkeepers, a delay in permits, a raised eyebrow at the synagogue's plans to expand.

But then came the propaganda: inflammatory newspaper columns blaming Jews for inflation, for crime, for everything wrong with the fragile postwar economy.

In 1926, nationalist student groups began staging public demonstrations. "Romania for Romanians!" they shouted, often with a hateful edge that no longer pretended to be about patriotism. In cities like Iași and Bucharest, Jewish students were harassed at university gates, and even sometimes not allowed in.

In Czernowitz, though the community remained more multicultural, however, tensions began to seep in. Posters were defaced. A Jewish tailor was beaten outside his shop on an ordinary Tuesday afternoon. The city's newspaper editor ran a piece questioning the "loyalty" of Jewish citizens to the Romanian nation.

For the Finkelthals, who had always believed in the advantage of education and community, these developments felt both surreal and frightening. Jetti, Esther, and Aaron began attending meetings at the synagogue not just for worship, but to discuss contingency plans. They stopped sending Berta and Rivka into town alone. Rivka was told not to wear her Star of David necklace. Kurti, who once proudly drew the synagogue dome for a project Mrs. Kohn assigned, was not allowed to share any religious art outside their home.

By 1930, the rise of the Iron Guard, a fascist paramilitary organization fueled by xenophobia and ultranationalism, confirmed their worst fears. Synagogues were vandalized in other cities. Jewish professors were dismissed from universities. Laws were proposed to limit the number of Jews allowed to study medicine, law, and engineering. Conversations at dinner tables grew more somber, more urgent.

Still, within the walls of the mansion, life pulsed on with reasonable resistance. Rituals became more than traditions... they became anchors. On Friday evenings, Berta, now twelve years old, lit the Shabbat candles like her mother, grandmother, and great-grandmother before her, with hands that trembled only slightly, whispering the ancient blessings while Esther and Aaron stood behind her, his kippah askew, eyes reflecting both reverence and worry.

The children watched the flames dance, their glow casting halos on the dining room walls, as if warding off the creeping darkness outside.

Songs were sung, lovely lullabies in Yiddish, psalms in Hebrew, as if their voices alone could preserve a vanishing world. Berta and Rivka often helped braid challah with Anka, their small hands sticky with dough and flour dusted across their aprons like snowfall. When the loaves came out of the oven, they were set reverently on the table, like twisted crowns, shiny, radiant, and defiant.

They clung to joy wherever it lived. In the fantastical wonder of a bedtime story, told while shadows lengthened across the reading room floor. In the treasures they gathered on forest walks, bunches of bright berries hidden in brambles, colorful mushrooms discovered within mossy alcoves, and the laughter that carried through the trees when Anka made up stories about squirrels and clever foxes. Kurti sketched their adventures on scraps of parchment, slipping the drawings into coat pockets like secret prayers.

But late at night, when the family had gone to sleep and the wind pressed gingerly against the windows, Jetti sat awake, her sewing projects untouched in her lap. The warmth of ritual could only reach so far. She listened to the rhythmic breathing of Berta in the bed next to hers, the ticking of the clock on the mantle, and the rising tide of questions in her heart.

How long could they hold on to this sliver of peace? How long before the knock came on their door? The world outside was changing, minute by minute, law by law. The very walls that kept them safe now felt like paper about to tear apart.

And though she smiled by day and praised her daughter with love, Jetti's heart carried the question that haunted so many mothers like her:

How would they survive?

Chapter Forty-two:
Cusp of Adolescence

By 1931, life in Czernowitz beat with a rhythm that felt, on the surface, almost jubilant. The city's cobblestone streets shimmered beneath the afternoon sun, alive with the sound of clattering horse hooves, haggling voices, and the occasional sputter of a passing motorcar. Vendors shouted from their stalls in what seemed like a dozen languages, offering ripe figs and dates, loaves, embroidered linens, and brass candlesticks. Women in patterned shawls bargained in German, Romanian and Yiddish, their baskets full of beets, fresh dill, and fragrant garlic. Street musicians played waltzes in the parks while young children darted between café tables in bursts of laughter.

To Berta, Rivka, and Kurti, now respectively thirteen and twelve years old, it was a playground of wonder. Every corner promised discovery: new pastries to try, alleyways growing with ivy painted with chalk, books waiting in crooked stacks at the foot of a cart.

They chased each other through the marketplace, skipped stones near the Prut River, and competed to identify birdsong in the early morning fog. Despite the slow tightening of restrictions on Jewish families, the children bloomed with a kind of stubborn joy.

They knew something was shifting—of course they did. There were always new rules. A shopkeeper no longer allowed Jews inside. A friend's father who returned from work early, his face tight with worry. Whispered conversations that halted the moment they entered a room. But that change hadn't yet settled into their bones the way it had for their parents. The fear had not hollowed them. Not yet.

For the children, life pulsed with promise. Their hearts were full of poems, and secret pacts sealed with sticky fingers and crusts of plum cake. They were allowed to be children. And somehow, within the growing shadows, they still found the light.

The children, on the cusp of adolescence, had grown into their interests with remarkable depth. Berta, with her flaxen curls and keen mind, was now fluent in both Romanian and German, eagerly teaching herself Russian, French, and Hebrew with the help of old texts in the library. She loved to sit at the window with a dictionary in one hand and a notebook in the other, jotting down new words and phrases.

Rivka, ever the historian, had taken her love for stories and turned it into a passion for genealogy. She spent hours interviewing family members about their ancestors, piecing together a family tree that sprawled across an entire sheet of parchment. Kurti, meanwhile, had become a prolific artist, filling sketchbooks with intricate drawings of cityscapes, animals, and the faces of his family. His work had matured, earning praise from visitors who often mistook his drawings for those of an older, trained artist.

But while the children thrived, their beloved teacher, Mrs. Kohn, was beginning to struggle. At 76 years old, the once-sharp tutor had started to show troubling signs of forgetfulness. She often misplaced her glasses or repeated the same lesson twice in a day. Worse yet, she began confusing the children's names, sometimes scolding one for something another had done.

"Kurti, stop doodling and pay attention!" she snapped one morning, only to realize moments later that it was Rivka who was drawing a map of ancient Persia.

The children found her forgetfulness amusing at first, giggling behind their hands when she mixed up lessons or called Berta by Kurti's name. "She's just getting old," Rivka said with a shrug, her tone dismissive. They teased her, never realizing the gravity of what they were witnessing.

One day, Berta came to her mother to share a particularly funny moment. "Mama, you won't believe what Mrs. Kohn said to Kurti today!" she began, her eyes sparkling with laughter. "She told him his drawing of the marketplace was 'too realistic' and asked if he had traced it from a photograph! Poor Kurti was so confused, he'd been sitting in the kitchen drawing for hours!"

Jetti laughed, wiping her hands on her apron as she helped Anka prepare dinner. "Oh, that dear woman. She always has a way with words."

But later that week, something happened that unsettled Berta deeply. Mrs. Kohn, in the middle of a language lesson, looked directly at her and said, "Rivka, why haven't you finished your assignment? You're too clever to be so lazy."

Berta froze. "But I'm not Rivka," she said dismayed. "And I already finished my lessons."

The teacher frowned, clearly flustered, and shuffled her papers. "Yes, yes, of course. My mistake," she murmured, but the moment lingered, the air heavy with discomfort.

That evening, Berta confided in her mother again, but this time her voice was tinged with worry. "Mama, something's wrong with Mrs. Kohn," she said, twisting the hem of her skirt. "She called me Rivka today and got upset with me for something I didn't do. It's not like her."

Jetti's smile faltered as she sat down beside her daughter. "Mrs. Kohn is getting older, my darling. Sometimes our minds don't stay as sharp as they once were. It doesn't mean she loves you any less."

"But what if it gets worse?" Berta asked, her blue eyes wide with concern.

Jetti stroked her hair. "We'll take care of her, no matter what. Just as she has taken care of you."

Berta nodded, though her heart remained concerned. She began watching Mrs. Kohn more closely, noticing the little things; the way her hands trembled when she wrote, how she sometimes trailed off mid-sentence. It was hard for a girl as empathetic as Berta to see someone she loved so much in decline.

Despite the challenges, the children continued to learn and grow under Mrs. Kohn's guidance. They adapted to her forgetfulness, sometimes helping her find misplaced items or reminding her of the day's lessons. For the three of them, this period marked a shift, not just in their studies, but in their understanding of life's complexities. They were no longer simply children; they were becoming young adults, learning that love often meant patience, and that caring for others sometimes meant stepping into roles they hadn't expected to fill.

Mrs. Kohn had become an integral part of the family over the years, her presence as constant as the ticking of the old grandfather clock in the hallway. She had been living in the Finkelthal home since the children were small, her room a cozy haven filled with books and mementos of a life dedicated to learning. Despite her recent struggles with forgetfulness, she remained a figure of stoicism and wisdom, her passing a heartbreak none had anticipated.

Chapter Forty-three:
Swan Pond

The Finkelthal estate was bathed in the rainbow hues of autumn, the air crisp and fragrant with the musk of fallen leaves and distant woodsmoke. Two days after Berta's fourteenth birthday, the leaves on the ancient oaks that framed the property had turned vibrant shades of red and gold, scattering like confetti with every breeze. The children, now accustomed to the rhythm of their studies and daily lives, were jarred from their routine by a somber event that would leave an indelible mark on their young hearts.

It was Anka, the housekeeper, who found her. The morning was unusually placid, the gardens blanketed in dew that shimmered under the rising sun. Anka had gone outside to collect herbs for the day's meals when she noticed Mrs. Kohn sitting in her favorite spot by the swan pond, a book of French poetry open in her lap. At first, Anka thought she was merely enjoying the tranquility of the morning, but as she approached, she noticed something amiss.

The book was upside down, its pages open. Mrs. Kohn sat completely rigid, her hands resting inside the leather-bound volume, her gaze fixed on the horizon. Anka's breath hitched as she realized the truth. A wave of sadness swept over her as she took in the scene: the old woman's peaceful expression, the herb garden, and the docile ripple of the pond where no swans swam that day.

"She must have passed away the day before," Anka whispered to herself, her voice trembling. Tears welled in her eyes as she considered the loneliness of it all. For all the love Mrs. Kohn had given and received in the Finkelthal home, she had died alone, her final moments spent in solitude.

When Aaron heard the news, his face fell into a mask of grief. He immediately set about making arrangements, knowing Mrs. Kohn's only living relatives were far away in New York. The family gathered in the kitchen, the atmosphere full of sorrow as they decided how best to honor the woman who had given so much of herself to their lives.

Aaron immediately drafted a telegram to Mrs. Kohn's relatives:

TO SAMUEL KOHN
MANHATTAN NEW YORK USA
REGRET TO INFORM YOU MADELINE KOHN PASSED
AWAY PEACEFULLY THIS MORNING AT ESTATE STOP
FUNERAL ARRANGEMENTS UNDERWAY
CZERNOWITZ STOP
KINDLY ADVISE REGARDING HER EFFECTS STOP
OUR DEEPEST CONDOLENCES STOP MAY HER
MEMORY BE A BLESSING STOP
AARON FINKELTHAL

That day, the family worked together to prepare for the funeral. Berta, ever empathetic, spent the morning gathering unique stones from the creek to adorn Mrs. Kohn's resting place. Rivka combed through the teacher's books and notes, selecting passages and poems to read during the service. Kurti, always with a pencil in hand, sketched a tender portrait of Mrs. Kohn to place beside the grave site.

As they prepared, memories of Mrs. Kohn filled their conversations. "Do you remember how she used to scold me for using my slate board as a doodle pad?" Kurti said with a small laugh, holding up a tiny pencil stub. "She'd always say, 'Kurti, your art can wait until after grammar!'"

Berta nodded, her voice saddened. "And how she would mix up our names? She called me Rivka just last week and scolded me for not finishing my Hebrew lessons when I had already done them." Her smile faltered as she added, "I think she knew, deep down, that something was wrong. But she kept trying for us."

The next day at the funeral it was overcast, a constant drizzle dampening the autumn air. The family and close friends gathered in the small synagogue in Czernowitz, the Rabbi's deep voice resonating through the room. Rabbi Cohen, a burly man with a booming laugh that had once been compared to a "jolly Krampus," led the service. The Rabbi, a beloved figure in the community, often lightened serious moments with humor, but today his voice carried a weight of solemn respect.

The children had grown to love Rabbi Cohen, who had been guiding Kurti through his Bar Mitzvah preparation. His stories, rich with history and myth, always captivated them, particularly his retelling of the weird legend of Krampus. Originating in Alpine folklore, the story was about a horned figure who punished naughty children during Christmas, a holiday they didn't celebrate, but a tale the children loved to hear anyway. "But if Krampus ever laughed," Rabbi Cohen would say with a twinkle in his eye, "he'd sound like me, HA HA HO HO HO!" And the children would roar with laughter, rolling on the floor.

Kurti had been studying diligently for his Bar Mitzvah, though his heart often strayed to his creative musings. He'd practice his Hebrew with Rabbi Cohen at the synagogue, and at home with Berta, who had grown fluent in the language. She corrected his pronunciation and patiently explained complex passages, her love for languages shining through.

"She's better than any teacher," Kurti had once muttered to himself out loud, earning a laugh from Berta.

As the service concluded, the family remained at Mrs. Kohn's grave, the rain drops mixing with their tears. Berta thought of all the lessons she had imparted, not just about languages or literature, but about kindness, patience, and perseverance.

Despite the drizzling rain, the Finkelthals stood united around Mrs. Kohn's fresh grave, the gray sky mirroring the heaviness in their hearts. Each of them carried a piece of her with them; a lesson, a memory, a kindness she had bestowed during her years as their teacher and guide.

Berta bent down, carefully placing the small stones she had gathered onto the grave, the rhythmic patter of raindrops blending with her soothing breaths. As she straightened, she glanced at Rivka and Kurti beside her. Rivka clutched the worn poetry book she had chosen from Mrs. Kohn's collection, her lips moving over the words she had recited during the service. Kurti held his sketchbook tightly, the tender portrait of Mrs. Kohn nestled within its pages, protected from the rain by his coat.

Rabbi Cohen stood nearby, his voice, so often jovial, overcome by melancholy as he murmured the closing prayers. Even his towering figure seemed subdued under the emotion of the moment. Yet, as the last words were spoken and the Rabbi stepped away, a blanket of calm seemed to settle over the gathering.

The family began to disperse, their steps squishing on the wet grass. Aaron placed a steadying hand on Berta's shoulder, his support a comfort. Jetti walked alongside Nurit and Ruth, all three women sharing a deep understanding of their loss, their bond strengthened by grief.

As the children stayed behind, Kurti's voice broke the silence. "Do you think she knew how much she meant to us?" His eyes were wide and searching, fixed on the blank headstone before them.

Berta nodded, though her throat tightened with emotion. "I think she did," she said, her voice steady despite the ache in her chest. "But maybe we should make sure the world remembers, too."

Rivka turned to her cousins, her brow furrowed in thought. "How?" she asked, holding her book closer as if it might provide an answer.

Berta glanced at Kurti's sketchbook, then at the other cemetery headstones, an idea sparking in her mind. "We could write her story," she said, her voice gaining passion. "About everything she taught us, about who she was. Your drawings, Kurti. Your notes, Rivka. And my words. We could create something that lasts."

Kurti looked down at his sketchbook, his lips curving into a small, determined smile. "A book?" he asked. "About her? About us?"

"Yes," Berta said, her blue eyes shining with newfound purpose. "For her. For us. For anyone who needs to know that she mattered."

The cousins exchanged glances, their grief momentarily replaced by the snapshot of something greater; an idea, a goal, a way to honor the woman who had meant so much to them. As they turned to leave the cemetery, the rain began to lift, and a glimmer of sunlight broke through the clouds.

But just as they reached the edge of the graveyard, Berta paused. In the distance, past the swaying willow trees and damp headstones, she noticed a figure standing alone, watching them. Clad in a dark long coat and hat, the person's face was obscured by the shadows of the clouded sky. The figure stood unmoving, as if rooted in place, their presence unsettlingly deliberate.

"Who's that?" Berta asked, her voice low.

Kurti and Rivka turned as they strained to make out the figure through the misty air. The stranger stood motionless for a heartbeat longer, as if debating whether to approach or retreat. Then, without a word, they slipped away into the maze of gravestones, their dark silhouette vanishing amidst the marble markers. The only trace of their presence was the fading rustle of damp leaves and the eerie chill that stuck around in their wake, leaving behind a shiver of unanswered questions.

The three children stood frozen, the lightness of their earlier conversation tinged with unease. "Maybe we should tell Mama," Rivka said, worried.

Berta shook her head, her jaw tightening with determination. "Not yet," she said. "Let's find out who it was first."

With that, the cousins exchanged a solemn glance, something mysterious pressing between them. Their shoes sank into the damp earth as they turned back towards the adults, the smell of wet grass and fresh-turned soil clinging to the air. The earlier drizzle had passed, but the heaviness remained, like decaying leaves settling in the hollows of bare tree roots, and the permanence of the headstones around them. Their plans to write about Mrs. Kohn, to preserve her memoir in stories and sketches, slipped away like following footsteps in a trickling stream. That spark of purpose that was so bright moments ago, now forgotten, as if it had never even happened. All that remained was the ghostly image of the stranger, a dark coat retreating between the old oak trees and marble graves like smoke dissolving in fog, and the unshakable feeling that something had been left unsaid.

Chapter Forty-four:
Uncle Yosef

The day following Mrs. Kohn's funeral carried a strange energy. The cousins spoke in hushed tones about the stranger in the graveyard, their imaginations weaving stories about the shadowy figure they had glimpsed. But as time passed, the mystery began to feel less menacing and more like an itch they couldn't quite reach. Life, as it always did, pulled them back into its rhythms; schoolwork, chores, and stolen moments of childish rebellion.

In the afternoon, the household stirred with an unusual commotion. Berta, perched at the parlor window with a book she wasn't truly reading, was the first to notice the carriage. Its sleek black wheels creaked as the driver pulled the horses to a halt at the gate. Her breath caught when the door opened, and a tall figure emerged.

He was dressed impeccably, his dark coat perfectly tailored to his broad shoulders, and his hat tilted at just the right angle. He moved with a confidence that spoke of a man accustomed to commanding attention. But his face...Berta froze. It was familiar in a way that made her heart skip.

"It's him," she whispered, her voice barely audible.

Rivka looked up from where she sat working on another history map. "Who?"

Berta didn't answer. She darted from the room, her feet skimming the floor as she ran to the front door. Rivka, abandoning her task, followed, and Kurti, who had been sketching a wilted rose, wasn't far behind. By the time Berta flung the door open, the man was already ascending the steps.

"Uncle Yosef?" she asked, the words tumbling out before she could stop them.

The man paused, his sharp features revealed as he removed his hat. His dark hair was neatly combed, but there was something older in his face, lines of thoughtfulness and shadows of experience. Then he smiled, and it was the same smile Berta had seen only once, years ago, when she and Mama had traveled to Bucharest to attend his graduation from high school.

"Hello, Berta," he said keenly. "You've grown into a beautiful young lady."

Rivka and Kurti skidded to a stop behind her, their eyes wide "It's you!" Rivka exclaimed. "You were that man we saw at the cemetery."

Yosef's brow furrowed, but his smile didn't waver. "I was," he admitted. "I wanted to pay my respects to Mrs. Kohn. She… she meant a great deal to me."

Berta stepped back, allowing him to cross the threshold. Her throat tightened with a mix of emotions—relief, curiosity, and the small sting of anger. "Why didn't you say anything? Why didn't you tell us you were back?"

"I arrived too late for the funeral," Yosef said, his voice measured but tinged with regret. "I didn't want to intrude."

Rivka opened her mouth to speak, but footsteps from the hallway silenced her. Jetti stood there, her expression frozen in a mixture of disbelief and something more fragile.

"Yosef," she said, her voice barely above a whisper.

He straightened, his hat clutched in his hands like a lifeline. "Jetti," he replied, and in that single word lay a world of apologies he hadn't found the courage to say.

Jetti approached slowly, her eyes scanning his face as if to confirm it was truly him. Her breath hitched, and she stopped just short of embracing him. "You've been gone so long," she said, wavering. "I thought…" She trailed off, shaking her head. "It doesn't matter what I thought. You're here now."

"Yes," Yosef said simply. "I'm back to teach the children."

The tension cracked as Aaron's booming voice called from the study, followed by the sound of his heavy footsteps. When he appeared in the foyer, his eyes lit up with recognition, his grin broad and genuine. "Yosef! My boy! It's so good to see you!"

Aaron embraced him with the kind of embrace that could erase years of distance. For a moment, the house buzzed with joy, laughter, and greetings filling the space. But even amidst the excitement, Berta couldn't shake the feeling that Yosef's return carried something more.

Later after dinner, when the cousins crowded into Jetti and Berta's suite to talk, Kurti leaned against the doorframe, arms crossed. "Why didn't he tell anyone he was coming back?"

"Maybe he didn't know how to," Rivka offered. "Sometimes it's hard to come home after so long."

Berta stared at the ceiling, her mind drifting back to the cemetery. "He's hiding something," she said inquisitively. "I don't know what, but I'm going to find out."

The cousins had barely finished whispering their theories when Aaron appeared in the doorway, his expression calm but purposeful. He leaned casually against the frame, his tone steady as he spoke.

"Yosef's moving in with us," he began, watching their curious faces. "I asked him to come home. He'll be teaching you here, just like he was doing in Bucharest."

"Teaching us?" Kurti asked, his brow furrowing in surprise.

Aaron nodded, a small smile playing at his lips. "He was tutoring Theodore Zissu, the son of A.L. Zissu. If Yosef's good enough for a student like that, he's more than capable of guiding you."

Rivka tilted her head. "Who's A.L. Zissu?"

"A man who's never short of an opinion," Aaron said with a chuckle. "He's one of the sharpest minds in the Jewish Party and a relentless critic of injustice. Yosef learned a lot from working with his family."

Berta, seated on the edge of the bed, stared at the floor. "Then why is he coming back?" she asked.

Aaron's smile faltered. "Because this is his home. And because he's bringing someone with him."

The room held its breath as the cousins exchanged glances.

"Someone?" Rivka asked, her curiosity clear.

"His wife," Aaron replied. "Her name is Lisa. They married in Bucharest."

"Wife?" Jetti's voice lifted with surprise, her hands gripping her lap as a smile began to tug at the corners of her lips.

Aaron met her eyes. "Yes. I thought it was time the family knew. They'll have their own suite in the east wing, and I've already spoken to Esther about a position for Lisa at the beauty salon, if she wants it."

Kurti raised his eyebrows. "A wife. So, is she staying here too?"

Aaron's lips twitched with amusement. "Yes, Kurti, that's usually how it works."

Berta remained pensive, her mind whirring with thoughts of this stranger who would now be part of their world.

The next morning, the house was alive with preparations. The staff bustled to ready one of the east wing suites, fluffing pillows and airing linens, while the cousins watched from the hallway, their excitement tempered by uncertainty. When the carriage finally arrived, they raced to the parlor window, their faces pressed against the glass as they tried to get the first glimpse of Yosef and his wife.

Yosef stepped out first, his familiar figure now more refined, his movements confident yet unhurried. Following him was a woman with dark curls pinned neatly under a hat, her posture elegant but approachable. Lisa carried herself with an astute confidence, her attention sweeping over the house as though she were already claiming it as her own.

"She's pretty," Rivka whispered.

Kurti squinted. "She looks serious."

"Of course she looks serious," Berta muttered. "Wouldn't you, walking into a house full of strangers?"

At the front door, Aaron greeted the pair with a handshake that turned into a long hug. "Welcome home," he said, his voice inviting. "Lisa, it's wonderful to finally meet you."

She smiled politely. "Thank you. Yosef has told me so much about Czernowitz and about all of you. I'm grateful to be here."

Inside, the cousins hovered by the staircase as Yosef and Lisa entered. Berta couldn't help but study them both. Yosef, who seemed at once familiar and distant, and Lisa, who carried herself like someone both confident and cautious.

Later that evening at dinner, the family gathered around the long table in the dining room, the air buzzing with anticipated curiosity. Lisa answered questions with confidence but seemed content to let Yosef take the lead.

"You worked with Theodore Zissu?" Aaron asked, breaking into a smile. "I hear his father's not an easy man to impress."

Yosef chuckled. "That's putting it lightly. Zissu demanded the best from everyone around him, but it was worth it. Working with his son taught me a lot, not just about teaching but about myself."

Lisa added, her voice flat but clear, "Yosef always said Theodore had a spark, an energy that reminded him of why he loves teaching."

As the conversation continued, Berta watched Lisa closely. There was something about her, something reserved but not cold, as though she were holding back until she found her place.

When the meal ended, and the family conversed over tea, Jetti audibly excused herself. She wandered outside to the garden, her mind swimming with thoughts. A wife. Yosef had a wife. And while Aaron's reassurances were meant to ease the adjustment, they hadn't entirely dissolved the unease surrounding this change.

From her seat near the window, Berta watched her mama retreat into the garden, the early evening shadows of the house stretching long across the grounds. Uncle Yosef's return had brought a whirlwind of excitement and curiosity, and Berta couldn't help but feel that this was the start of something new and full of possibility.

Chapter Forty-five:
New Lessons

Morning crept into the kitchen, not with noise, but with comfort and routine. Aromas drifted from the stovetop of fried eggs sizzling in the pan, a loaf of fresh rye resting on the counter, its crust whispering steam, and the sharp, familiar tang of pickled herring layered on a nearby plate. These were the smells of home, of a life built around tradition and convention.

A low fire crackled in the hearth, its flame casting shadows on the stone surrounding it, wrapping the room in a blanket of comfort. The air felt thick with a kind of sleepy calm, the kind that dwelt in serene moments before the day fully woke.

Wooden cabinets stood along the walls, their worn surfaces bearing the stories of years past. Scratches from knives, water rings from cups, burn marks from too hot pots placed haphazardly, like little trophies of time.

At the center of it all stood the kitchen table, long, scarred, sturdy, and lovingly set. Clean plates waited patiently, a jar of plum preserves beside a half-filled pitcher of milk. A woven basket sat in the middle, holding freshly picked apples. Slices of recently baked bread sent steam curling upward from its browned crusts like tiny spirits vanishing into the air as quickly as they rose.

Berta sat at the edge of the bench, her small fingers picking absently at a piece of bread. She didn't butter it. Didn't reach for the preserves. She only tugged at the soft center and let the doughy part ball up in her palm. She let her thoughts drift completely unfocused, toward the kitchen window, where a blur of trees bent swaying in the breeze. The nervous flutter in her chest dulled her appetite, though the comforting aroma of breakfast clung to her clothes.

In that peaceful room, nothing was urgent, but everything felt poised, on the edge of something just beginning to stir.

She glanced at her cousins, her own unease mirrored in their faces. Rivka sat with her chin propped in one hand, the other aimlessly nudging a forkful of eggs across her plate. Kurti, perched on the edge of his chair, stared at the table, his leg bouncing in restless anticipation.

"I don't know what to expect," Rivka murmured. Her voice was low, almost drowned out by the clink of cutlery on plates.

"Neither do I," Berta admitted, her fingers now fidgeting with a piece of crust. "Mrs. Kohn was so… easygoing. She never pushed us too hard."

Kurti sighed, shoving a piece of herring into his mouth and grimacing at the sharp and sour brininess. "Yeah, and now we've got Uncle Yosef, who went to the fanciest school in Bucharest. What if he expects us to already know everything?"

Rivka wrinkled her nose, stealing a piece of bread from Berta's plate. "Mrs. Kohn didn't even care if we mixed up our numbers. I don't think Uncle Yosef will let that slide."

Berta heard something and looked toward the back staircase, the wooden steps creaking as if in anticipation. "I just hope he's not too strict," she said, her voice barely above a whisper.

The soft shuffle of footsteps on the stairs broke the conversation. The cousins turned as one to see Uncle Yosef descending, his dark coat draped neatly over his arm, his movements steady and composed. Behind him came Lisa, her black curls peeking out from beneath a mauve headscarf. She held onto the rail, her eyes bright with curiosity as she took in the kitchen.

"Good morning," Yosef said, his voice calm as he stepped into the room. He glanced at the table, a wide smile tugging at his lips. "It seems like this is the best spot in the house."

Lisa followed him. "And clearly the most inviting," she said, her tone uplifting. "I can see why everyone gathers here."

She moved toward the counter as Yosef gestured to the coffee pot. "Help yourself," he told her. "There's fresh bread too. The herring... well, that's a matter of taste."

She chuckled as she poured herself a cup of coffee, the nutty aroma filling the air. "Noted."

Yosef turned to the children. "And you three; Berta, Rivka, Kurti. Did you sleep well?"

They nodded, offering polite murmurs of agreement, though their apprehension was palpable.

Yosef pulled out a chair and settled into it with an easy grace, his hands resting flat on the table. "So," he began, "tell me what you've been learning. I'd like to know what Mrs. Kohn taught you."

Berta hesitated, glancing at her cousins before answering. "She let us pick what we liked best," she said finally. "She said it was important to enjoy learning."

Yosef tilted his head, his interest genuine. "And what did you enjoy most?"

"Languages," Berta said quickly, her fingers brushing against the edge of the table. "She taught me German, and Hebrew."

"I like History and maps," Rivka added, her voice gaining confidence. "Mrs. Kohn had this big atlas, and I learned to memorize where all the countries were."

Kurti shifted in his seat. "I like drawing and art," he muttered, his voice barely audible. "She said it helped me focus."

Yosef leaned forward. "It sounds like Mrs. Kohn understood how to make learning meaningful," he said thoughtfully. "That's a gift that not every teacher can do."

Lisa returned to the table with a coffee cup cradled in her hands. "And what about the things you found difficult?" she asked. "Were there subjects you didn't enjoy as much?"

"Math," Rivka and Kurti said at the same time, earning a laugh from Berta.

"Figures," Kurti grumbled. "Too many rules."

"Math can be tricky," Yosef agreed, his tone wise. "But it can also be fun, once you understand the patterns. We'll take it slow, I promise no one will be overwhelmed."

Rivka perked up. "Really? You won't give us exams right away?"

Yosef smiled, his eyes crinkling at the corners. "Not right away. First, we'll see what you already know. Then, we'll build from there."

Lisa leaned forward. "Learning is about growing, not just memorizing. It sounds like you already have wonderful foundations."

The cousins exchanged glances, the tension between them easing. Kurti smirked, Rivka grinned, and even Berta felt a tickle of excitement creep into her chest.

As the conversation flowed, the sunlight streamed lazily through the kitchen window. By the time breakfast was over, the children weren't just prepared for their first lesson with Uncle Yosef, they were curious and excited about what it might bring.

Chapter Forty-six:
Curiosity

The library held the majesty of being a sacred place to the familiar students. Morning sunbeams slanted through the tall windows, dancing across polished floors and illuminating motes of dust that drifted like tiny snowflakes. Along the towering bookshelves, row upon row of weathered spines leaned together like old friends, each one a gateway to another world. Though the room had been visited many times, it always seemed to greet its students anew. The hush of turned pages, the faint scent of parchment, and the inviting sprawl of new books laid out for exciting discoveries. The central table, long and stately, bore fresh parchment and inkwells that shimmered like obsidian, while the new globe at its corner gleamed, as if waiting for young hands to spin it and dream.

This was where Mrs. Kohn had taught them, where she had read aloud from thick books, her voice carrying the magic of faraway lands and forgotten histories. The room still felt like hers, and the children couldn't help but tread lightly as they entered, their footsteps barely making a sound on the polished floor.

Berta ran her hand along the edge of the table as she took her seat, the cool wood grounding her in the present. Rivka settled beside her, setting her notebook down, looking excitedly at the shiny new globe while Kurti waited by one of the shelves, his fingers grazing the spines of the books as though seeking reassurance.

When Yosef entered, his presence filled the room with a palpable energy. He paused at the door, taking in the space with a mix of nostalgia and purpose. He placed his dark coat neatly over the back of a chair and carefully laid a stack of new notebooks on a low coffee table for the children.

"Good morning," he said, formally, his voice steady. "It's good to see you all here."

The children giggled at his obvious joke, mockingly playing round with polite greetings to each other, their apprehension melting away with every second. Yosef moved over to the coffee table, rearranging the notebooks into three neat piles, one for each of them. "This room," he began, gesturing to the towering bookshelves, "is one of the most special places in this house. Do you know why?"

Berta glanced at her cousins, then raised her hand hesitantly. "Because it has all the books?"

Yosef smiled. "That's part of it. But it's more than that. This room holds ideas, stories, questions and answers. So many questions. It's a place where learning can take us anywhere we want to go."

He picked up a piece of chalk and moved to the large slate board that stood against one wall. In clear, deliberate letters, he wrote the word:

Curiosity

"This is where we'll start," Yosef said, turning back to face them. "With curiosity. Mrs. Kohn taught you the value of exploring what interests you, and I want to continue that. But I also want to challenge you. To push you to think deeper, to ask questions, so you find your own answers."

Kurti shifted in his chair, his pencil tapping against the table. "What kind of questions?" he asked, his voice skeptical.

"Any kind," Yosef replied, his tone inviting. "Questions about the world, about history, about yourselves. For example…" He walked to the globe at the end of the table, spinning it so it turned beneath his hand. "If you could visit anywhere in the world, where would it be, and why?"

Kurti sat up straighter, his skepticism giving way to interest. "Paris," he said without hesitation. "For the art. I want to see the paintings and sculptures."

"Paris," Yosef repeated, writing it on the chalk board. "A wonderful choice. And you, Rivka?"

Rivka hesitated, then spoke with obvious determination. "Egypt. I want to see the pyramids and learn how they were built."

"Egypt," Yosef said, adding it to the list. He turned to Berta. "What about you?"

She glanced down at her hands, then looked over at the towering shelves of books. "New York," she said boldly. "I want to see the Statue of Liberty."

The room hushed, her words hanging in the air. Yosef's expression softened, his eyes meeting hers with perceptible understanding. He nodded, turning to the board and writing **New York** next to **Paris**, and **Egypt**, with deliberate care. "That's a wonderful choice, Berta," he said.

Lisa appeared, carrying a tray with cups of tea and a plate of biscuits. She set it down on the side table with a sideways smile. "I thought you all might need a little energy."

"Thank you, Lisa," Yosef said, his tone full of gratitude. He turned back to the children. "You see? Learning isn't just about books and chalkboards, it's about moments like this, about sharing ideas and building something together."

The children exchanged glances, their initial trepidation melting into cautious excitement. The room, once tinged with the ghost of Mrs. Kohn's absence, began to feel alive again.

As the lesson unfolded, Yosef wove stories about each of the destinations the children chose into his teaching, drawing connections between the their interests and the world around them. By the time the session ended, the air buzzed with a sense of discovery, and even Kurti seemed eager for what tomorrow might bring.

When they were packing up their notebooks and pencils, Berta delayed for a moment, her eyes scanning the shelves. Since Mrs. Kohn's passing, the library didn't feel like a relic of the past. It felt like a door to something new, and Berta couldn't wait to see what was on the other side.

Rivka and Kurti had already bounded off, but she stayed behind, her notebook open on the table. Yosef, busy wiping down the chalkboard, seemed lost in thought, the chalk dust clinging to his sleeves.

"Uncle Yosef?" she began hesitantly, her voice breaking the silence.

He turned and noticed her still seated. "Yes, Berta?"

She fidgeted with her pencil, clicking it against the edge of her notebook. "Can I ask you something? About where you went to school?"

Yosef smiled, setting the chalk down on the tray. "Of course. What would you like to know?"

Berta straightened in her chair, her curiosity overcoming her shyness. "Why was it so special? Uncle Aaron talks about it like it is the best school in the world."

Yosef pulled out a chair across from her and sat down, his hands resting in his lap. For a moment, he seemed to be weighing his words, gazing briefly to the window where the afternoon light spilled across the room.

"It isn't the best school in the world," he said finally, his voice thoughtful. "But it is one of the finest in Romania. The **Iulia Hasdeu National College** is more than just a school. It is a place where ideas flourish, where we were encouraged to think for ourselves, to develop new ideas, and explore options that challenge the status quo."

Berta's eyes widened. "What kind of ideas?"

"All kinds," Yosef replied, his tone brightening. "We explored politics, science, history, literature, and mostly ideas about how to make a change in the world and our place in it. The professors there are extraordinary. They don't just lecture; they pushed us to investigate, to dig deeper. They believed that knowledge wasn't just something you memorized, it is something you live."

"What was it like?" she pressed, leaning forward. "Your first year, I mean."

Yosef distant as he recalled the memory. "My first year. The world outside the college felt like it was unraveling, war was close by in the Balkans. But inside those walls, it was different. There was a sense of excitement, of purpose. The halls were lined with books, more than I've ever seen in my life. The classrooms were filled with students from all over Europe, each one eager to learn, to dream of something better."

"Was it hard?" Berta asked, her voice tinged with awe.

"It was," Yosef admitted with a small smile. "The standards were high, and the professors demanded a lot from us. But it was worth it. Every lesson felt like a step toward understanding the world more clearly. And the friends I made there, they are some of the brightest, most driven people I've ever met. We pushed each other to be better, to think bigger."

Berta's fingers traced absent patterns on the table as she listened, captivated. "Do you think we could ever go somewhere like that?"

Yosef's smile widened, a hint of pride in his expression. "Why not? If you're curious, if you're willing to work hard, there's no limit to where you can go. That's the beauty of learning, Berta. School and education will open doors you didn't even know existed."

Berta nodded slowly, her thoughts swirling with possibilities. The towering shelves of books surrounding her didn't feel overwhelming, they felt like an invitation to her future.

"Thank you, Uncle Yosef," she said eagerly.

He reached across the table, giving her hand a squeeze. "Never stop asking questions, Berta. That's where all great journeys begin."

Chapter Forty-seven:
Beneath the Elms

The garden stretched out in green waves behind the servant's entryway, bordered by low stone walls and several unruly shrubs that caught the morning dew. Jetti stepped carefully onto the gravel path, a red paisley shawl wrapped loosely around her shoulders, breath forming miniature clouds ahead of her in the chilly air. The autumn morning was brisk, the leaves turning the color of flames, and the sky above Czernowitz was pale, as if not yet fully awake.

Yosef was already outside, his hands clasped behind his back, his posture thoughtful as he strolled beneath the gnarled arms of the elm trees. When he heard her approach, he turned, his face lighting up, not with the polite calm he wore for the children, but with something more vulnerable.

"Do you remember this path?" Jetti asked, falling into step beside him.

Yosef glanced down at the stones beneath their feet, at the roots that poked through the earth. "I think I remember chasing butterflies with you," he said with a half-smile. "Though, I must've been no more than four or five."

"You were barely walking," she laughed. "But you were so determined. You never gave up, even when you fell face first into a gooseberry bush."

He chuckled, unguarded. But it faded quickly.

They walked together for a time, listening to the rustle of dry leaves and the distant clatter of a wagon down the lane. The mansion behind them growing more distant from the clinks of breakfast dishes and children's voices, but out here, it was just the two of them, the sister who had mothered him once, and the brother who had grown into a man far away from home.

"I missed you," Jetti said finally, her voice yearning. "All those years. We were told it was for the best, that Bucharest would shape you into something greater, but it never felt right to me. You were still so young."

Yosef stopped walking. His eyes were darker than hers, shadowed by things she hadn't seen. "I know," he said. "I never blamed you, or Aaron. I think he did what he thought was necessary. Maybe he was right. Maybe not. But I missed you, too. And sometimes I hated that school."

Jetti's eyes widened.

"Not the learning," he added quickly. "I loved the books. The challenge. But it was lonely. I was always the only Jew in my class. At first, they mocked my name. Then my accent. And later… well. By the time I was sixteen, there were clubs I couldn't join. Professors who stopped calling on me. Graffiti on the school gates."

Jetti felt her chest tighten. "It's getting worse, isn't it?"

He nodded slowly. "Since the Iron Guard started gaining support, it's become dangerous in ways I didn't expect. You've heard of them, yes? The Garda de Fier?"

She shook her head side to side, grimly.

"They recruit from the universities now," Yosef said. "Some of my classmates wore their pins. Green shirts, the Archangel Michael badge. They talk about purity. About cleansing Romania of foreign influence." He paused. "And by that, they mean us… Jews."

Jetti looked away, her arms crossed tightly over her chest. "Here in Czernowitz, we've always lived beside the Ukrainians, the Germans, the Romanians. But it's changing. Everyone can feel it."

"Yes," Yosef said. "It's not just politics. It's in the community too! They've started refusing Jewish students at certain colleges. The *numerus clausus* laws are discussed openly now. At the university in Iaşi, some Jews were beaten in the lecture halls. In Bucharest last winter, a synagogue was vandalized during Hanukkah. Broken windows. Torah scrolls were thrown and burned in the street."

A shiver ran through Jetti despite the morning sun. "What are we going to do?"

Yosef was speechless for a moment. He turned to the old stone bench beneath a tall elm and sat, hands clasped between his knees. "I don't know," he admitted. "But we can't pretend anymore. This place, where we live, it isn't safe. Not really. Not for much longer."

Jetti sat beside him, brushing a leaf from the hem of her skirt. "But the children... they're thriving. They're innocent to it. They don't understand how quickly it could all disappear."

"Which is why we need to prepare them," he said. "Not frighten them, but make them strong. Make them curious. Let them question everything so they can think clearly. If they ever have to leave... someday... they must know who they are. What they stand for."

A single yellow leaf fell between them, spinning slowly to the ground.

"I can't bear the thought of them growing up in fear," Jetti whispered.

Yosef reached out, covering her hand with his. "They won't Jetti, not if we're honest with them. And not if we act now while they are young, but old enough to understand."

They sat in deep thought for a long time, the cold stone of the bench beneath them, the wind carrying with it the acrid smoke from a chimney across the avenue.

Somewhere inside the mansion, Berta's voice rang out in laughter.

It was a beautiful morning. And also, a terrifying one.

Chapter Forty-eight:
The Lesson They Didn't Expect

The children were basking in the fullness of their breakfast, sugary tea still cloying on their tongues, crumbs of crusty bread brushed from their sleeves, as they filed into the library again. The air held that comforting mix of old pages, chalk dust, and yesterday's firewood, like a promise of stories that were waiting to be told. Berta plopped into her seat with a familiar bounce, Rivka adjusted her notebook just so, and Kurti spun his pencil between his fingers, all three assuming they were in for another pleasant dive into geography or ancient legends.

But today, Yosef didn't write anything on the slate. He didn't touch the globe. He simply stood at the head of the table, his hands clasped before him, something somber settling into the classroom.

"Today," he said after a moment, "we're going to talk about history… but not the kind you can memorize from a textbook. Today we're going to talk about the kind of history that lives in people's bones. The kind that changes how we walk through the world."

The children looked at each other, puzzled but intrigued.

"Do you know how the Great War began?" Yosef asked. "I don't mean the rumors you may have heard. I mean the real reason—why it happened at all."

"I think someone was assassinated," Rivka said, her brow furrowed.

"Yes, Rivka that is right… Archduke Franz Ferdinand. His assassination was the trigger, but the war had been brewing long before that day. Think of Europe like dry straw in a barn, in the governments at the time tensions were running high everywhere, and it only needed a spark to ignite."

He continued, pausing to let the silence settle. "This war didn't just start with a single shot," he said, raising a finger. "It had been building for years." He stepped toward the chalkboard, tapping it once with the edge of his hand. "Every country thought it was the greatest—its people, its culture, its armies." He let the words hang, then spread his arms wide. "All shouting at once."

He turned back, pacing slowly. "Huge empires like Austria-Hungary and the Ottoman Empire—" he drew a line on the slate, "—they were like patched-up quilts, stitched from too many fabrics of life. But the stitches were coming loose." He snapped his fingers. "Serbia wanted freedom. Rebels inside Austria-Hungary wanted power."

He stopped then, looking each of them in the eye. "And Germany…" He let the pause stretch, his voice dropping low. "Germany was pacing like a caged animal, restless, demanding its place in the center of the world."

Yosef paused, letting the children absorb his last word. Then, he leaned forward slightly, lowering his voice. "Militarism," he said, drawing the word out on the slate behind him. "It added fuel to the fire." He mimed an explosion with his hands, fingers splaying wide. "Every country was building massive armies, stockpiling weapons, drafting young men of every religion and race, even in peacetime." He tapped the table for emphasis, each word falling like a drumbeat. "It was an arms race. No one wanted to fall behind."

He straightened, then lifted one finger, as if letting them in on a secret. "And there were alliances too—kind of like quiet promises." He paced over to the chalkboard, sketching two rough triangles. On one side he wrote the members of the 'Triple Alliance: Germany, Austria-Hungary, Italy.' He tapped each name. Then, he did the same with the other triangle. 'The Triple Entente: France, Russia, and Great Britain.'

Turning back to the children, he let his gaze linger to make sure he could see understanding in their eyes. "Everyone was watching each other nervously," he said. He crossed his arms, shoulders tense. "Promising that if war came, they'd back each other up." He held the silence, letting the unease sink in.

They were fixated on him.

Yosef watched the children carefully, then pressed on. "June twenty-eighth, 1914," he said slowly, letting the date settle. "In the city of Sarajevo." He drew a small circle at the top of the board. "A young Serbian nationalist—his name was Gavrilo Princip—stepped out of the crowd." Yosef wrote his name in the circle and mimed someone pushing through bodies, then lifted an invisible pistol. "Two shots." He clapped his hands together, sharp and loud.

The children jumped.

"Archduke Franz Ferdinand," he said, voice firm, "the heir to the Austro-Hungarian throne. Dead. His wife, Sophie—dead." He let the silence hang. "Two lives ended in a heartbeat." He drew in a breath, holding it in, and lowering his hands. "And for weeks afterward, it was as if every nation held its breath too..." He leaned forward, his eyes narrowing. "Until suddenly—," he spread his arms wide—"they all started shouting."

He scanned the room to be sure they followed, then went on, his tone slower, deliberate. "Austria blamed Serbia, and declared war." He jabbed a finger toward the floor. "Russia didn't want Serbia crushed, so they stepped in." Another jab. "Germany was furious, and as Austria's ally, they declared war on Russia." He pivoted, pointing in the opposite direction. "France was Russia's friend, so they began to mobilize."

He took a step back, his voice quickening now. "Then Germany did something no one expected." He dragged his hand in a sweeping motion across the air. "They marched straight through Belgium to surprise France." He paused, looking around at their faces. "But Belgium was neutral. Attacking them made Britain furious. And so..." He straightened, his voice ringing in the room. "Britain entered the war, too."

Sitting at the edges of their seats they were intently listening, especially Rivka who had a love for all things historical.

"In just a few weeks, all of Europe was tangled up in battle. One decision after another, one country pulling in the next, until it became the biggest war the world has ever seen."

"But it wasn't just a war of soldiers and generals. It was a war of trenches and poison gas, of freezing mud and unspeakable loss. It was a war that changed the shape of the entire world... and one that left deep scars all over the countries that never fully healed."

He paused again to make sure they were understanding the full effect of what he was saying.

"You must remember this," Yosef continued, his voice low and steady, his eyes holding theirs. "War doesn't begin or end with one moment. It's like a slow avalanche, with pressure building over time until it all comes crashing down. And when you look at the world around you now, with the current events happening right here in our town, look at the posters, the speeches, the violence that's creeping into everyday life here in Romania... we can feel the ground shifting again. Even though it is a different time, it holds the same tensions."

He stopped talking for a moment, letting the silence settle around the room.

"We study history," he said, "not just to honor those who came before us. But to learn to see the signs... so we know when it's time to stand up, before it's too late."

Walking slowly around the table, his voice sounding urgent. "By the end of it, nine million soldiers were dead. Another seven million innocent civilians with them. The world was redrawn. Empires collapsed. And little countries, like ours, were left to figure out who we are now."

Kurti looked down at his notebook. "But that was a long time ago."

Yosef stopped. "Not long enough. The scars are fresh for many adults. And the anger that fed that war? It didn't disappear. It just changed shapes and is lying low."

He turned to the window and gestured toward the town beyond. "In 1918, Greater Romania was born. We united regions, gained land, grew stronger, but at the same time it was also more divided. Our new borders included millions of minorities: Hungarians, Ukrainians, Germans, and over 750,000 Jews. We were told we were part of the nation, but we were treated like strangers."

Rivka raised her hand, hesitant but steady. Her voice trembled. "But why, Uncle Yosef? Why do they hate us?"

The room fell silent. Yosef sat at the edge of the table, folding his hands together. His voice, when it came, was softer, composed, yet heavy. "Because fear is powerful," he said slowly. "Fear can paralyze people, keep them from thinking clearly... from acting justly." He let the words hang, then leaned forward, his eyes intent. "And people—people are easy to convince when they're afraid."

He drew in a breath. "I saw it in Bucharest with my own eyes. After the war, jobs were scarce. Homes were broken. Families hungry. And someone needed to be blamed." He spread his palms on the table. "So, the government, the newspapers, even the schools... all began to whisper the same lie." He dropped his voice to a near whisper. "That Jews were the problem. That we were greedy. That we didn't belong."

He looked at each child in turn, his eyes dark, his words deliberate. "In 1927, just a few years ago, the Iron Guard was formed." He straightened, his voice hardening. "Do you know what they did?" He let the pause stretch, then answered his own question. "They murdered Jewish professors." He lifted a finger. "They attacked synogogues." Another finger. "They threw acid in people's faces." He lowered his hand, the silence in the room now absolute.

The children gasped, Berta's hand flying to her mouth.

"In Iaşi, in 1929, Jewish students were beaten for trying to sit in the same lecture halls as their classmates. The police did nothing. In fact, they watched. And worse, some of them joined in. In the city where I studied, you couldn't wear a kippah without someone spitting at you in the street."

Kurti's pencil had stopped on the page. "Why didn't people stop them?"

"Some tried. But not enough. And others..." Yosef's jaw clenched, "...others agreed with them."

The light coming through the window had shifted, now casting long shadows across the table.

"I am not telling you this to frighten you," Yosef said, his voice steady. "I am telling you because I love you. Because you need to know that history isn't something that happens behind you. It happens around you. And you are... right now... living through a moment that will be long remembered."

He rose, walking slowly to the chalkboard, where he wrote three words in thick, deliberate strokes:

TRUTH   COURAGE   MEMORY

"These are the tools you must carry," he said. "Not just in your books or your lessons. The truth of who you are, and where your roots come from. The courage to stand up when it's hard. And to carry the memory of those who came before you in your hearts... because we owe them that."

Rivka reached for Berta's hand under the table. Kurti sat upright, his face pale but resolute.

Yoself's gaze softened as he looked around the table. He drew a long breath before speaking. "I cannot tell you what tomorrow will bring." He let the silence rest there, the weight of it pressing into the room. Then his voice steadied. "But I can tell you this—none of you will face it alone." He leaned closer, his hand resting flat on the table. "If we meet what's ahead with courage in our eyes and compassion in our hearts..." His words slowed, deliberate. "then this world is still ours to shape."

Outside, the wind stirred the last of the fallen leaves on the elm trees. Inside, three children sat a little taller in their chairs, their childhoods shifting, ever so slightly, toward something more resilient. Toward something braver.

Chapter Forty-nine:
Midnight Mystery

As the grandfather clock struck midnight, its deep chime reverberating through the halls of the mansion, Berta stirred in her bed, the resonant sound pulling her from the edge of sleep. At first, she thought she'd imagined it... the nutty aroma of freshly brewed coffee and the rich, sugary scent of chocolate babka. It was a combination she loved, evoking mornings filled with celebration and indulgence. But as her eyes adjusted to the darkness, reality set in. This was no morning, and the comforting smells seemed oddly misplaced in the late hour.

She sat up slowly, her heart quickening as she strained to hear muffled whispers coming from below. Her mind raced, trying to make sense of it. Who was awake at this hour, and what could possibly require such a clandestine gathering in the heart of their home? The household was large, its routines predictable, even in times of strife. Midnight was for sleep, not hushed conversations and strange stirrings in the kitchen.

Sliding her feet into slippers, Berta crept toward the bedroom door. Careful not to wake her mama, she took very small steps, and waited to hear the repetitious rhythm of her breathing, but it was not there. *Where was she?* Berta wondered, concerned. She walked quickly to the door and pressed her ear against the wood, listening intently. The whispers were hushed, distorted by the thick walls, but they were there, insistent and urgent. She hesitated, torn between returning to the safety of her warm bed and satisfying her gnawing curiosity.

Outside, the moon floated pale and distant above the dark trees of the orchard, and the house creaked with the settling cold. Berta rested her cheek against the door again. Hearing voices drift up through the floorboards… low, serious tones, impossible to make out but serious enough to twist unease into the silence. She knew she should go back to bed, but her thoughts wouldn't surrender.

Uncle Yosef's lesson returned to her in sleep, not as words but as a world she could not grasp. She had tried to be brave in class, scribbling notes, pretending the war was something distant, long gone. But in her dreams it came alive—and it felt too real.

The earth split open, trenches carved like serpentine wounds bleeding mud. Boys no older than Kurti crouched inside, their bodies pressed against the walls, their faces pale masks. Their eyes were hollow, aged beyond years, staring straight through her, unblinking. Rifles too large for their frames rattled in fragile hands, the cold black metal seeming to reject their touch.

Then the air thickened. A yellow haze slithered across the ground, curling upward with a hiss. It wasn't fog at all—it was alive, malicious—wrapping itself around throats, forcing screams, pulling blood from eyes and noses.

Horses thrashed and whinnied in the distance, their cries so sharp they might have been human. Eyes rolled white, they stumbled, collapsed, their bodies crashing into the earth. Even the sky seemed to sag, buckling under the weight of it all.

And then—Kurti. His face wavered in the smoke, his hand reaching for her. His mouth moved, shaping words she couldn't hear. She tried to call back, but her voice dissolved in the yellow haze. At that instant, his outline broke apart—piece by piece—until nothing remained but choking silence.

The nightmare had jolted her awake in the darkness, and since then, the images haunted her like smudges in the corners of her vision. Uncle Yosef had said that the world had changed after that war… and now it was changing again. She felt it, even in her bones. Something was coming.

Her eyes wandered the familiar shapes of her room: the carved wardrobe with the brass handles, the embroidered blanket that had once belonged to her grandmother, the shelf of folded paper animals someone had given her when she was small, perched like sentries above her desk. What would she miss most, if war were to come here? The warm kitchen mornings with fresh braids of challah dough rising on the hearth? The library that smelled like ink and musky leather from the books in sunlight? The apple trees, the garden path, the slow way twilight fell across the parlor floor?

Berta's throat tightened. She didn't want to be afraid...but how could she not be, with so many secrets whispered in grown-up voices and so many new rules appearing like shadows where sunlight used to be?

A sudden creak from the settling mansion snapped her back to reality. She turned her head sharply, listening... then quietness again.

She stood up and padded across the floor, her slippered feet barely audible. Her heart pounded, not with fear exactly, but with curiosity.

She didn't know what she would do, or what was coming next. But she knew she wanted to remember everything...every scent, every voice, every bit of the life they had now... before the world shifted again.

Berta moved cautiously down the back staircase, avoiding the creaky sixth and seventh steps with practiced precision. The familiar smells grew bolder, the tang of tobacco smoke and the sweetness of beeswax candles. As she neared the bottom, the sounds became clearer. She heard the distinct clacking of spoons against china, the scrape of a chair against the floor, and low voices exchanging words too dampened to discern.

She crouched at the bottom step, peering around the corner into the kitchen. The glow of lamplight spilled into the hallway, casting shadows that crept like specters on the walls. Her mother sat at the long wooden table, her head bowed, hands clasped tightly in her lap. Surrounding her were Aaron, Avi, Yosef, and Joseph. Each looking grave, their expressions etched with worry. The sight of her family gathered in secret sent a chill down Berta's spine.

"Jetti," Aaron's voice cut through the air. "We must act now. The situation is deteriorating faster than we anticipated."

Jetti raised her head, her face pale and drawn. "I know, Aaron," she said, her voice trembling. "But she's just a child. She's only fifteen."

Berta's heart lurched. They were talking about her. She leaned closer, her pulse quickening, desperate to hear more.

Aaron sighed heavily, his fingers drumming against the table. "Fifteen is old enough, Jetti. You've seen the news, heard the reports. The violence is spreading. It's no longer just rumors Jetti, it's here. We can't wait until it's too late."

Jetti shook her head, her eyes glistening with tears. "And what am I supposed to tell her, Aaron? That her childhood is over? That she must leave everything she's ever known and marry a man she's never met? How do I explain that to my daughter?"

She could hear the persistent ticking of the grandfather clock in the hallway. Berta pressed a hand to her chest, her breath coming in shallow gasps. *Married?* The word echoed in her mind, loaded and foreign. Her fingers gripped the edge of the step as she struggled to make sense of what she was hearing.

"It's not about what she wants, Jetti," Avi said. "It's about survival. Solomon is a good man. He has means... connections. He can take her to Palestine, where she'll be safe. Do you want her to stay here and risk...." He stopped abruptly, his voice faltering.

"Risk what?" Jetti snapped, her voice rising. "Risk the same fate as the others? As their children? Do you think I don't know what's at stake, Avi? Do you think I haven't thought of every possible way to protect her?"

Joseph reached out, placing a hand on Jetti's shoulder. "We're all trying to protect her," he said. "This is the only way, Jetti. You know that."

Berta's stomach churned as she listened to their words. She felt like a pawn being moved across a chessboard, her future decided without her consent. The mention of Palestine brought a trace of recognition. She'd heard her uncles speak of it before, a distant land of promise and freedom for Jews. But the idea of leaving her home, her mama, her family, and everything she knew was unbearable.

Aaron's voice cut through her spiraling thoughts, steady and unyielding. "We'll tell her tomorrow," he said. "The preparations are already in motion. Solomon is already on his way. The marriage will take place here, in the house, in a few days. There's no time to waste." He leaned forward, his fingers drumming on the table, his brow furrowed in a mix of determination and unease.

"After they marry, Solomon will take her to Odessa first," he continued, his words precise and methodical, as though he had rehearsed them. "That will be her new home for the time being. He needs to settle his affairs; liquidate his business, secure the sale of his property, and arrange for the journey to Palestine. Everything must be handled discreetly and swiftly. Once the way is clear, they'll travel to Palestine together, where they can start anew."

The room seemed to grow heavier with each word, the intensity of the plan settling like a shroud over the air. Aaron's voice slowed a bit, though the urgency remained. "It's the only way to ensure her safety, Jetti. Solomon is ready to protect her, to provide for her. This isn't just a marriage…it's her chance at survival."

Jetti's trembling hands flew to her face, trying to stop the raw sobs that broke free from her chest. Her shoulders shook violently, each breath jagged and filled with anguish. The words had barely left Aaron's lips, but their magnitude hung in the air like an iron veil. Her voice cracked as she managed to whisper, "I don't know if I can do this. She's my only child… my 'only' child."

Aaron's steady presence didn't waver as he moved closer, his expression stern but not unkind. He reached out a hand, placing it on her arm. "Jetti," he said, his tone measured, almost pleading. "You have to understand. We don't have the luxury of time. Berta needs to hear this. She needs to understand what's at stake."

Jetti lifted her tear-streaked face, her eyes bloodshot and brimming with despair. Her voice trembled, but there was steel in it now, a defiance that cut through her grief. "No, Aaron. Not you. This is not your place. If anyone is to tell her, it will be me. I am her mother." She straightened her gait, her breath steady as she tried to compose herself. "Do you hear me? Me! Not you."

Aaron's brow furrowed, but he nodded solemnly, understanding the depth of her discomfort. "I only mean to help," he said, his tone edged with concern. "You shouldn't have to carry this alone."

Jetti's voice hardened, the fierce protectiveness of a mother shining through her despair. "She's my child, Aaron. My responsibility. I brought her into this world, and I will be the one to prepare her for what's coming. Not you. Not anyone else." Her hands clenched into fists, her body convulsing with the force of her emotion. "Don't take this from me."

The tension in the room was palpable. Aaron drew back surprised, his lips pressing into a thin line as he nodded once. "As you wish, Jetti," he said, humbled. "But don't wait too long. Every minute counts." Again, he pressed the truth she couldn't escape: *Solomon was already on his way.*

Jetti turned away, clutching the edge of the table for support. Her tears fell freely now, hot and relentless, but her love for Berta burned brighter through them. This was her burden, her role as Berta's mother. And no matter how much it hurt, she would be the one to tell her daughter the truth...because no one else could. No one else should.

Berta couldn't listen anymore. Her vision blurred with tears as she retreated up the stairs, each step a struggle against the gravity of what she'd just heard. By the time she reached her room, her legs were quivering, and her mind was racing with questions and fear.

Chapter Fifty
Fractured Trust

Berta wandered the halls in a daze, avoiding her mother and uncles as much as possible. She couldn't bring herself to face them, not after what she'd overheard the night before. Her mind churned with anger, uncertainty, and a sense of betrayal. How could they do this to her? How could her mother agree to send her away, and marry a man she did not know?

That evening, as she sat by the window in their suite, her thoughts were interrupted by the creak of the door. She turned to see her mother standing there, her face pale but resolute.

"Berta," Jetti said, stepping inside. "May I sit with you?"

She nodded stiffly, her hands gripping the folds of her dress. Berta watched as her mother crossed the room and sank into the chair beside her. For a moment, neither of them spoke, it felt as if a taut wire stretched between them.

Jetti took a deep breath, her hands trembling as she reached for Berta's. "I need to talk to you," she began. "About something very important."

Berta pulled her hands away, her voice sharp. "I already know, Mama. I heard you and the uncles last night."

Jetti's eyes widened in shock. "You… you were listening?"

"Yes," Berta said, her voice trembling with emotion. "I heard everything. About the marriage, about Odessa, and Palestine. How could you make this decision without telling me?"

Jetti's face crumpled, tears spilling down her cheeks. "Because I am trying to protect you," she said. "I didn't want you to be afraid."

Berta stood up abruptly, she started pacing the room. "Afraid? You've already decided my fate, Mama! How am I supposed to feel anything but afraid?"

Jetti rose, her voice determined despite her tears. "You're supposed to feel grateful, Berta. Grateful that we have a way to keep you safe. Do you think I want to send you away? Do you think this is easy for me?"

Berta turned to face her, her eyes blazing. "Then don't send me! Let me stay here, with you!"

Jetti shook her head, her expression pained. "You can't, my sweet girl. Staying here is too dangerous. You've heard the stories, seen what's happening. We have no choice."

The significance of their argument hung heavy in the air. Berta sank back into her chair, tears streaming down her face. "I don't want to marry him, Mama," she whispered. "I don't want to leave you."

Jetti knelt beside her, taking Berta's hands in hers. "I know," she said. "But sometimes, we have to do things we don't want to do to survive. I promise you, Berta, this is the only way."

Berta stared at her mother, her heart breaking. She wanted to believe her, to trust that this decision was for the best. But as she looked into her mother's tearful eyes, she already felt a deep, aching sense of loss.

As dawn broke over Czernowitz, Berta sat by the window, watching the first rays of sun pierce the darkness. The world outside looked unchanged, yet she knew everything was different. Her life, once predictable and secure, now felt like a fragile thread ready to snap.

The chimes of the grandfather clock drifted through the house, marking the start of a new day. For Berta, though, it was a day weighted with uncertainty, shadowed by the knowledge that her life would never be the same again.

Chapter Fifty-one
Letting Go

The air in Czernowitz carried something sinister, a tension that clung to the streets like an unseasonable fog. Romania's political tides were beginning to shift ominously, and the shadow of Hitler's Germany loomed threateningly to the west. Though the city's cobblestone streets bustled with the familiar vibrancy of merchants hawking their wares and street musicians filling the air with lively melodies, an undercurrent of unease wove itself into the fabric of daily life.

For the Jewish families of this cosmopolitan enclave in Bukovina, the once-welcoming city began to feel precariously perched on the edge of something darker. Anti-Semitism and the rumblings of impending war turned even the closest family dinners into solemn debates. Eyes darted toward doors and windows during conversations, as if the walls themselves might betray the fear growing in their hearts. Some neighbors began to vanish without explanation, their homes left eerily empty, and it wasn't long before people started making secret preparations to flee the storm they all knew was coming.

In the grand mansion, a sharp current of anxiety hung in the air. Gold-framed mirrors reflected the dim of candlelight as Berta, just fifteen, stood in the parlor, clutching a linen handkerchief to her lips. Her mother, Jetti, knelt before her, smoothing the hem of her beautifully embroidered silken dress.

For so long, Berta had been all limbs and laughter…bare feet on marble stone floors, tousled curls escaping her braids, a high, bell-like voice echoing through the halls of the mansion. But tonight, in the dimness of this chamber, Jetti saw her daughter not as the child she'd raised, but as a young woman on the precipice of something irreversible.

Her breath seized in her throat.

The swell of Berta's chest, barely noticeable just months ago, now filled out the bodice of her wedding dress with pleasing rounded curves. Her waist had narrowed too, subtly but unmistakably, and her once boyish hips had begun to suggest the shape of a woman. Even her collarbones seemed more defined now, peeking delicately above her neckline, like fragile wings beneath her skin.

Jetti's hands, weathered by time and years of sorrow, trembled against the silk fabric as she tried to adjust the cuffs, her mind already wandering. She remembered the time she bathed Berta after a long fever, years ago, how small her limbs had been then, how weightless. Now, she could feel the womanhood blooming in her daughter's frame, the repressed dignity in the way she held herself, the self-conscious grace of someone who had become aware of her body but didn't yet know what to do with it.

But to Jetti, she was still a child. Her child.

She'd ignored the signs for as long as she could. Pretended she hadn't noticed the way Berta began to tilt her face toward the mirror at odd moments, studying the new slope of her cheek line or the way her hair fell across her shoulders. Pretended not to see the smudges of blood on the linen cloth in the washbasin last spring; another unmistakable marker that the time for innocence was closing. Even now, Jetti's heart clung to the little girl who used to braid daisies into her apron ties.

But there was no denying it tonight. Not in that gown. Not under the grace of the pearl necklace, fastened with a yellow diamond clasp that glittered like the sun with memories Jetti had buried deep.

Her fingers lingered at Berta's neck longer than they needed to, trembling slightly as they secured the clasp. "Berta, stand tall," she said again, her voice thinner this time, frayed at the edges.

The necklace rested just above her daughter's heart.

Jetti thought of her own wedding day… the way her stomach had churned with a strange mix of anticipation and excitement, the foolish hope that love could be coaxed from duty. She hadn't known then how cold a bed could feel when it was shared with the wrong man. She had wanted better for Berta.

She wasn't ready for Berta to marry. Especially not to a man three times her age with yellowing teeth, streaks of silver in his hair, and a hunger in his eyes Jetti had tried not to notice. But the world wasn't asking if she was ready.

She knew this was the only choice left that might save her daughter.

She swallowed the lump in her throat and stepped back to take in the full image: her daughter, beautiful and elegant under the candlelight, dressed not for joy but for surrender. And in that moment, Jetti realized she wasn't just sending Berta into a new chapter—she was letting go of the last piece of her own.

Chapter Fifty-two
Ketubah

B erta's dowry was both a financial lifeline and a social declaration, meticulously prepared by her mother and uncles as they negotiated the terms of her marriage to Solomon. In the Jewish tradition, a dowry was an essential element of arranged marriages, symbolizing the bride's family's investment in her future and the establishment of a secure household. For the Finkelthal family, the dowry also carried desperation, a final effort to ensure Berta's survival in an increasingly hostile world. It was a display of their immense wealth but also a tool to protect her against the uncertainties she would face as a young bride leaving the safety of home.

The Jewish marriage contract, or Ketubah, was central to these negotiations. This legally binding document served as much more than a ceremonial declaration; it outlined the financial and personal obligations of the groom to his bride and detailed the terms of the dowry.

The Ketubah held immense importance in all Jewish marriages, especially during times of social and political instability. Rooted in Jewish law, this document was far more than a symbolic artifact; it was a legal contract enforceable by rabbinical authority. Written in Hebrew, it detailed the groom's obligations to provide for his wife, including food, clothing, housing, financial stability, and marital rights, as well as outlining provisions for her support in the event of Solomon's death or divorce.

The Ketubah also formally recorded the bride's dowry, listing each item and its approximate value. In Berta's case, this included an array of small family treasures; engraved silver Shabbat candlesticks that were passed down through generations, fine linens embroidered with the family crest with two moons facing east and west and a star of David above them, a high-quality German camera, a symbol of modernity and sophistication, a modest amount of gold coins for immediate needs, an assortment of finely crafted jewelry, a war medal which was her fathers, and valuable loose facet cut gemstones that could be traded for money or goods. Each item was meticulously cataloged, ensuring they could be reclaimed if the marriage dissolved under the agreed terms. The presence of the Ketubah lent a sense of permanence and dignity to what was otherwise a pragmatic, even sorrowful, arrangement.

Once signed, the Ketubah could only be nullified by a rabbi, underscoring its binding nature. This authority emphasized the religious and communal oversight of marriage, making it almost impossible for either party to break the agreement without cause. For Berta, this added another layer of complexity to her predicament. Her life was now governed not only by the will of her new husband but also by the unyielding constraints of Jewish law, and she was scared.

In Berta's case, the Ketubah was written with extraordinary care, and was specifically drawn up to prevent her from leaving the marriage, this was very unusual at the time, but her family wanted to make sure that she always had a home, and would never be destitute. If she ever sought a divorce from Solomon, the document stipulated she would forfeit all rights to the dowry. However, if Solomon initiated the divorce, Berta was entitled to reclaim every item and asset provided by her family, ensuring her financial security. These terms, while unusual, reflected the precariousness of the arrangement and the family's determination to safeguard Berta's future as much as possible under the circumstances.

For the Finkelthals, the carefully inked words on that parchment were both a last vestige of survival and a painful farewell.

Berta's dowry was a reflection of her family's social standing in Czernowitz. While many Jewish dowries of the time were modest, often including items like household furniture or small sums of money, the Finkelthal's contribution was opulent, intended to attract a man of means and stability who would protect Berta during their voyage and relocation to Palestine. The small chest Solomon received for this arrangement was filled with valuables that spoke of a very privileged life.

The size and quality of this dowry made Berta a desirable match despite her youth and the looming threat of war. For Solomon, accepting the dowry also came with the burden of responsibility. It was not merely a financial transaction; it was an acknowledgment that he was now entrusted with Berta's safety and future.

Jetti looked directly in to Berta's eyes and whispered "You must look like the lady you were raised to be."

Berta tasted the salt of her tears at the corners of her mouth, as she bit her lip to try to keep from crying. She glanced toward the doorway, where her Uncle, Aaron, stood with Solomon Abramovich, the man who had agreed to marry her.

Solomon was tall, broad-shouldered and graying, his thick hands calloused from years as a grain merchant were clasped in front of his body. He could have been her father…or even her grandfather. Berta could tell that he too was nervous about this arrangement. She knew nothing about the man she was about to marry, and he knew nothing of the life she was about to leave behind.

"He will protect her," Aaron muttered to himself, as if trying to convince his own heart. He turned to Solomon, forcing a smile. "She is a good girl, kind, well educated, and bright. She will make a very good wife."

Solomon said little, his face unreadable. Aaron motioned toward the ornate polished mahogany chest placed carefully on the table, its brass hinges gleaming in the gaslight. As the lid opened, the room filled with the shimmer of wealth, inside were silver Shabbat candlesticks, strands of pearls, glittering gemstones, and even a German-made camera nestled among embroidered linens, and more they couldn't see underneath. Each item told a story of a prosperous life now distilled into a dowry that had once belonged to Jetti years ago. Aaron's hands held the candlesticks as he said, "These were my great-grandmother's. They will bring you both light." His voice caught, the air thick with trepidation he didn't dare speak.

Berta stood frozen as Aaron deliberately closed the lid of the chest. The metallic click of the brass latch felt final, like the closing of a door she hadn't meant to walk through. Her hands were clenched at her sides, her delicate lace gloves damp with sweat. She didn't remember putting them on.

Jetti had stepped back into the shadows near the window, her face half-lit by dusk. She had said everything she could say, and it hadn't been enough to ease the ache that now hollowed her chest. This was the right choice. The safest path. The one that would give Berta a home, a future, a name that would protect her in a world that had grown too dangerous for girls without one.

And yet... she remained her little girl.

Jetti swept over Berta's silhouette, looking carefully at the graceful line of her neck, the way the dress clung to her changing figure, the stubborn tilt of her chin that hadn't changed since she was three. A rush of memories surged forward: Berta chasing butterflies in the vineyard with her cousins, falling asleep in her lap with sticky jam fingers, asking if she would ever be old enough to have her ears pierced.

Another time she found Berta giggling with a runny nose and wild braids, chasing hens barefoot through the back garden, once asking, "Mama, when I'm a lady, will I have to stop climbing trees?"

Jetti took one step forward, then another, until she was in front of her daughter. She didn't speak. She couldn't. Instead, she reached out and placed her hand over Berta's heart. Through the thin fabric, she felt the wild flutter of a frightened bird trapped in its cage.

Berta looked up at her mother; what passed between them in that glance would never be spoken aloud.

Jetti leaned in and whispered, "You are not alone." Her voice trembled. "You will never be alone."

Tears slipped wearily down Berta's cheeks, tracing delicate paths along her skin. She made no move to brush them away. They fell hastily, vanishing into the depths of her bodice... absorbed like secrets into the fabric of a life she hadn't chosen, yet would carry with grace.

From the hallway, the old clock began to chime the hour. Six slow, mournful bells.

Jetti took one step back. Then another. Until the space between them was filled with everything that could not be changed.

Chapter Fifty-three
Wedding Night

R abbi Cohen arrived at dusk, his prayer book clutched tightly under his arm, his face etched with an egregious and reasonable fear. He entered the parlor with an air of ceremony, the future of the times heavy on his shoulders. There was no canopy, no jubilant gathering of friends and family, no music to celebrate the union. Instead, the room held a sweet essence of honey from the candle wax, and the only sounds were the rustle of prayer shawls and the rabbi's steady chanting of blessings.

Jetti, her eyes brimming with tears, poured wine into delicate handblown glasses engraved with swirling vines. Her hands quivered as she passed the glass to Berta, who sipped the bitter wine without flinching. The tartness stung her tongue, sharp and jarring, a contrast to the subdued sweetness of her childhood now left behind.

Solomon took Berta's unsteady hand as the rabbi recited the blessings of the ceremony. The simple gold band, unadorned and smooth, caught the dim light as Solomon carefully placed it on the index finger of her right hand. This act, rooted in ancient Jewish tradition, carried deep symbolism. The index finger, believed to be the closest to the heart according to the Talmud, was supposed to signify the direct connection of the couple's union to their deepest emotions. The right hand, associated with contracts and testimony in Judaism, underscored the binding nature of the marriage as a sacred and legal covenant.

The plainness of the ring, free of gemstones or ornate designs, was intentional. Its simplicity represented a pure and honest relationship, unmarred by excess or false pretenses. The unbroken circle symbolized the perfection of marriage, an aspiration for a bond that, despite the hardships surrounding them, might endure with the same seamless continuity.

Berta glanced down at her hand, the ring's presence foreign yet significant. She knew that, as tradition dictated, she would later move the band to her left ring finger, but for now, it rested where generations of Jewish brides had first worn theirs. This was a solemn marker of a commitment forged not just between two people, but before their faith and community.

After the hurried ceremony, Berta and Solomon were ushered upstairs to a private guest suite in the sprawling mansion. To Berta it felt as if the grand marble staircase would eat her alive, the sound of their steps as they ascended echoing through the hushed mansion like a reminder of the perishability of her innocence.

The suite was opulent but cold from the spring rains, its tall windows draped with velvet curtains that failed to block the early evening chill. A chandelier cast a muted radiance over the room, illuminating a massive canopy bed dressed in embroidered linens and a matching settee arranged near a marble fireplace. A tray of untouched delicacies; figs, spiced almonds, and a crystal decanter of ruby colored wine, sat on a table in the corner. Berta barely noticed the finery as she stood near the door, her hands clasped tightly in front of her to prevent them from trembling, while Solomon, equally out of place, stared into the small fire.

Jewish tradition held the consummation of a marriage as both a physical and spiritual act, a sacred union symbolizing the beginning of a new household and the fulfillment of the marital bond established under religious law.

But for Berta, the very idea of intimacy was shrouded in fear and mystery. At fifteen, she felt like she was still a child, she was timid and inexperienced, her understanding of marital relations was limited to whispered conversations overheard between older women in her community. She had never kissed a boy, much less imagined herself in the arms of a husband. Her innocence, once a source of pride for her family, now felt like something foreign pressing down on her chest as she avoided Solomon's stare.

Solomon, a widower in his mid forties, was no stranger to the intricacies of marriage. He had once loved deeply and lost, a grief that was fresh in the lines of his face. He understood the enormity of what had been asked of Berta, to leave her family, to marry a man she didn't know, and face an uncertain future. He turned from the fire and met her wary eyes, his expression bleak. He could see the fear in her, the way she stood rigid and uncertain, and he knew he had to tread carefully.

"You don't need to be afraid, Berta," he said, his voice steady but kind. "This is a marriage of safety, of protection. Not of demands."

Berta's hands twisted the fabric of her dress. "I don't know... I don't know what's expected of me," she whispered, holding back tears, her voice barely audible

Solomon took a tentative step closer but kept his distance, his movements deliberate and unthreatening. "What's expected is that we survive, together. Nothing more."

Tears welled in Berta's eyes, and she quickly brushed them away, her cheeks flushing with embarrassment. "I don't know how to be a wife. I've never even kissed anyone."

Solomon gave her a small, reassuring smile. "Then let's take our time. There's no need for us to do anything tonight, or even tomorrow. Let's focus on the journey ahead. When we're safe, when we've reached Palestine and found a home, we can talk about what it means to be husband and wife."

Berta nodded, her shoulders easing. Her fear didn't vanish, but Solomon's words gave her a sense of control in a situation where she had felt powerless. Solomon returned to the fire, adding another piece of wood to warm the cold room. Berta moved to sit on the settee, then she got up and walked closer to the door, thinking she might try to go back to her own suite where her mama was. She looked over at Solomon by the fire and realized that the space between them may have been filled with an assumed understanding.

For now, survival was their shared goal, and the rest could wait for a safer tomorrow.

Solomon got up from the fire and considerately gestured to Berta to go toward the grand canopy bed, its frame carved from dark mahogany and draped with embroidered linens that seemed almost too fine to touch. The over sized feather-stuffed mattress, layered with silky sheets and an intricately quilted coverlet, was a luxury Berta knew about living in the mansion, but had never experienced because she was a child. The bed promised a comfort that felt out of reach in her current state of turmoil.

Solomon, sensing her unease, stepped forward and spoke clearly.

"The bed is yours tonight, Berta," he said. "I'll sleep here by the fire."

He gathered a few pillow cushions from the chaise and arranged them on the thick Persian rug near the hearth. The fire casting shadows on the walls as Solomon removed his jacket and lay down, tucking himself in with one of the richly embroidered throws that had been folded at the foot of the settee. Though he tried to make himself comfortable, it was clear he expected no true rest on the floor.

Berta stood frozen near the door, her fingers clutching at the folds of her dress. The bed loomed in front of her like a foreign thing, too grand and too intimate all at once. She couldn't bring herself to change into the nightgown her mother had carefully folded and left on the bed for her. The idea of undressing in the same room as Solomon, even with his back turned, filled her with dread. He was a stranger to her, and though he had shown only kindness, the mere fact of his presence made her chest tighten with fear.

She hesitated for so long that Solomon glanced over his shoulder from his place by the fire. "Berta," he said, "you needn't worry. I'll keep my eyes closed until morning if it helps. You're safe here."

Safe. The word was a bitter comfort, for Berta felt like safety in this house, in this bed, would not last. She finally slipped off her shoes and sat on the edge of the feather mattress, fully clothed, her trembling hands smoothing the coverlet beneath her. The plushness of the bed was unlike anything she had ever known, and yet it felt wrong... a luxury made meaningless by the prevalent anxiety of her fears.

She reluctantly climbed into the bed and pushed her little body under the covers.

She lay stiffly in the feather bed, her fingers instinctively tracing the smooth band that now circled her left ring finger. The simplicity of the ring seemed both a comfort and a cruel irony, its meaning laden with obligations she had not chosen. This was her wedding night, yet it bore none of the joy or romance she had once imagined.

In her most private dreams, Berta had pictured a wedding to someone she cherished, a man she adored with every part of her heart. Someone she would have a family with, and hold dear. She had imagined an extravagant celebration, the estate alive with music and laughter, the rooms filled with family and friends adorned in their finest attire. A canopy of fresh flowers hung overhead, their delicate fragrance mingling with the aromas of the feast below—roasted meats, braided loaves of challah, exotic fruits, and sugared confections spilling over silver trays.

Her dress would be the finest her family could commission, a gown of ivory satin with intricate lacework, adorned with real pearls, its long train spilling behind her as she walked toward her beloved beneath the chuppah. The groom, a man of her choosing, would stand tall and proud, his eyes shining with devotion. There would be dances for hours, beneath a sky lit by a thousand stars, and the glory of klezmer music would carry across the estate, a joyful testament to their union. She had pictured the way her uncle Tata would beam with pride as he offered his blessing, the way her mother would fuss over her veil, and how her cousins would giggle and steal glances at the other guests gathered to celebrate.

But now, clutching the plain gold band, Berta felt that dream had completely slipped away, as though it had never belonged to her at all. This ring symbolized safety, not love; a contract, not companionship. It bound her to Solomon, a man she didn't know, an old man that could be her grandfather, under circumstances no young girl could have ever prepared for. The stark contrast between her childish fantasies and her current reality was almost too much to bear. Where was the joy, the music, the perfume of roses, and the promise of a life shared with someone who adored her? All she had now was the coldness of a ring against her skin and the empty feeling that it might, one day, come to mean something more than survival.

Berta stared up at the canopy, her mind racing. She couldn't sleep. Every creak of the floorboards, every whisper of wind against the windows set her nerves on edge. Her thoughts turned to her mother, to the unconditional love of her embrace and the soothing sound of her voice. Berta's throat tightened with grief as she realized how far she had already drifted from her family, and they were only steps away. The paralyzing thought that she might never see her mama again made her chest ache, and tears slipped down her temples, soaking into the silk pillow beneath her head.

She was terrified, not just of Solomon, but of the world that awaited her outside the walls of the mansion. She feared the long walking journey to Odessa, taking a ship to Palestine, the dangers she might face along the way, and the guarantee of being sent to a land she had only heard of in hushed prayers, with a new husband, a total stranger. The thought of being so far from everything familiar, from her family, her home, her faith, left her feeling small and untethered. Stress a fifteen year old should never endure.

By the fire, Solomon shifted heavily, trying to find a comfortable position on the rug. He didn't look at her, but his presence was oddly steadying. Berta knew he was trying to make this easier for her, but no amount of kindness could erase the vast unknown that stretched out before her. As the hours crept by, she remained motionless in the feather bed, her body tense beneath the blankets, eyes wide and unblinking. The question repeated in her mind with relentless persistence... would she ever feel safe again?

Chapter Fifty-four
Journey

By the time they left Czernowitz, the fog had rolled in low and heavy, curling around the wheels of the cart like fingers reluctant to let them go. The morning air smelled of damp earth and smoke from last night's hearths. It clung to Berta's clothing, to her lashes, to every part of her that wanted to stay.

She walked beside the wagon, her delicate shoes soaking through with dew. The road ahead, barely visible in the haze, felt like it belonged to another world. Even the trees stood still, their branches veiled in mist, watching her departure like witnesses to a crime they could not stop.

The wagon creaked forward under the weight of two oak trunks, both hers. One held clothing and personal items carefully packed by Anka and her mother. The other, linens and her dowry. The trunks were monogrammed with the Finkelthal crest, two opposing crescent moons and a star of David in the center, highly polished and proud, as if the family name alone could keep her safe in a city of strangers.

She had not cried when they left the gate.

Not when Rivka clutched her sleeve and refused to let go.

Not when Nurit placed a spool of yellow ribbon in her palm, and whispered, "So you don't forget your cousins," before closing her fingers around it.

Not even when her mother, standing perfectly still on the front step, called her name just once, the sound already fading before it reached the road.

But now, walking through the mist, her eyes stung. And not from the cold.

The cart seemed to groan under the heft of more than trunks. Beside it walked Anka and Solomon's manservant... both overlooked, both carrying burdens of their own. But only Anka knew the full meaning of what lay hidden in the folds of Berta's gowns.

In the days leading up to the wedding, Jetti had sewn late into the evenings, her hands calloused and precise. In the lining of sleeves and hems, she had tucked all her family heirlooms. A gold locket, tiny coin pouches, and diamond studs wrapped in gauze. A ruby necklace set sewn into the crimson hem of a formal ball gown.

"I don't know where she'll end up," Jetti had whispered to Anka as she stitched. "But I know what she'll need."

Each needle prick was an act of premeditated defiance. A mother's way of saying: you will not take her from me completely.

Anka had sworn to keep the secret, even from Berta. Especially from Berta until the right moment. And now, as they moved farther from Czernowitz with every step, Anka's fingers tightened occasionally around the strap of her satchel, her eyes looking over toward the girl she had helped deliver into this uncertain world, a girl who she helped raise. She would know when it was time to tell her. But not yet.

The mist began to lift slowly as the sun struggled to break through the veil. Pale dawn shimmered through the trees, catching on the brass buckles of the trunks, glinting off the blonde curls that spilled down Berta's back. She hadn't spoken in hours.

Solomon walked ahead, his coat soaked with damp, his voice low as he murmured something to his manservant. He hadn't looked at her since they left.

She didn't want him to.

Berta's feet already ached. Her wet shawl clung to her shoulders. But her thoughts… her thoughts ran hot and jagged, clawing at her from the inside.

She kept seeing her mother's face.

Not the one she kissed goodbye.

The face from the night before… the one that crumbled when she begged to stay.

And then came the memory of Uncle Tata, who had said nothing but placed a wrapped bundle in her hands at the last minute. Inside was a set of pencils and a leather-bound journal, blank except for the first page, where he had written:

"Write it all down. So you remember who you are."

That journal was now tucked into the depths of one of her chests, where the memories of her past were on a journey to make her future.

They passed a lone traveler on the road. A man in a coat too thin for the cold, pushing a cart of empty jugs. He didn't meet their eyes. He simply tipped his hat, and Berta wondered what his story was. Who had he left behind?

What would she look like to him? A runaway? A prisoner? A daughter? A granddaughter? But certainly not a newly married bride.

When they stopped just before noon at a clearing by a willow tree, Solomon said only, "We'll rest here." Then walked off toward the woods.

Berta sat down on a flat rock and took a bite of the bread Anka handed her. She imagined that it was warm and crusty, but it was already stale and tasted of nothing.

She didn't speak.

She didn't cry.

She stared at the clouds as they drifted across the open sky, curling upward, thinning slowly like feathers.

And then, just before she looked away, she thought she saw something at the edge of the trees.

A shape? An animal?

A movement barely visible through the branches.

Gone before she could blink.

Her breath caught.

Anka noticed it too, looked up quickly—but said nothing.

The road to Odessa stretched ahead like a wound, raw and unhealed.

Behind them, Jetti stood alone at the entryway of the estate, her heart pounding like a drum in her ears. She hadn't slept. She hadn't moved.

Somewhere, deep in her chest, Jetti felt something shift—slowly at first, like the grinding of tectonic plates beneath the Earth's surface. It wasn't just the distance growing between her and the stranger that took her daughter away. It wasn't even the fear of what lay ahead for Berta on the road to Odessa. It was something else. Something final. A formidable breaking that left her hollow and trembling.

She imagined Berta now, walking beside the cart in the damp morning mist, her curls limp from the fog, her small shod feet growing heavier with each muddy step. Jetti pictured the way she'd pull her shawl tight around her shoulders without complaint, the way her eyes would dart from tree to tree, not out of wonder like they once had, but in search of something steady. Something familiar. Maybe even someone coming to stop all of this.

And then... what would she do when Anka finally told her? When the moment came, days or weeks from now, when they were alone in some unfamiliar room, and Anka, steady and sentimental, began to lift the hems of her dresses to reveal what Jetti had sewn in secret? The coins. The rings. The bloodline of their family legacy disguised as simple seams. Would Berta cry? Would she feel betrayed? Or would she finally understand how deep her mother's love went. A love that could be stitched into fabric, hidden beneath thread, and sent along the road surreptitiously?

Jetti pressed her hand to her mouth, the ache too sharp for sound. She had done everything she could. Everything. But now, as the fog swallowed the last outline of the wagon, a darker fear crept in... one she hadn't allowed herself to name until now.

Could she trust Solomon?

He had said all the right things. Promised protection, stability, the illusion of a future in a place with fewer threats and more fences. But what if that was just talk? What if, when the doors closed and no one was looking, his tone changed? What if he punished Berta for the parts of her that refused to be obedient... her wit, her stubbornness, the fire Jetti had fought so hard to preserve?

Jetti's arms felt suddenly too empty. Her fingers curled around the fabric of her apron like it was the last thing tethering her to this world. She had not cried when Berta left... but now, in the hours that followed, the tears came. Violently. Unrelenting.

Because in letting her daughter go, she had not just given her a future... she had given her to fate.

And fate, Jetti knew, could be cruel.

By the time the hints of dawn stretched over the hills of Czernowitz, Berta and Solomon had already been gone for hours. Their small caravan moved slowly through the misted countryside, wheels creaking, hooves striking drumming rhythms into the damp earth. The road to Odessa stretched out before them like a question with no answer. Behind them, the Finkelthal mansion, once a symbol of safety...now a house of parting, shrank into the blue-gray morning.

Solomon walked ahead, his broad back upright, his boots disturbing the damp pathway. Anka followed behind the wagon, lips pressed tight, her pace measured. The manservant kept to himself. Neither of them spoke. The road demanded reverence now.

What Berta didn't know—what only Anka and Jetti had shared —was that her trunks carried more than dresses and linens.

They were not gifts. They were weapons. A mother's last defense in a world she no longer trusted.

"Don't tell her yet," Jetti had whispered to Anka, her voice rasped from sleepless nights. "Not until you leave her in Odessa. Not until she understands why I did what I did."

Each stitch had been a prayer. Each knot a goodbye.

And now, the wagon slipped beyond the rise. Her daughter was gone—not just down the road, but into a life Jetti could no longer reach.

She had done what she could. She had handed over her child with a steady hand and a shattered heart.

And still, the question clung to her like mist: Would it be enough?

Could Solomon be trusted with something so precious?

The wind offered no answer, for there was none, no elusive rustle of leaves, no breath from the earth to mourn her absence, and the echo of wheels had already slipped into the unknown.

A Note to Readers

T hank you for taking the time to journey through the pages of *Bright One*. Writing this story was an act of love, memory, and imagination —and if it moved you, lingered with you, or sparked reflection, then it has fulfilled its purpose.

Books find their way into the hands of new readers because of the voices of those who have read them. Reviews—whether a few heartfelt lines or a thoughtful reflection—are one of the most powerful ways to help a story live on. They lend visibility to the work of authors, especially those of us without large marketing machines behind us.

If this story meant something, please consider leaving a review on Amazon or Goodreads. It doesn't have to be long—just honest. Your words have the power to open the door for others.

BOOK TWO of the BRIGHT ONE SERIES,
***GOLDEN FLIGHT* will be released Spring 2026.**

Acknowledgments

First, to my partner Jon, who endured every twist, turn, and plot idea I threw your way (and there were many). Thank you for being by my side, when I was waking up at 5 a.m. every morning to write or edit, and for being my favorite "Rock." Everyone who knows me knows how much I love rocks... and you're the best one I've got.

To my parents, Ruth and Chuck: thank you for filling in all those little details I couldn't quite remember. Your stories and memories brought depth and authenticity to this book, and the next four.

To my sister Tracie, who kept me smiling (and laughing) through it all. Your humor is unmatched, and your support was just what I needed to keep going.

A special thank you to my Aunt Joy for caring for O'ma in her later years with so much love and dedication. Your selflessness inspires me, and because of you, I knew she was always safe.

To every friend and reader who cheered me on, thank you for believing in me and this story. You helped turn this dream into reality, and I'll forever be grateful.

To Kerry, Eric, and their friend Marilyn—thank you for igniting the spark under me when I needed it most. Your encouragement helped me break through the wall of that elusive first fully written chapter, which, in a twist of irony and magic, ended up becoming one of the final chapters of this book. I'll never forget that moment of momentum you gave me.

Here's to many more books, more laughs, and plenty of early mornings filled with coffee and creativity!

With love and gratitude,

Lisajoy

A Reader's Guide

This novel explores themes of resilience, family, and identity through the experiences of a Jewish family navigating the turmoil of the early 20th century. Set against the backdrop of World War I, the rise of antisemitism, and the impending shadows of World War II, *Bright One* weaves history and imagination to illuminate the enduring strength of the human spirit and the complexities of survival and hopefulness.

Discussion Questions

- Joel returns to Czernowitz haunted by the war and unsure of his place in his family and marriage. How does his relationship with Jetti reflect the tension between personal survival and family responsibility?

- The story takes place at the end of World War I, but the looming threat of World War II and rising antisemitism adds layers of tension. How does the historical setting shape the character's fears and hopes?

- The Croix de Virtute Militara serves as a tangible reminder of Joel's wartime experiences. How does his conflicted relationship with the medal mirror his feelings about his survival and return?

- How does Jetti's demeanor and her words reflect her resilience and determination to create a stable life? How does she act as a counterbalance to Joel's uncertainties?

- What do the letters represent for Joel? How do they serve as a bridge between his past and the uncertain future?

- How do you think Jetti views her role in the marriage now that Joel has returned?

- Does her attempt to recreate their suite "the way it was" show an optimism about their relationship, or does it suggest something else?

- Jetti experiences profound grief after Joel's disappearance. How does her response to his absence reflect her emotional dependence on him and her sense of identity?

- The dowry chest holds both sentimental value and painful reminders for Jetti. How does its presence in the story symbolize the state of her marriage and her own self-worth?

- How does the Jewish concept of 'Chai' (life) intertwine with the broader theme of renewal?

- How does Jetti's decision to dress up and descend the grand staircase symbolize her tentative steps toward reclaiming her place in the world?

- How does the author use the contrast between Jetti's inner turmoil and her family's joy to explore the complexities of grief and resilience?

- After Joel leaves, what does the dowry chest represent for Jetti, and how does her decision to move it reflect her emotional state?

- How does the act of moving the chest serve as a turning point in Jetti's journey?

- How does Jetti's decision to transform her suite symbolize her emotional journey?

- What significance do the changes she makes—such as the new furniture and lighter drapes—hold for her identity and healing process?

- In what ways does the act of reimagining her space parallel her desire to reclaim her life and move forward?

- Miriam becomes a maternal figure for Jetti. How does her guidance help Jetti find a sense of belonging and purpose?

- What does Miriam's approach to both life and dressmaking teach Jetti about resilience and creativity?

- How does Jetti's growing bond with Miriam and her involvement in the Singer family's work contribute to her healing process?

- How does Jetti's work at the Singer gown shop help her redefine her identity after Joel's departure?

- What does the contrast between her meticulous work on Nina's dress and her earlier struggles to find purpose suggest about her emotional growth?

- How does Jetti's reaction to the news of her pregnancy reflect her emotional state and her journey toward self-reliance?

- What role does Miriam play in helping Jetti come to terms with her new reality?

- How does Jetti's resolve to protect her child and build a better future signify her personal growth since Joel's departure?

- In what ways does her strength contrast with her earlier feelings of powerlessness?

- How does the arrival of the flu epidemic shift the tone of the story? What emotions does Jetti experience as she witnesses the devastation around her?

- How does Jetti cope with the overwhelming grief and silence that surrounds her?

- How does the author use imagery, such as the blooming lilacs, to contrast the beauty of the outside world with the desolation inside the Finkelthal mansion?

- What does the death of the Singer family symbolize within the larger context of the story?

- How does the birth of Jetti's daughter represent a turning point in the narrative?

- In what ways does the scene in Jetti's bedroom, surrounded by her family after the birth of Berta, emphasize the themes of hope and renewal amidst grief?

- How does Jetti's journey throughout the chapter reflect her growing strength and determination?

- What does the act of naming her daughter "Berta" signify for Jetti's character development?

- How does the Finkelthal family adapt their businesses to the changing economic and social landscape of Czernowitz after the Great War?

- What does the consolidation of their enterprises say about Aaron's leadership and vision?

- How do the descriptions of the family members who were lost highlight the importance of their contributions to the Finkelthal legacy?

- What hints are given about potential challenges the family may face in the future?

- In what ways does the family's commitment to education and storytelling reflect their enduring strength and optimism?

- How do the children's actions in the aftermath of Mrs. Kohn's passing demonstrate their understanding of her influence?

- How do Berta, Rivka, and Kurti's initial fears about Yosef as a teacher highlight their unique personalities and concerns?

- What role does their shared bond play in easing their anxieties about this change?

- What does the word "curiosity" on the chalkboard symbolize for both the children and the narrative?

- How does Yosef's emphasis on curiosity set the tone for his lessons?

- What do Yosef's stories suggest about the challenges and opportunities that lie ahead for the children?

- How does Jetti's decision to arrange Berta's marriage illustrate the sacrifices parents make for their children?

- Do you think Jetti was justified in making this decision without consulting Berta? Why or why not?

BEHIND THE STORY

This novel was inspired by a massive collection of letters, documents, hundreds of photographs, and oral histories passed down through generations of my family. These artifacts included correspondence from my great-grandparents and stories shared by my grandmother, Berta, and her relatives. While some of the characters and events in **Bright One** are fictionalized, they are deeply rooted in the emotions and struggles of those who lived through these extraordinary times. Writing this book is not only an act of storytelling but also a way to honor the resilience and legacy of my ancestors, whose lives continue to echo in our present.

ABOUT THE AUTHOR

L isajoy Sachs is a dedicated writer and passionate advocate for preserving history and culture through storytelling. With her schooling on Long Island and weekends in New York's Catskill Mountains, her early years were shaped by the striking contrast of sea and mountains. Growing up in a family deeply rooted in community and tradition, Lisajoy developed a lifelong appreciation for connection, creativity, and cultural heritage.

Her professional journey is as dynamic as her personal interests. With a career that spans Fine Arts, Interior Design, Metalsmithing, Lapidary, and the craft beer and hospitality industries, Lisajoy has cultivated a rich and diverse foundation of knowledge and experience.

She holds several distinguished degrees and certifications, including a Master of Fine Arts from the City University of New York and a Bachelor of Fine Arts from Alfred University. Additionally, she is an Accredited Jewelry Professional through the Gemological Institute of America. In the beer world, Lisajoy is a graduate of Yakima Chief Hops' Hop & Brew School and a Cicerone® Certified Beer Server, reflecting her expertise and passion for the craft.

As a writer, Lisajoy explores a wide range of topics; from beer culture and community engagement to historical fiction, which remains closest to her heart. Her work reflects a deep respect for the past and a fascination with how personal stories intersect with larger historical movements. She has published multiple articles highlighting how the craft beer industry promotes diversity and unity and continues to inspire readers with her thoughtful and emotionally resonant storytelling.

Lisajoy's fiction is driven by a passion for history and family heritage, often set against vividly imagined backdrops and featuring characters navigating profound social and personal change. Whether capturing the resilience of refugees in the years leading up to World War II or highlighting the plight of individuals during times of upheaval, her stories bring authenticity, emotion, and depth to the page.

Outside her professional life, Lisajoy is an avid cyclist and skier. Alongside her partner Jon and their dog Hops, she travels in their camper van to explore new landscapes and seek out adventure.

Through her creative pursuits and professional endeavors, Lisajoy Sachs continues to bridge the gap btween history, culture, and the shared human experience—bringing voice and visibility to the stories that matter most.

Follow the author at:

www.historiumpress.com/lisajoy-sachs

www.historiumpress.com